D0241639

TO SEE A FINE LADY

By the same author

NORAH LOFTS

To See a Fine Lady

HODDER AND STOUGHTON
LONDON · SYDNEY · AUCKLAND · TORONTO

Copyright 1946 by Norah Lofts. First printed in Great Britain 1946. This edition 1973. ISBN 0 340 16810 2. Reproduced by arrangement with Corgi Books. All rights reserved. No part of this publication may be reproduced or transmitted in any form or by any means, electronic or mechanical, including photocopy, recording, or any information storage and retrieval system, without permission in writing from the publisher. Printed in Great Britain for Hodder and Stoughton Limited, St. Paul's House, Warwick Lane, London, EC4P 4AH by Compton Printing Limited, London and Aylesbury.

Contents

★

PART ONE

Araminta Is Led Into Temptation

In the year 1817, Mr. Pollard, of Uplands Farm, reaped and harvested a corn crop which surpassed everything in his experience. And he had farmed in his own right for twenty-seven years, and been aware of crops, good and bad, for a much longer time, in fact since his prattling childhood. True, the crop was a little untimely, for the wars with Napoleon had ended and prices were tumbling; but all the same, to the true farmer, there was something exciting in the sight of the good sound grain turning golden in the fields and then being cut and carted in a spell of such beautiful weather that the last sheaf, the "Maiden," was solemnly carried and laid upon the peak of the last stack as early as the middle day of September.

Also, in that year—though Mr. Pollard would have been ashamed to admit that he even remembered the fact—he and his plump little wife had completed twenty-five years of married life. So, taking one thing with another, he decided to make the Harvest Supper, which he and everyone else called a "Horky," a memorable affair. And because Mrs. Pollard could not drink ale, which engendered wind and made her tightly corsetted figure acutely uncomfortable, he ordered, for the benefit of the ladies, three bottles of the best port wine. Fortunately, neither he nor Mrs. Pollard ever guessed or suspected that because of that rich fruity beverage, their dairy lost the best worker it had ever seen.

Araminta Glover, at the time of the Horky, was just seventeen and a half years old, and at Michaelmas she would have completed her two years' term at Uplands. It was incomparably the best place she had ever worked in; both the Pollards were kind, easy-going folk; she was earning two pounds a year and her keep, and had not known a pang of hunger since the day of her arrival. She knew, because she had measured herself on the barn door and weighed herself on the sack scale, that in two years she had grown ten inches in height and gained a stone and a half in weight, although she had worked hard in the dairy and in the kitchen and lent a hand anywhere else about the farm where her services were temporarily needed.

She could not read or write, and had never even visited the local market town, but she was an intelligent girl and knew when she was well off, and when she sat down to the Harvest Supper she had every intention of renewing her contract with Mrs. Pollard when Michaelmas came round; but, since she had been acting as head-dairymaid since Agnes' marriage in June, she also intended to ask, with tact, and with firmness, for a rise of ten shillings a year. She would then be able to send two pounds a year, instead of thirty shillings, home to the little clod cottage on Minsham Green, from which she had set out to make a living at the age of ten. She reckoned—and that was a phrase often upon her tongue and in her mind, for she was a foresighted girl who liked to plan for the future—that, having managed with ten shillings "spending money" for the past two years, she could do it again. This year she was certain that she could, for at Easter Mrs. Pollard had given her an old gown to make over, and she had found a way of getting shoes for nothing. Shoes were the most expensive and worrisome item of a girl's equipment. When your body grew you could let out a tuck, or put in a gusset, or lower a hem, or when such devices would no longer serve, you could go about in a dress that was too tight and too short; but when your feet grew you were helpless, and nothing could make you so miserable, or so impede your speed, as last year's shoes cramping your toes. However, at last, she had solved that problem. Old Snappy, the cobbler, had a good bit of garden which this year he had been unable to dig on account of his rheumatism. Araminta had dug the garden—and a hard old job it was, all ground elder and great spreading branches of horse-radish—and put in the potatoes on Good Friday, and on Easter Monday Snappy had measured her for a pair of shoes, chalking the outline of her foot on a sheet of leather and even measuring around her ankles, as though she were his best customer. When she sat down to the table on the evening of the third Saturday in September, she was, in a way, still in debt; for the finished shoes were on her feet and the cobbler's potatoes were still in the ground. However, she reckoned to dig and store them between tea and supper on the next Saturday. That was a space of time which she could always call her own. So it was all right to wear the shoes. Now and then, during the afternoon of the festivities, she lifted the smoothly-ironed skirt of the made-over lilac-coloured print dress and admired the neatly-finished, beautifully-fitting shoes at the ends of her slim, brown, stockingless legs, now much scratched from harvest work amongst the stubble. If only her feet would stop growing the shoes would last her six or seven years, with care. Of course, there was a belief in the countryside that if you beat a child with an elder stick it would stop his growth . . . would it work with feet? The picture of herself industriously thrashing her own feet with an elder twig amused her, and she smiled. The smile was at once humourous and derisive, for her wide, firm-lipped mouth had a quirk at one corner and lifted higher on that side. Her sneer was lopsided too, and easily provoked: possibly on that account some few of the people with whom she had worked, had accorded her a respect more than was due to her age and status.

Mr. Pollard's lavish suggestions regarding food and drink had been infectious, and this year even the barn was decorated. Mrs. Pollard, her Cousin Sarah who was staying for the occasion, Araminta and the other girl, Cissie, had worked hard during the golden mellow morning to make the place look festive. They had hung great boughs of fir and copper beech along the nail-studded walls and looped yards and yards of brightly-coloured horse-braid from side to side. They had cleared the floor in the barn's centre by the simple process of having everything movable pushed away into the corner, and Araminta herself had fetched the stiffest broom and swept the dust and the chaff and the little bits of string and bent nails and old wizened turnips and the granary key which Mr. Pollard had dropped round about Christmas time last year, out into the stackyard. The landlord of "The Sword In Hand" had lent a long trestle table, and when Araminta and Cissie (supervised by Araminta) had scrubbed the boards of it, the other table, which went across the top in a T-shape and was covered with Mrs. Pollard's second-best damask cloth, was hardly whiter. Down the centre of the table, linking the jars of purple knapweed and yellow sunflowers and dusky velvet snapdragons, ran a long trail of ivy. Araminta, whose idea this was, admired it intensely, and was very sorry that it stopped short at the tablecloth, because Mrs. Pollard had expressed a definite opinion that, shake it how you might, ivy still held dust.

At one end of the table was a vast, an incredible sirloin; roasted to a brown glaze outside, succulent and pink within. At the other a huge ham, garnished with parsley, and a whole loin of pork sat side by side. For those who preferred a hot dish there were two great beef-steak puddings which had been boiling slowly for a whole night and a day; and there were two of Mrs. Pollard's milk-pans, one holding a mound of mashed potato, the other full of pickled onions. At intervals along the table were boards of golden-crusted home-made bread, each loaf cut into slices and then replaced in shape, to look tidy, dishes of butter, little pans of salt and mustard. Afterwards, for those who had not eaten to satiety there was to be apple-pie and cream and a noble cheese.

The meal was timed for five o'clock, and as the barn began to fill the late afternoon sun came slanting in by the wide open doorway, and through innumerable chinks and crannies, sending long slanting beams of golden, dust-shimmering light upon the mustering company. There were several Pollard relatives, five or six neighbouring farmers with their wives and children, the landlord of "The Sword In Hand," the village blacksmith, the two old brothers who had carried their fiddles to every rustic festival worth mentioning for the last forty years, and a pale young man who played the flute, as well as every permanent and seasonal worker at Uplands, down to the humblest little horse-leading, rook-scaring, stone-picking boy or girl. Only the Parson, whom Mrs. Pollard would have been glad and proud to see in a place of honour by the damask-covered table, was absent. Even at this heart-opening moment, Mr. Pollard could neither forget nor forgive the quarrel which he had inherited from his father over a matter of tithe. But despite the absence of the Church's representative, a spirit of good-will was abroad in the barn, and one of the visiting farmers, a staunch Methodist, said a solemn and impressive Grace before the meal began, laying great stress upon the Heavenly goodness which had provided the "kindly fruits of the earth" and sent the fine harvest weather.

Perhaps no one in all that washed and tidy, excited company saw any irony in the groaning table of food or the Grace which was spoken above it. It would have been silly to sour one's stomach at such a moment by reflections about the unfairness of the division of those "kindly fruits." The feasters drew their chairs close, or jostled into position along the narrow benches, Mr. Pollard took up his carving knife, Uncle Fred Pollard at the other end of the table copied the action, plates upon which there was scarcely room for a helping of potatoes or a couple of pickled onions were passed rapidly from hand to hand, and in a short space of time everyone had settled down; even Araminta, who had kept popping up whenever the slightest hitch was threatened. The greater part of the company was earnestly engaged upon filling their bellies with the best for once in a while, and prepared to forget that they were engaged in a relenting and unrewarding war, not only against poverty and hunger and overwork, but against the genial, booming man who sat at the head of the table, stuffing his mouth with food and looking about him with complacency, as though he did not know that within a week or two all these wicked idle rogues and scamps would be demanding eight shillings a week as a winter wage and trying to extort that preposterous sum by threats and violence.

Araminta was thoroughly enjoying herself. Long years of privation had given her an appetite for food which was almost insatiable, and here was food in abundance. She enjoyed company too, especially in her leisure time, and here was company of all kinds. She had purposely seated herself next to Mrs. Thatcher, wife of the Uplands head-man, Bob, because Mrs. Thatcher was also a native of Minsham, and often, now that her family was grown up, went over for the day to visit a sister who lived quite near the Glover cottage. She was always careful to ask after the family and to relay every bit of news and gossip to Araminta. Upon her other side sat the landlord of "The Sword In Hand," a cheerful man, quick with a joke. He had never seen Araminta before, and the first time he won a smile from her he was interested to watch the way her mouth curved, so he made another and another, rough and simple and homely, but good enough to win a smile at such a moment. And it was while she was still laughing at one of the landlord's jokes that her eye wandered along the table and she found herself smiling straight into the eyes of Jan Honeywood, who immediately smiled back, and lifting his mug of ale, held it towards her for a second and then drank, looking at her boldly over the rim of it.

Her face, which had been relaxed and merry, hardened instantly. I'm a fool, she thought. Why did I look that way? He'll think I done it a-purpose.

On and off all day, as she had run to and fro between the house and the barn, she had thought about Jan. Lately, indeed, he had been often in her thoughts and frequently in her dreams. Until three weeks ago, at the beginning of the harvest, she would have laughed at the idea of being in love with him, but now she was no longer sure.

It was a pity, she thought ruefully, that people made merry at the end of the harvest, not at the beginning; three weeks ago she would have enjoyed dancing and laughing and fooling about with Jan; to-night she must keep out of his way.

She had always regarded him as Agnes' fellow, and had some-times wondered what such a merry, well-set-up chap could see in that great limp "yard of pump water," and thought it a shame that he had chosen for his woman somebody who actually boasted of the fact that she'd never do a stroke of work more than she must once she was married. In those days Araminta had been too virginally untouched, too ignorant of the workings of her own mind to suspect that the pang which she felt whenever she thought of Jan wearing an unmended shirt, or going home to a dirty hearth, or eating a slovenly-prepared meal, was a sign of any feeling warmer than friendship. And then Agnes, all in a hurry, had announced that she was going to marry ugly, cross old Crummy Gathercole, and wanted a June wedding. Privately Araminta thought this a far more suitable match—if a final proof of Agnes' stupidity; she thought Jan had had a lucky escape, and wondered if he minded at all. He gave no sign of heart-break; and he still hung about the dairy, looking in at the window and chatting until Mrs. Pollard would hear the sound of voices and laughter and bustle in, pretending to be angry, and say, "Jan Honeywood, if the master can't find you a job, I can. " Sometimes indeed she would pounce on him with some job, like harnessing up the gig for her, or catching a young rooster whose neck she wanted wrung. That had all been fun; but then, coming back along the lane from the harvest field, in a lovely twilight three weeks ago, Jan had put a hand on her elbow and restrained her swift pace until at last they were away behind everybody else and alone in the lane. And then, drawing her aside, into the hedge, which was sweet with late honeysuckle, he had kissed her. Araminta had been dreadfully scared; not of the kiss, for she had been kissed before, and always got out of it, laughing or cross: no, this time she had been frightened of herself, by the wild feelings roused in her by the touch of his hands, the nearness of his big warm sweaty body inside the thin shirt, the pressure of his lips on her own. Goodsakes, she had thought, suppose I went and got sloppy about *him*, and him earning nine shillings a week at best. I must be daft!

She had torn herself away, and for the rest of the evening, for that part of the night which was wakeful, and for all the next day, she felt as though she had done herself a physical violence, ripped off a limb, as rats were supposed to do if they were trapped. But even if she had known for certain that to tear herself away would

13

cost an arm or a leg . . . or even her head, she would still have done it. Better he dead than the wife of a labourer. That was the paramount lesson which seventeen years of living had taught her. Her dad was a labourer, and she was the eldest survivor of fifteen children.

So, for the rest of the busy harvest time she had, not without cost to herself, avoided Jan like the plague. It had been easier than it would have been at any other time of the year, for he had no time now to lean against the dairy window, he was busy all day in the cornfields; and when Araminta went into the field to help with the stooking and binding, she worked with the other women; and at the end of the day's toil she scuttled back ahead of everybody else under pretence of being anxious about the supper.

But to-night, she knew, would be a teaser. Even if he made no special advances towards her she was practically certain to meet him somewhere in the whirling round dances; and if once he touched her all those peculiar feelings would begin again. And already—quite apart from Jan, Araminta had a distrust of feelings. They wasted your time and your energy. If you had your living to earn and always as much work as you could manage, you couldn't afford to get angry, or frightened, or homesick, to pity either yourself or anybody else very much, or to be in love. So she had determined, with regret, for she loved a dance as well as any other light-footed young creature, that she would sit out by the wall with the older women, and avoid looking at Jan and whatever partners he chose. He could even dance with Silly Cissie and she wouldn't take a bit of notice.

And now, in the very first hour, there she was, looking at him and grinning like a trollop.

Abruptly she quenched the smile; and as she did so the curious muscular tension in each honey-brown cheek, which might have been a dimple had her face been plumper and which did look very like one when she smiled, changed its shape and seemed to pull inwards and downwards, so that her young face looked lined and hollowed. Mrs. Pollard, who was looking along the table in order to relieve the boredom of Cousin Sarah's story of a Horky which

14

had been ruined by a cloudburst, a story which she had heard many times before, caught a glimpse of her favourite maid's face and thought little Araminta looked tired and glum.

Mrs. Pollard had motherly instincts and no family, and so she was in constant danger of spoiling any young maid who was fairly biddable and clean in her ways. Of Araminta she was especially fond; and now she could not bear to see the girl, who had worked so hard and so merrily all day, looking so harshly unhappy. She looked round for some remedy, and her eye fell upon the port wine. She whispered that Araminta's glass was to be filled—and, not to make favouritism too obvious—Cissie's as well. Nobody else's, mind. After all, Araminta and Cissie were house-servants, almost part of the family in a way.

It was Araminta's first taste of real intoxicating liquor; for the mild, bitter-tasting home-brewed ale which was plentiful as water about the farm, and which counted as "drink" when computing wages and allowances, was brewed with such cautious economy that it had thirst-quenching qualities and flavour and nothing more. Young Billy Friar who had been sent with the bottle, had not brought a wine-glass, so he had poured a good generous measure into Araminta's ordinary glass, and she drank the lovely glowing stuff as though it had been the home-brewed for which she had been waiting. It brightened her eyes and deepened the faint carnation colour which lay under her honey-tinted tan. And it lightened her heart. After a few minutes she felt equal to anything; even to sitting out amongst the old women and watching Jan dance with Cissie. And she wished that it were a little nearer Michaelmas, because to-night she could have tackled Mrs. Pollard about the ten shillings rise without a single tremor.

The long meal came to end at last. There was just enough food left to show that everyone had had a bellyful, and not so much as to make Mr. Pollard feel that he had catered extravagantly. Bob Thatcher, the Uplands head-man, helped by a little prodding and whispering, rose to his feet, shy and embarrassed, and after clearing his throat several times, expressed his thanks and the thanks of everybody present. He said they were all glad that the harvest had been so good and the weather so fine; he said they were all grateful to Mr. Pollard for the fine feast he had provided, and to Mrs. Pollard for the sight of trouble she had gone to to get it ready. He was sure that they all wished the Master and Missus long life and prosperity.

He sat down amidst a murmurous, hand-clapping, foot-stamping hubbub of agreement. In seven weeks' time, at Uplands, as all over England, the vexed question of the winter reduction in wages was going to arise with more than usual bitterness; and through one week in November big booming Mr. Pollard was going to spend the raw cold nights in the stackyard, guarding, with his old rook gun, the stacks of that fine harvest from the hands of the temporarily crazy incendiarists who had built them. But the only sign of social consciousness which was revealed on this evening, came in his own return speech, when he said, perhaps from tact or from caution, or just by way of a joke, "And don't you chaps run off with the notion that the Missus give me a feed like this every day. This is a special occasion, and as much of a treat to me as anybody." This palpable untruth was swallowed with laughter because the meat and the ale had prepared the way for it.

The sun had wheeled round behind the belt of elms which marked Mr. Pollard's boundary, and the long golden fingers had ceased to probe through the chinks of the barn. Bob Thatcher rose and with a nod to those whom he had appointed to help him, began to light and set in place the lanterns which had been cleaned and fitted with new candles earlier in the day. In their muted light the barn took on a different, almost an enchanted air. Araminta found her breath catch unaccountably as she looked round.

·Now the benches and chairs were being pushed and lifted aside. The trestle boards were cleared quickly and set on end. The cloth-covered table was carried to a corner, and near it Mrs. Pollard and the visiting ladies took their seats. Cousin Sarah, in the middle of one of her dreary stories, had knocked her glass and spilled some wine which had left a stain that Mrs. Pollard's fingers itched to be after. If only she could catch the eye of either Cissie or Araminta she would beckon and send for some salt. A pinch of salt, unobtrusively applied, might save the cloth without offending Sarah. Mrs. Pollard looked about earnestly. In a minute she saw a sight which made her smile. Araminta had rescued two of the jars of flowers, and with one in either hand was moving towards a ledge in the barn wall, apparently unaware that Jan Honeywood had crept up behind her. In his big hands he held a wreath which he had twisted from one of the trailing strands of ivy. He reached out and set it, like a coronet, on her curly head, and then, dropping his hands to her shoulders, twisted her round, as though to judge the effect. Mrs. Pollard watched the little business with a smile far more doting than she knew; it would be all right for Jan to marry Araminta; it would keep her at Uplands and she could pop in often to lend a hand in the dairy; and she was a steady, contriving sort of girl, just the kind he needed. . . . Not for anything would Mrs. Pollard have disturbed the pair just then, and she was about to avert her gaze when Araminta's eyes, looking about wildly, met those of her mistress. Mrs. Pollard saw her lips move, saw her reach out and set the jars in safety on the ledge and then turn and come rapidly towards the table.

"Did you want something, ma'am?" she asked, quite eagerly.

"Well, it didn't really matter. But since you are here, Araminta" . . . she lowered her voice, "Run fetch me a little salt and come and put it in my hand without making a song about it. And"—she raised her voice again—"get hold of Cissie and remind her about the tea-tray."

"I'll bring that too." Surely, if she waited to boil the kettle the dancing would have started and Jan would be tired of waiting for her. The ivy wreath weighed like lead on her hair.

"No, no. I want what I told you at once. Let Cissie do the tea. She's done nothing all day."

Half-way across the yard Araminta heard the first wailing sweet notes of the fiddles and a second after the icy aching call of the flute. When she returned, and under pretence of a whisper slipped the salt into Mrs. Pollard's hand, the first dance was in full swing.

She edged along the wall and took a seat on the bench between old Mrs. Thatcher, an active octogenarian who could still pick a bushel of stones with the best, and Agnes, whose figure was already betraying the secret of her reason for choosing a June wedding. It had nothing to do with the roses, Araminta thought grimly.

She was feeling a little less happy now. For one thing she knew she was conspicuous, sitting here between an old woman and a pregnant one. Not another young woman on the whole bench. But being beside Agnes gave her a certain wry comfort. The silly ninny had been earning fifty shillings a year and living like a lord; but sometime or other she'd let her feelings get the better of her and look at her now! She'd be lucky if she ever had fifty pence for herself in a single year again. Remember that and forget the way the music makes your toes twitch inside your new shoes, Araminta Glover.

She saw Cissie, dawdling thing that she was, bring the best tea-tray and set it on the table. And then—for in some matters Cissie could be brisk enough—she saw her slip into the circling ring, resolutely joining the chain of girls, not caring who lost her partner so long as she got one as soon as the music changed. It changed, the ring broke, and there was Cissie face to face with Jan, who immediately lifted her so high that her feet left the ground and made a great sweep through the air. With a sick feeling Araminta imagined what it must be like to be lifted like that, pressed against Jan's chest, held in his arms. . . . She had to battle with herself so fiercely that the lines cut into her cheeks again and there was a scowl between her thin dark brows and the quirk at the corner of her mouth was like a groove.

At that moment old Mrs. Pollard, whose interest in all matters connected with breeding—in its less genteel sense—had not been dulled by sixty-five years of living close to the open mysteries of farmyard life, looked across to the bench of sitting women and saw Agnes. She leaned forward and said to her daughter-in-law, in the special voice she reserved for such subjects:

"Nellie, that gal of yours that married in June lost no time a-quickening."

"Aggie," said Mrs. Pollard, looking towards the bench, "oh, she always was too slow to say no." Her attention drifted. Why on earth was Araminta sitting there, looking so sick and sorry for herself?

"ARAMINTA," she called on a rising note in a voice which could, if necessary, make itself heard across two fields.

"Ma'am," said Araminta, jumping to her feet. That Cissie, no doubt she'd forgotten something from the tray, counted the cups wrong as like as not.

"What ails you, girl?" Mrs. Pollard asked, anxiously, kindly, putting a hand on Araminta's brown arm. "New shoes hurting?"

Araminta shook her head. The muscles in her cheeks twitched into dimples at the idea of anything so absurd.

"Are you sick then? Did you get tired too early in the day?" Mrs. Pollard persisted.

"No ma'am," said Araminta, who took pride in her physical endurance. Immediately she was sorry that vanity had tricked her into saying that. It would have been so simple to murmur that her head ached a little.

"Well, I can't have you sitting there with all those old women looking like a death's head," said Mrs. Pollard. "You fair turn my supper." She spoke irritably, a little annoyed with herself for caring whether Araminta enjoyed herself or not. But she couldn't help it. Araminta was such a good, hard-working, clean little girl, and so pretty too.

"Where's your wreath?" she asked.

"Reckon I dropped it in the yard," said Araminta, who had slipped it under her pillow when she went for the salt, and had then regretted doing so and planned to throw it out of the window as soon as she returned to the house.

Perhaps that was what was upsetting her, Mrs. Pollard thought. Girls were so funny when they'd got a chap in tow. Perhaps she didn't want him to see that she had lost his favour—thought it would have been more like the resourceful Araminta to have rigged up another. She looked at the table. Araminta was a wonderful one for tea, perhaps a cup would cheer her up now. But all the cups were in use, and the only other thing upon the table was the glass which Mr. Pollard had filled, despite Mrs. Friar's giggling protest that she couldn't take a sip more.

"Here," said Mrs. Pollard, taking it up so hastily that another stain went to join Cousin Sarah's, "drink this, Araminta, and put it out of danger. That *should* make your toes tingle."

Araminta took the glass and, knowing her place, stepped a little aside from the ladies and drank it slowly, making it last and planning her next move. If it annoyed Mrs. Pollard to see her sitting with the other women she would watch her opportunity and slip off to bed. Bed was like food, something you could never have too much of; and once there she would be safe, and out of the way of the temptation to get up and pull Cissie away from Jan by brute force.

She tilted back her head, draining the last drop of wine from the glass, and then, straightening up, had a momentary fear that the action had turned her brain. She was as dizzy as a duck, her head was swimming, her whole body felt as though it were floating, and her feet were a long way away.

She set the glass back on the table with exaggerated carefulness, and said "Thank you ma'am" from what she judged to be a respectful distance, but actually so close to her mistress' ear that for a second brown curls and grey frizz mingled. Then she turned, and upon unmanageable feet, set out to cross the barn. There was only one idea left in her head—to get to the big doors quickly and unaccosted and see what a breath of fresh air would do for her. But the spinning of the dancing couples made her so dizzy that she couldn't walk straight, so putting a hand behind her she backed against the wall, and stood there, leaning against it for a moment, grateful for its sturdy support and wondering why, feeling so strange, she did not feel ill. For despite the dizziness and the distance from her own feet she felt happy and excited, better than she had ever felt in her life. So light, so carefree. She saw tall Bessie Hemp being swung round by little Jim Stubbings, and the sight, which would have amused her at any time, was now so extremely funny that she burst out laughing, and made no effort to check her laughter, though ordinarily she would have done so, knowing that to laugh or talk to yourself was a sure sign of madness.

The fiddles gave a sudden whoosh of sound, the spinning couples broke apart, each man turning to his left, each woman to her right, hands extended to the new partner. Araminta saw Cissie cheat, for the second time that evening. She turned right, pretended to stumble and twisted round, falling, with apparent loss of direction, between Jan and little Mary Hemp who was as stunted as her sister was overgrown. That was too much. Araminta swooped forward like a swallow and shouldered Cissie aside. Jan's big hands, burnt to a rich brown, hard as wood and chipped and scarred all over by a lifetime's manual labour, closed on hers, a warm dry clasp which struck sparks of feeling all over her body. He swung her in silence for the few seconds the fiddles, with another whoosh, announced another change of partners, and then, still spinning, to the great confusion of the other questing couples, thrust an inconsiderate path through them until he was near the big door, just an oblong of dusky blue twilight against the glowing yellow of the lanterns. Quickly he dropped her hands and with one arm about her waist drew her outside.

"Oh," she said, stiffening and resisting the pressure of his arm, "why'd you do that, Jan? I wanted to dance."

"I'd have lost you in a minute," he said frankly, "and I mightn't have got you back. Way you've been behaving. Going to sit with all them owd crones. Reckoning on me making a mawkin of myself coming to ask you to stand up, huh?" He laughed down at her, teasingly. Held so close she could feel the thud of his heart.

"I'd bin running about all day, Jan. I wanted a bit of a rest. But I'm rested now. I want to dance. Listen, they're doing Fiddlers' Jig. We could dance that straight through, together. Let's get back."

"Whass dancing for?" he asked scornfully. "For them as hain't made up their minds yet, or them like Bessie Hemp as no chap'd go near if it worn't for the music. Not for us."

Something at the very core of her melted, hearing him say "us" in that special, meaning way. Probably the mental slackening affected her muscles, for in the next second he had moved her away from the door and sideways. They were near the stacks now, and between the great four-square bulks there were narrow passages of genuine darkness.

She made another effort. "Jan I gotta get back. S'pose the Missus want something and look for me. What'd she think?"

"Damn her and what she'd think," Jan said without violence. He bent his head and kissed her. The kiss began just where the one in the lane had broken off. Mingled waves of fear and delight engulfed Araminta, mind and body. She knew that he was dragging her towards the darkness between the stacks; and she knew that if once she went there she was lost.

"Oh," she said weakly. "Let me go, Jan." And then, as the high nettles stung her bare ankles, "Jan, you're pulling me through a nettle-bed."

He lifted her, stepped lightly over the weeds, and then, still carrying her, rounded a stack and came to a narrow place between it and a tall hawthorn hedge. Some loose straw had fallen upon the sun-bleached grass; overhead the sky was pricked with stars and the harvest moon was rising in glory. It was a sweeter bed than many that Araminta had known.

As old as the human race, this meeting of male and female in the covering night; this press of the desirous flesh; this groping of hands; this mystery of separateness for ever seeking to lose itself in unity: old, but fresh and new to-night—as it is always fresh and new for some reason or another—because for Jan it was the first time that he had mingled tenderness with his passion; because for Araminta it was the first time in her memory that she had given rein to her senses and forgotten all about industry and carefulness and earning money.

Afterwards, in a great peace, with the clean scent of new straw in their nostrils and the sound of the fiddles coming plaintively from the barn, they lay side by side, their clamorous senses stilled. And then Jan said the words which so many girls in Araminta's place would have been glad to hear, words which indeed he owed in several other places.

"We'll get married, come Michaelmas, sweetheart. They reckon owd Theo can't last out more'n a week and I'll speak to Master about us heving his cottage."

Sanity and sobriety came rushing back. She'd known it all along; she'd told herself so time and again in the last three weeks. You began with kissing and cuddling and the joy you took in these pleasures was just the bran that baited the trap. Because where did you end? In a clod cottage, with a tired, worn-out man, and a swarm of hungry little children to feed on nine shillings a week. It had happened to her mother, nobody knew better than Araminta the full grinding horror of her mother's life; and she had seen it happen, or begin to happen to several girls with whom she had lived and worked. And now, because she had been a fool for less space of time than it took to dance the whole of Fiddlers' Jig, it was going to happen to her. At Michaelmas, too. Just when she had planned to improve her prospects. A hasty, improvident answer rose to her lips, to be checked there by a cold stab of fear in her vitals. Suppose by—she reckoned hastily—next Wednesday, thank God, not long to wait and wonder; suppose that by Wednesday, only she'd wait till the week's end, she was in such a state that she'd be humbly glad to take Jan at his word. Oh God, oh dear loving Christ, that couldn't happen to her; not to Araminta Glover, always so busy and sensible and proud. But she mustn't dash away what might be her one hope.

"D'you want to get married, Jan?"

"Not till about three weeks ago I didn't," he admitted. "But I'm right mad for you, Minta, and thass the truth. Now more'n ever."

Oh, to be able to say—and I'm right mad for you, Jan. Oh, if only he was somebody you could hope to make something of. If he'd got a trade of some sort. If he'd been a blacksmith, how she would have helped him, blowing the bellows and keeping the forge bright and holding the horses so that where he'd shoed one horse before he could now shoe two, and make double money and get to be known as the best and quickest smith in the district. Or if, say, he'd been a cobbler. Wouldn't she have looked after the leather and handed him the brads as they were needed, and done the simple jobs and carried the orders home so that he wasted no time but could make and mend from dawn to dark and gather in the shillings. But what could anybody do with a labouring chap and a feckless one at that? He could work his guts out and he'd never have more than nine shillings in summer and eight in winter. And he'd never be even head-man, like Bob Thatcher, with certain privileges and a chance of making a bit extra taking the bull round, or getting a present because the calves did so well. Jan wasn't the sort to become head-man, too happy-go-lucky. And they were the ones who turned sourest afterwards, when there were too many children and not enough to eat. She knew: Dad had been "one for a laugh and a joke," Mum always said. And look at him now. Not a word to throw to a dog.

"Reckon I ought to get back," she said. "You go in first, Jan. We don't want folks talking about us."

"Let 'em," he said. "If we get married at Michaelmas they can think and say what they like. Anyway, I ain't going back in there. I'm going home. Reckon I'll dream about you, Minta."

He stood up beside her and caught her to him in a great bear's hug. For a moment she was frightened again. But he set her down after a hearty kiss or two. Then, with unwonted consideration, he remembered the belt of nettles and turned back to lift her over. Araminta waited until his step—still light and lithe for a labourer's— had ceased to sound in the yard, and then she turned and scuttled into the house. There'd be straw in her hair for certain, and she couldn't face anybody until she had seen whether the recent experience had left any sign upon her face.

The house was dark and silent and every familiar thing in it seemed to have a reproachful look—what've you done since you were here last? The kitchen had not been tidied since the last happy bustle of preparation; and the bedroom was untidy too, Cissie's clothes and her own just flung down anywhere when they changed at the last minute.

Holding the candle close to her face she studied it intently in the dim, rather spotty little mirror which, so short time ago, had gladly assured her that she looked her best. She looked paler and rather tired and her eyes seemed bigger; but she often looked like that after a hard day.

She took the wreath of ivy from under her pillow and went to the window, intending to throw it out. Then something halted her. Suppose the worst happened and she had to settle down like all the other women; and suppose there came a time when Jan didn't love her any more, by then she might be so humbled, so like the other women that she might be glad to have something to remember this night by. It didn't seem very likely, but after all, to-night had proved that she was no more sensible than the rest. And her mother, through all these years, had cherished a scrap of red ribbon which she had been wearing in her hair at the moment when Tom Glover had asked her to marry him. It was kept in a screw of paper, and once, with a soft look which had seemed strange upon her battered face, she had shown it Araminta and told her about it. And that's what I'm likely to come to, Araminta thought desolately; if I ain't lucky on Wednesday, in twenty years' time I'll have a great hungry family, and I'll be looking at this old wreath and thinking to-night was the happiest night of my life.

"Be damned if I do," she said aloud with sudden violence, and wrenching the window open she flung the spray of leaves as far out as she could. Then she went back and sat on the edge of the bed, wishing that she could cry. But she had finished with tears at her first place. She'd been ten then, and so homesick, so frightened of the other servants, so frightened of doing something wrong, so frightened of the dark stairs and the long passages, that if she hadn't taken herself in hand she would have been howling like a dog all the time. So she had taken herself in hand and restrained tears so often that the source seemed to have been sealed, and now, when tears would have been a relief, she could not cry at all.

Nor could she go back to face the gaiety of the barn. Presently she got up from the edge of the bed and tidied her half of the room. Yesterday, scolding and scornful, she would have tidied Cissie's half, too; but now she felt a grudge against the silly giggling, cheating creature. If she hadn't provoked her. . . . But oh, what was the good of thinking if, if, if. She must wait and see what happened this week. After all, she wasn't finally doomed yet.

Her feelings having sunk as low as possible, took a faint upward turn. She undressed and got into bed. The sagging old feather mattress fitted itself to her body, receiving her kindly, holding her safely. She was warm and comfortable, and very soon asleep.

On Wednesday, at about a quarter to five, having set upon the table the substantial cold meal which Mr. Pollard needed to greet him when he came in at five o'clock, and put the kettle on the hook over the fire, Araminta asked with great diffidence, "Do you mind, ma'am, if I run down now and start on Snappy's potatoes. That get dark so quick these days, I reckon they'll take me two evenings."

"*It gets,*" said Mrs. Pollard, "and quickly, not quick. Nobody would think, to hear you, Araminta, the pains I have taken with you."

Mrs. Pollard, before her marriage, had been governess to the family of a corn-chandler in Baildon; and though twenty-five years of rustic company had so affected her speech that she was now almost bi-lingual, she had her pernicketty moments and would make these little corrections genially, or tartly, according to her mood. Araminta, being bright and intelligent, often roused the slumbering demagogue in the farmer's wife and had received a good deal of instruction which had mystified her at first but which was now beginning to make sense.

"It gets dark so quickly," she repeated. "May I then?"

"You may," said Mrs. Pollard graciously. "And while you are there remind him about the Master's winter boots. He'll be needing them soon."

Winter was coming on; and this year, she promised herself, she would start to teach Araminta to read and write. It had been impossible last year because Agnes had a jealous nature and would have wanted to learn as well, and the labour of teaching that great stupid lump of nonsense anything would have been too much like the old days.

Araminta departed with alacrity, arranging her shawl as she ran down the lane. She wasn't really worried yet, but the worry lay there at the back of her mind, waiting to pounce. A good hour's hard digging and then hauling a sack or two of potatoes into the cobbler's shed wouldn't do any harm, and it might do good. Anyway, it would be a relief to get out of the house. The last four days had been a torment. She was beginning to learn that she knew nothing at all about Araminta Glover, who appeared to be capable of folly upon folly. Twice, once on Sunday and once on Tuesday, Jan had come up to the dairy window. On the first occasion Cissie had been there and Araminta had stayed in the background, just saying a word now and then and turning a stony, disregarding eye upon Jan's significant glances. The second time she had been alone, but she had had the presence of mind to call out loudly, "I'm just bringing it ma'am," and dart away into the passage. And each time the mere sight of him, the sound of his voice and the sense of his nearness had set her pulses throbbing madly. There was no sense in blinding herself any longer to the fact that she was head over ears in love with him. Heaven only knew what might happen if she found herself alone with him and he started his tricks again. And that, despite the worry and the iron determination that, unless forced into it, she would never marry him.

I reckon I'm a trollop after all, Araminta thought, setting her hand upon the cobbler's latch, decent girls either marry a chap or else live without one; I shall have to take myself in hand.

When, in the last, rather misty moment of twilight she ran back up the lane, the worst of her fears was over. It was all right. She wouldn't have to marry Jan and live in old Theo's cottage and never be able to send another penny home. If she had sinned—and she had known a certain amount of sporadic religious training, so that she knew sin when she saw it—if she had sinned then God had forgiven her and was washing away her guilt; if she had been a fool—and there was no doubt at all in her mind as to the grossness of her folly—then the final payment for it was not to be exacted. Both her heart and her feet were so light that as she ran she took occasional little skipping steps. Everything was all right again, and now she could begin to think and plan what to say to Jan next time she saw him. She'd make it all quite plain and tell him, as pleasantly as possible, that she couldn't marry him. She needn't say why.

And then, out of the mist, came the sound of steps and voices. She recognized them, Crummy going home to Agnes, Jan going home to his funny foreign mother. Too late to do anything about it, the lane had a high thick hedge on either side, and if she had heard their step they must have heard hers, so if she turned and ran they'd be suspicious and run after her. Anyway, Jan was sure to be hungry and have his mind on his supper; he'd probably shout "Good night" and walk straight past.

But of course he did no such thing. He said, "Hullo, Minta. G'night Crummy," and stopped.

"I hoped I'd meet you," he said. "I looked in at the house and Cissie towd me where you'd gone."

"They took a bit longer than I'd reckoned for and I'm late," said Araminta sternly, beginning to step out again. He fell into step beside her.

"Here," he said, "don't be in such a hurry. I ain't seen you since Saturday. But I've thought about you a lot." He said the last sentence in a significant way, so that despite herself she felt the blood beginning to run quickly and warmly in her veins. "Maybe you've been too busy to give me a thought."

"Oh no," she moved to one side, increasing the distance between them, and lengthened her stride, "I've thought about you." She was beginning to search for words which would convey the result of her thinking in the least hurtful manner, when he said:

"Owd Theo is unconscious to-day. I asked on my way up this morning. They reckon he'll never speak again. Ted Hemp promised to drop me word the moment he's dead so that I can speak for the cottage before anybody else, see?"

"But," said Araminta—and now there was a painful lump in her throat, not to be banished by all her firm determination. "But Jan, I'm sorry . . . I can't marry you after all."

"Not marry me," he said. He sounded quite stunned. "Why Minta, you as good as promised. Why, only Saturday . . ."

28

"I never said it," said Araminta in a voice gruff with emotion. "I never said I'd marry you. Never once. All I said was did you want to get married. I never said how I felt at all."

"What about the way you acted?"

"If i acted wrong, I'm sorry. You'd best forget all about it. And about me."

He was puzzled. He knew—for he had not lacked women to tell him so—that he was the best-looking, most attractive young man in four villages; he had had a good deal of experience, and he had known Araminta for two years. He knew that she was neither light nor wanton and he had known that her response to him was genuine. And blast it he had done her the high honour of mentioning marriage with the first breath he drew *afterwards*. What on earth had come over her? Words failed him; but then he had never been handy with words; he knew a better way. He reached out and took her by the shoulder, and the thin squareness of it under his hand spurred passion in him, though always before he had liked plump women, what he called a "tidy armful."

"Here," he said, pulling her towards him, "what are you talking about? Forget you? Why Minta, Saturday night you loved me right well. I took your maidenhead: and if I was to forget that you ain't likely to. Maybe you've been hearing summat not much to my credit . . . but I swear I worn't first with Agnes and she arst for all she got. Besides, I'm going to settle down. I'll make you a good husband, I promise you."

The lump in her throat was strangling her. She tried to speak, and failed; tried to tear herself away, and was dragged closer. He bent his head and began to kiss her. All the old treachery waked in her blood. She twisted her head free and tried to speak again. This time it was better.

"Jan, it you let me go I'll think about it again. There's a lot of things you don't know. I have to think about my family. I send home most of my money and they'd miss it. I got to do a lot of thinking before I can be sure. Just let me go now, there's a dear. I'm that late already. We'll talk about this another time."

"You could still earn money," he said, letting her go and standing back a little. "The Missus'd keep you on and be thankful. You could send what you made home just the same."

Oh, but that was generous! And he'd been frank too about Agnes. He really was set on it, no doubt about that. But how long could she work when the children started coming?

"I'll think it over," she said again. "But now I must go. That'll be as dark as a pit before I'm in."

"I'll walk back along with you."

"Go along and get your supper," she said lightly. "I don't mind the dark. Thanks all the same."

"Will I see you to-morrow?"

"I should think so. Or next day."

"I shall speak for the cottage." She let that pass. She couldn't argue any more to-night.

"Good night, Jan."

"Good night, sweetheart."

Speeding up the lane she knew what she must do. Leave this place where she had been so happy and go right away. Out of the reach of temptation.

Before she had even begun to worry how to break the news to Mrs. Pollard, an opening was made for her. Mrs. Pollard, alone in the kitchen, was standing up to knit, a thing she only did when she was what Araminta called "savage." As the girl entered she ceased the ferocious clicking of her needles, and the angry expression of her face cleared a little at the prospect of sharing her grievance.

"I'm not keeping that Cissie," she said. "Of all the awkward, clumsy good-for-nothing mawkins I've been bothered with, she is the worst." She put down the knitting—a long speckled stocking for Mr. Pollard to wear with his winter boots—and reached for the tea-caddy.

"We'll have a cuppa tea," she said companionably. "You're a silly thoughtless girl yourself, running off without your tea, Araminta."

"Whass Cissie done now?"

"Broke my best cream pitcher. All the cream for to-morrow's

churning is now on the dairy floor. At least she's clearing it up. I gave her a good box of the ears and told her she can go at Michaelmas."

She poured boiling water into the pot and stood it on the hob for a moment to draw. Araminta, deeply thoughtful, took two cups down from the dresser and set them into their saucers as though her life depended upon their meticulous symmetry. Mrs. Pollard rattled on:

"I shan't have another half-trained girl. They get into slummocky ways in their other places and then expect to be paid for *experience*. I'll get right a youngster, Araminta, and you can train her."

Now, if ever, it must be said.

"I shan't be here, ma'am."

"What?" Mrs. Pollard's pink face flushed to bright crimson. She could hardly believe her own ears. "What on earth are you talking about, Araminta? Of course you'll be staying. Weren't we talking about making quince jelly on All Hallowse'en, only the other day?"

"I gotta go home," said Araminta, whose brain had been pecking around in search of a good excuse and had—she believed—found an irrefutable argument. "I towd you my mother was in the family way again, didn't I? Well, now it seem she's took queer. I sat by Mrs. Thatcher Saturday night, and she towd me Mum hadn't been to Mrs. Whistler's to work all last week."

But, of course, if Mrs. Pollard knew anything about the secret life in the labourers' cottages, she would know that the threat of a new baby and the loss of a week's work, was no reason for recalling an elder daughter home; it was a reason for keeping her in a good place and sending a younger one out, if possible. But apparently Mrs. Pollard didn't know that. She said, with the innate good nature which made her occasional little flashes of temper so endearing, "Well, Araminta, I'm downright sorry to hear that. To tell you the truth I never had a girl I took to so well. I shall miss you a lot."

"And I shall miss you, ma'am," said Araminta, with complete sincerity. "This is the best place I've ever had; or likely to get either." Wasn't it hard, she thought, that she must leave a pleasant home and a kind mistress, just because she couldn't trust herself?

"There isn't another sister old enough to manage?" suggested Mrs. Pollard helpfully. "I was going to give you fifty shillings next year, Araminta. And I had thought about teaching you to read and write in the long evenings. You never know when that mightn't be handy to you."

So there was another blessing she was losing. She wavered a little. But immediately she knew that, even if she succeeded in discouraging Jan entirely, she couldn't bear seeing him in the yard, or going past the window, or meeting him in the lane. One day . . . sooner or later . . . she was bound to break out and make a fool of herself. Oh, she had been right to distrust feelings; nothing else in all her life had got her into a muddle like this.

"Betsy's only ten, and not quite bright at that."

Mrs. Pollard did a little thinking about babies; incidentally, reflecting with as much bitterness as her nature would sustain, how strange it was that she herself, who had longed for a baby and could have given one a good home, had never had even the promise of one, whereas this unknown Mrs. Glover should fill a cradle time and again. And on nine shillings a week, or less. Sometimes she wondered how on earth such people managed to bring up their children at all.

"I could keep the place for you," she said, at the end of her pondering. "Suppose I kept Cissie after all, and got a real good girl as well, and then you could come back next year and I'd sack Cissie. You'd like a better girl to work with, Araminta?"

Araminta's tough little heart was dangerously near softening. In another minute, if she wasn't careful, she'd be blurting out the whole story. But that wouldn't do. Mrs. Pollard would either take offence at being given notice for so silly a reason, or else, in her kind, muddle-headed way she'd start a lot of schemes for making a match of it. She was the nicest woman Araminta had ever known, but she wasn't to be trusted where what Araminta called "real sensible" matters were concerned. She'd had life too easy.

"Thass wholly kind of you, ma'am; but I wouldn't like you to make any arrangements counting on me. I might have to get a job where I could sleep at home for a bit. Anything might happen."

"Maybe you're right," said Mrs. Pollard, heavily. "But I am downright sorry, Araminta, that I am." She poured the last cup of tea out of the pot. "Here, take this in to that soft idiot and tell her to stop howling. Tell her she can stay on if she'll mend her ways."

Araminta, carrying the tea to the puffy-eyed Cissie in the dairy knew that it was not, despite the look of it, the fear of being left without a maid at all which had brought about this change of mind upon her mistress' part. That was just Mrs. Pollard's way. Besides, Uplands was known as a pleasant place, Mrs. Pollard could have her pick of twenty girls. But would she, Araminta, find it so easy to get another place?

Thursday and Friday passed uneventfully. A good deal of the two days Araminta spent in drying slices of windfall apples which could not be stored on account of their blemishes, and in making damson cheese. That was one thing she had liked about Uplands; it wasn't, like her last place, all dairy work, which she liked well enough in itself, but which became tedious day after day. She had chosen to be a dairymaid because butter-making was skilled work, and better paid than most things; but she could do almost anything in a kitchen and enjoyed displaying her prowess.

Saturday was Colchester market day, and Mr. Pollard, who had abstained from attending the market during the harvest weeks, went off in high good humour, knowing that this would be a great day, with all the farmers gathering to eat the *Red Lion* Ordinary, comparing crops and speculating about prices, cursing the government and encouraging one another to be obdurant about the winter wages. Jan, who had given the horse an extra grooming, polished the harness and dusted the gig, had a lucky moment for the request he was about to make.

"Poor owd Theo died this morning, sir," he said. "And I'd like to speak for his cottage if you hain't promised it elsewhere."

"You aiming to get hitched?" Mr. Pollard asked amiably, taking the reins.

Jan nodded.

"Do I know the lucky wench?"

"Thass Araminta, out of your dairy, sir."

"Well, I'll be damned. The Missus did say summat about her quitting, but I bet she didn't know the reason. That'll be a bit of news for to-night. Take the edge off her tongue in case I'm late."

"And will that be all right about Theo's cottage, sir?"

"Aye. Of course, my boy. Tell you what, I'll hev it whitewashed for ye. She's a tidy little creature and Theo was a dirty old varmint. Giddap Slicer!"

Jan watched the gig bowl away, conscious of his own good luck. His mother had already promised him a bed, a table, a couple of chairs and a rug. Unlike most widows with only sons, she was not in the least resentful of his leaving her. She had a tiny pension from the lady who had brought her from France as a personal maid, long ago; and she was getting old enough to feel that it was time a younger woman took on the job of getting Jan's breakfast in the dark winter mornings and having his supper on the table when he came home. Left alone, she could stay in bed until the day was aired; besides, she looked forward to seeing her grandchildren. So that was settled; and now he had the promise of the cottage, white-washed into the bargain; and it only remained for him to see Araminta and talk, or kiss her, into agreement. Three Sundays must be allowed for the asking of the banns; and inside a month they could be married. He forgot that he had often wondered at the alacrity with which other, simpler chaps put their heads into the noose.

All day he whistled about his work; and twice contrived errands which would take him past the dairy window. But he caught no sight of Araminta. So at the end of the day's work, confident because of his honourable intentions, he crossed the cobbles and knocked on the kitchen door. Mrs. Pollard answered it, and was pleased, without knowing it, because he took off his cap instead of plucking at it as the other men did; and because he gave her the smile which so often got him his own way with women.

"Could I hev a word with Minta, please ma'am?"

34

"Certainly," said Mrs. Pollard. "You can go into the dairy if you like; or shall I send her out?"

"I'd like her to step out if it's all the same to you, ma'am."

"Araminta, there's someone to see you," Mrs. Pollard shouted, and Araminta, seeing Jan's figure in the doorway, with the autumn dusk behind him and that eager expression on his face, knew that the bad moment had come. She closed the door carefully behind her.

"Owd Theo died this morning and Master promised me the cottage afore he went to market," Jan burst out. Araminta said nothing for a moment, she was anxious to put a little distance between them and the house. Then, trying to free herself from the long arm which Jan had placed round her waist, she said:

"Jan, I promised to think it over, and I hev. I can't marry you, not at Michaelmas nor at no other time."

"But thass what you said th' other night and then you promised to think it over. Why can't you, Minta?"

"Because of what I towd you then. My mother is going to hev another baby and I got to go home and see to things. I towd you I'd got to think about my family."

"You said," Jan pointed out with careful patience, "that you'd got to send 'em money and I towd you how you could still manage that."

"Yes, there's that too. But I've got to go home, Jan. I'm sorry. I towd the Missus and she saw there wasn't ought else I could do."

"Well, that *is* a facer," he said, and was silent for a few seconds, pulling her close and meditatively rubbing his cheek against the top of her head. Then he said, "Minta, when's she expecting?"

Araminta thought rapidly. Mrs. Thatcher had told her the news after she'd been home round about Lammas time. Two months gone she'd said.

"About February, I reckon. Might be a little before."

"Well then; thass a job soon over. We could get married at Easter. Master hev promised to whitewash the place, and I'll get the garden round. Right pretty that'd look with some daffodillys and stocks in the garden. I don't mind waiting for a good thing," he added magnanimously.

Even now, in her present distress of mind, the old spell was working. And she could see the little cottage, its white walls shining, its two windows sparkling, the garden a-blow with flowers and Jan coming home to a bright fire on a clean hearth. And she could run across the meadow and work in the dairy and maybe take in a wash or two as well. And there were couples who contrived somehow to have no children, or only two or three. Like that they could manage. Especially as there was a garden; nobody knew what a difference a garden made to a labouring man. It might be possible. And it would be lovely.

But no; she daren't risk it: she simply daren't risk it. Every other woman who got married hoped that things would be all right; they wouldn't do it if they knew what they were in for. And she did know. She'd had her own mother and her own home as an object lesson, and even if it broke her heart she wouldn't take the first step towards bringing a similar fate upon herself.

"I'm sorry," she said again. "But when I said not Michaelmas nor at no other time, that was what I meant. I've told you that, and I've given you a reason. Now will you let me go?"

He did then drop his arm, but as he did so he caught her wrist between his fingers and held it, almost cruelly.

"There's one thing you ain't told me," he said. "And thass that you've changed your mind since Saturday and you ain't fond of me arter all."

Every instinct save one urged her to protest, but she stood silent. He must think what he liked. She couldn't argue or hedge any more.

"For the last time, Minta, are you going to marry me, any time next year you like to say?"

"No, Jan."

He flung her hand back at her.

"Then you know what I think of you, Minta Glover. You're a loose, lying little trollop, and I wish I'd cut my tongue out before I mentioned marriage to you."

He swung round on his heel and began to walk away.

They had been so much engrossed in their own affairs that they had not noticed Mr. Pollard's arrival in his gig. But he had seen them standing together, and had seen Jan leave Araminta hastily. He was a little tipsy, for he had been mixing his drinks considerably, and as Jan's first few angry strides brought him level with the gig, he climbed down, calling out heartily, "Waiting to put the horse up and doing a bit of courting at the same time, eh? Thass the way, my boy, thass the way! Mix your business with pleasure. Nothing like it."

Not noticing the man's silence, he moved fumble-footedly into the house, found Mrs. Pollard, who had heard the gig, dishing up supper, and kissed her heartily on both cheeks, at the same time pressing into her hands the little presents he had brought her to mark the first market day after harvest. Then, dropping into his chair and beginning to unfasten his boots, he said, "Heard the news?" He was afraid, from finding Araminta and Jan together in the yard, that the matter was already made public, and was pleased to see that her face was expressive rather of curiosity than of knowledge.

"No. What news? Old Theo's dead, but you're not meaning that, are you?"

"No, no. I mean the news about Minta and young Honeywood. Fixing to get married and take the owd chap's cottage."

"What rubbish!" Mrs. Pollard exclaimed sharply. "Why, I told you she'd given me notice; but you were so sunk in your old paper you didn't listen. She's going home to look after her mother. In the family way *again!*"

"No, you musta got it wrong, Nellie. Honeywood asked about the cottage this morning and said they was fixed to get married. And there they was just now in the yard, cuddled up together till they heard the gig. Arst her if you don't believe your own husband." He laughed, reflecting that, between the gifts and the bit of news no word had been said about his being so late or smelling so strongly of liquor. He pulled his chair to the table and started his meal.

"I *will* ask her," said Mrs. Pollard dryly. "And I'll ask her what she meant by telling me all that yarn about her mother. How on earth did she think she could marry Jan Honeywood and have me not know. She must have taken leave of her senses. ARAMINTA!"

Araminta was standing with her back to the dairy door. She had shot into that place of refuge, partly because it was nearest and partly because Cissie was in the bedroom putting her hair in curlers for Sunday. And never before had Araminta been in such need of peace and privacy. She was shaking all over as though smitten with an ague and the tears which she could not shed were hurting her throat and her chest so terribly that she had to press both her hands to the pain. It was really over now; she would never see Jan again; and he would think evilly of her every time he remembered her. And she loved him, loved him, loved him. She knew now that she had loved him since the first time she saw him; it was love that had made her not want him to marry Agnes . . . and now, as like as not, he'd go off and pick just such another; and they'd live in Theo's little white cottage. . . . It was unbearable. She'd done it herself, but it was unbearable all the same. And all because she didn't want to go hungry or see her children go hungry. . . . It wasn't fair. There was no justice in the world.

She heard Mrs. Pollard's rousing call, and did her best to gain some control of herself. Before she had done so Mrs. Pollard called again. Keeping her arms close to her sides and trying to hide the shudders which vibrated down her body and along her limbs, she walked into the kitchen. Oh, so Master was back and Missus was cross because she'd had to dish his supper.

"Yes, ma'am," she said meekly.

"Now," said Mrs. Pollard, "perhaps you'll be good enough to tell me what's all this I hear about you going to marry Jan Honeywood and me all the time thinking you're going home to a sick mother, Araminta."

"I ain't going to marry him. I am going home," Araminta said in a wooden voice.

"There you are," said Mrs. Pollard, wheeling upon her husband.

"You've been drinking, and don't know what you're saying. Or is this your idea of a joke?"

The mention of drinking ruffled Mr. Pollard's temper. He said quite sharply, "I ain't drunk, and I ain't joking. First thing Honeywood said to me this morning was could he hev Theo's cottage. I arst him if he was aiming to get hitched and he said yes. I arst him if I knew the female, and he said it was Minta outa the dairy there. If that ain't plain talking I never heard none." He loaded his fork and filled his mouth, looking from one woman to another as he did so, as though to convey that from now on he was out of the discussion and they could wrestle it out between them.

"Well?" said Mrs. Pollard stonily.

Araminta's face took on a hunted expression. If only she could speak out and explain. It would have been quite easy to do so to the Master, he'd just say, "Thass right, Minta, you take your time. Pretty little gal like you don't want to go rushing inta anything in a hurry." But there was a daft streak in Mrs. Pollard; Araminta had watched it in action many times. She'd start saying what an upstanding chap Jan was; and what a pretty little cottage they could have; and there was an old rug in the attic and enough odds and ends of china at the back of the stairs cupboard to start up two people and Araminta could have them and welcome. That was the kind of thing nice women always said if there was a prospect of a wedding; and that was just the kind of thing Araminta didn't want to hear to-night. It would take so little to weaken her finally and fatally. So she said again, stubbornly:

"I ain't going to marry him."

"Then you'd best let him know," said Mr. Pollard mildly, tempted back into the argument because Nellie looked so savage and Minta seemed so utterly unlike herself. He'd never seen a little wench look so distressed. "I mean to say, if Jan don't want the cottage, there's plenty that do. Thass about the soundest little place on the farm." (Yes, and it was to have daffodillies and sweet-scented stocks in the garden, and the windows would wink in the sunset. . . .)

"I . . ." she said, struggling again with the pain in her throat,

"I . . ." She wanted to say that she had just told him, but the words would not come.

"So you're deceiving him too," said Mrs. Pollard, unkindly, because secretly she was cut to the quick that Araminta had not taken her into her confidence. After the way she'd been kind to her, too.

The strain was too much; either Araminta's fortitude or her patience must snap. It had come to the point where she'd either break down and make a regular fool of herself or fly out in self-defence. And both fortitude and patience had been trained and tempered in the same hard school of poverty and servitude. There was a brief struggle. Then she said hotly, "I ain't deceived nobody. I give you notice, as was your right ma'am. And I towd Jan not ten minutes ago that I wasn't going to marry him. So you've both had your dues and I reckon the rest of it is my business and nobody else's."

She felt better. Anger acted on her festering self-pity like a hot poultice.

Mrs. Pollard also rushed into anger as a palliative for all her thwarted affection.

"So that's how you answer me, do you?" she demanded. "That's what I get for taking an interest in your affairs and offering to keep a job open for you. A nice ungrateful little baggage you've turned out for all your mealy-mouthed ways."

She had used the one adjective which Araminta could not bear.

"I don't know what you're raging about," she said rudely. "I bin a good servant to you."

"A good servant that I shall be thankful to lose at Michaelmas," snapped Mrs. Pollard.

"I wish I could go this minnit."

"Now, now," said Mr. Pollard in the voice he sometimes used to a restive horse. Neither woman heeded him.

"You can. That's just what you can do. Go to-night. Make your bundle and I'll get your money. Not that you're entitled to a penny, breaking your time in a temper."

She flounced out of the kitchen; and it was Mr. Pollard who saw the sick, earthy pallor which poured into Araminta's face as sanity poured back into her mind. Her money; her precious, precious money. Ten shillings; a whole quarter's wages. Suppose Mrs. Pollard changed her mind, as she was so dreadfully apt to do, and withheld it after all. The thought of going home without her money turned her bowels to water and her knees to wool. What in the name of God had happened to her lately? First she lost her senses and gave up her place and now she'd lost her temper and risked her money. A wild demented look came into her face.

If he hadn't been quite certain that in a moment Nellie would come rushing back, almost in tears, demanding apologies from Araminta, but actually making them herself, Mr. Pollard would have said a word of comfort to the girl. As it was, avoiding her eyes, he went stolidly on with his supper. Nellie was so apt to go off half-cocked, he thought to himself. As for him, he couldn't see that the girl had done anything so dreadful—except, of course, to speak so rudely at the end. And even that was under provocation. Araminta turned and dragged herself upstairs.

Mrs. Pollard was back in the kitchen first. By that time she had lashed herself into real fury through the simple human need for self-justification, and if anyone at that moment had asked for Araminta's character they would have heard that she was deceitful, insolent, ungrateful, wanton, playing fast and loose with the men and making a laughing-stock of her mistress.

"I'm going to give her eight shillings, Mr. Pollard. Not a penny more. Why should I? She isn't entitled to anything, not staying to the end of the quarter."

"She've worked hard," said Mr. Pollard, surprised and concerned to see that for once Nellie's temper had lasted for five whole minutes. "If you mean to let her go, give her the lot. You'll be sorry in the morning."

"So will she, I should hope."

Araminta stepped off the back stairs and closed the door behind her. She had her bundle—a very small one, for she had felt forced to leave Mrs. Pollard's made-over dress spread out on the bed, a mute reproach—tied up in an old checked handkerchief. The new shoes, linked by their laces, hung over her arm and her old faded shawl covered her head and shoulders.

Like Mr. Pollard, she had remembered the sudden waxing and waning of her mistress' temper, and had known a half-hope that, with a sufficiently humble apology the thing might be patched up. Not that she wanted to stay here a moment longer, for every moment would be a torment, inevitably, with Jan so near; she had said no more than the truth when she said that she wished she could leave at once. But she did want her money.

However, Mrs. Pollard looked, if anything, angrier than ever, as, with a defiant glance at her husband, she pushed eight shillings across the table.

"There you are, and it's more than you deserve after such insolence!"

No denying the truth of that. She was only withholding a fifth of the money and she might have kept it all.

Araminta took the money in her hand and said, "Good-bye, ma'am; good-bye, sir." She wanted to add—you've been very kind to me, and I hate to leave like this. But she knew that the soft words would choke her.

"Wait a bit," said Mr. Pollard. His face set in a manner which showed that he was thinking that there were times when a man should be master in his own house. And nobody had ever polished his boots as Araminta had done. With some difficulty, for he was seated, and thick-thighed, and his market breeches were well-fitting, he pushed his big hand into his pocket. After a fumble and a tussle he brought out two half-crowns, fitted together to look like one, and pressed them into her hand amongst the other silver.

"There you are. I was going to whitewash the cottage and mend the fence."

The two coins changed everything. Colour came back into Araminta's face, cheer and confidence into her heart. Five shillings. So she had her quarter's money, and more; and she had a fortnight in which to look for a job, and she wouldn't have the torment of seeing Jan go past the window or across the yard. She smiled at her master and her dimples flashed, surprisingly seductive.

"Oh, thank you, sir. Thank you, indeed."

A real little hussy into the bargain, thought Mrs. Pollard, who had often sunned herself in that very smile. A good thing that she was going.

Araminta closed the door softly behind her; and in recognition of her good fortune Mrs. Pollard sat down by the table and burst into tears.

PART TWO

Araminta is given her daily bread

I F there had been the slightest real doubt in her mind as to the wisdom of her decision, it would have been dispelled before she had been home for a quarter of an hour.

It had been dusk when Jan knocked on the kitchen door; dark when she had closed it behind her. There were ten miles between Uplands and Minsham Green, and when she arrived at the cottage— one of a row, so dilapidated that they seemed to stand only by leaning against one another—it was long past bedtime. Beating upon the door with the heel of her shoe brought no answer, and she had flung several handsful of grit and small stones at the tiny upper window before it opened and a sleepy, timid voice which she recognized as her mother's, asked through the one pane which would open, who was there and what they wanted.

"It's Araminta, Mum."

"Araminta!" said Mary Glover in a stunned voice. "Why, what are you doing here at this time a'night."

"Let me in and I'll tell you."

There was a short pause, and then the bolt of the door screeched and the door opened. Mrs. Glover held a farthing dip in her hand, and she lifted it to Araminta's face and looked at her earnestly as soon as she had crossed the threshold.

"Whass the matter?" she whispered.

"Nothing. I got the chance of a bit of a holiday and come right away."

The cottage was peculiarly planned. Just inside the front door was a slip of passage, too small to take a bed, too small to be furnished at all. At its end rose the steep, ladder-like stair which led to the single upper room. Almost opposite the front door was another which opened into the only room on the ground floor, and this, where the family must wash and cook and eat and sit was, by the width of the passage, smaller than the one above. Often Mrs. Glover had said that she wished it had been the other way round, because you didn't move about much when you were asleep.

It was five years since Araminta had slept under the sagging thatched roof of her home, and eighteen months since she had been home at all; but instantly she recognized the scent of it; sad and sour, a mingling of dampness and dirt; the accumulated effluvia of old clothes and unwashed bodies, of smoky fires kept going by any fuel that came handy, of potatoes sticking to the bottom of the thin saucepan as they boiled. Yet it was, in its way, a clean cottage, for Mrs. Glover was a good worker, and her family better behaved than most. There were some on the Green from which ordinary people, even upon charity visits, were forced to back away, holding their handkerchiefs to their noses.

In the living-room the fire was out, and it was stuffily chilly. Araminta laid her bundle and her shoes on the table and sat down on a broken-backed chair. She was exhausted and extremely hungry. She and Cissie would ordinarily have taken their supper as soon as the Master and Mistress had finished, and she had, of course, missed the meal. Mrs. Glover put the dip beside the shoes and leaned against the edge of the table, looking at her daughter. In the dim, undiscriminating light their relationship was very obvious. Araminta was exactly what her mother had been at eighteen; Mary Glover was exactly what Araminta would be at forty-two unless life treated her more kindly. They had the same square thin build of body, the same high cheekbones and long firm mouths, the same delicate brows and wide foreheads. But Mary Glover looked like an old woman; her face was grey and sunken, her hair scanty and almost white, her mouth had fallen in upon the few remaining stumps of teeth, and her figure was so distorted by continuous pregnancies that it was difficult to tell with certainty whether she were carrying a child or not. But to-night, looking at Araminta, there was about her ruined face, despite its anxiety, a kind, maternal look, and when she voiced her most urgent fear, "Minta, are you in any sorta trouble?" Araminta knew that, even had she been forced to confess the worst possible thing, she could have counted upon her mother's help and support in the face of shame and gossip and anything her father might say. It was with a great soaring of the heart that she heard herself saying:

"No, Mum. I've left Uplands but not on account of trouble. Look, I got my money and three shillings for a present."

Mary Glover looked at the silver which Araminta—who had carried it clenched in her hand through all that ten miles over rough roads and field-paths—laid on the table. Her face quivered.

"Minta, thass a real answer to prayer. Ther ain't a bit of food in the house, and when Betsy went to Clark's for taters to-night he said no more credit till we'd paid his bill. Jackie went and borrered the heel of a loaf from Mrs. Gable, and him and the little 'uns et it. But your dad went to bed hungry. And now, bless you, my gal, I ain't got a bite to offer you and you walking all that way, I *am* sorry."

"Thass all right," Araminta lied stoutly. "I had my supper before I left. And to-morrer I'll knock up Clark, Sunday or no Sunday, and give him my money and a piece of my mind as well."

"You marnt rile him, Minta. There ain't no other shop handy."

"I shan't rile him. But I'll tell him I'm surprised at him. We're dealt with him all my time and always paid him, haven't we?"

Mrs. Glover nodded; but she added, "Times are getting worse, Minta, and everybody's getting close. You see your dad put a fork in his foot a fortnight back and been laid up since. And Mr. Whistler never give him a penny for the time he was sick. Now in the old days the old man would have paid him and sent him over summat tasty to hearten him into the bargain. Thass what I mean. Folks are getting closer and closer."

"Mrs. Thatcher didn't tell me nothing about Dad being sick."

"I towd her not to. No sense in fretting you with what you couldn't help. But you see that was how we got behind with

Clark's money. There worn't no call for him to be so mean, though. I'd paid him all but four shillings."

They were both silent for a few seconds; both thinking, in their different ways, Mary with resignation, Araminta with fury, of the perilously narrow margin which divided them, and hundreds of others like them, from debt and genuine belly-empty hunger. The older woman changed the subject. She said, a little diffidently, for after all, who was she to question the actions of this good, good daughter of hers?

"Minta, Mrs. Thatcher said you was fixed to stay on along of the Pollard's. She said she reckoned you knew when you was well off."

"So I do," said Araminta. "But you can stay *too* long in a place. I'm going to get fifty shillings where I go next."

"You got a place in mind, Minta?"

"One or two," Araminta lied again, cheerfully. No sense in worrying poor old Mum before you need.

"That go to my heart Minta, not to hev a cup of tea for you," said Mary Glover, changing the subject again.

"We'll hev one in the morning. I'll hev that owd Clark up that early he'll think the Militia is after him. We'd best get off to bed. now."

"You'll hev to push in between Betsy and Sarann, Minta." It went through Mrs. Glover's mind that she ought to have something better to offer this good, good daughter, than a third share of a straw-stuffed palliasse heaped with rags and sacking; but it went through almost painlessly; she was still alive and still sane because years and years ago she learnt the way of resignation.

"Thass a pity. I'm used to a four-poster," Araminta said with a smile that lifted the corner of her mouth.

"You oughta hev one if anybody did," said her mother, carefully scooping up the silver and placing it in a little pill-box which stood on the cluttered shelf over the hearth.

The stairs opened direct into the bedchamber where, sunk in slumber, the greatest solace of the poor, lay the rest of Araminta's family. On one side of the room was a feather mattress, all that remained of the bed which Mary Glover's mistress had given her, with her best wishes, for a wedding present. The rest of it had been sold for four shillings during a hard winter long ago. Tom Glover lay asleep in the middle of it, looking pathetically defenceless, with his mouth open and his sparse grey beard and moustache moving with each breath. He was a thin, shrivelled little man, though Mary remembered him as handsome enough, and even now his face with its weather-beaten tan had a spurious look of health which made him seem younger than his wife. Araminta respected her father; he was a good workman and never sought to find solace for his woes in the alehouse, and, although surly and glum in the home, he was an unusually kind parent. Since she had reached the point of thinking about things she had felt a certain pity for him, too; but there was no secret bond of understanding between them as there was between her and her mother.

Between Tom Glover and the greyish-green wall from which all the whitewash had long been worn away by friction and by dampness, Tommy the three-year-old, slept with his thumb in his mouth. He had been a chubby little boy when she was home last, not long enough weaned to have felt the pinch of hunger much; but a glance told her now that he was conforming to the Glover pattern, a thin pale child with neat features and bright brown hair. The third place in this bed was Mary's; and the corner of the hastily thrown-back cotton quilt showed where she had been sleeping when the last clod had called her back to consciousness.

In the middle of the room, Jackie, who was twelve years old and already had three years' service in the Whistler cowsheds to his credit, slept peacefully and with apparent ease upon an old piece of matting, folded into four thicknesses. Mrs. Glover had been lucky over that matting. It had lain in the Whistler kitchen until one day, when Mrs. Whistler, in a hurry, caught her foot in one of its many worn places and lost her balance. She had lost her temper, too, and said that she would have a new floor-covering if it took a month's egg money to pay for it; as for the old Mrs. Glover could have it if it was of any use to her. Jackie was covered by an old horse-rug and a sack, which should both of them have been reposing in Mr.

Whistler's barn; and the farmer, who regarded Jackie Glover as an honest little boy, if a bit stupid, would have been hurt and angry had he known that they had been smuggled home for bedcovers. Araminta extended to Jackie the respect she felt for her father; he was a good steady little boy at his work; but he was getting to be more like his parent every day, monosyllabic to the point of surliness, an industrious automaton.

In the remaining portion of the room lay a straw-stuffed palliasse, covered partly by a checked shawl, partly by a worn black cloak which in really cold weather, Mary Glover wore out of doors. Here slept Betsy, eight years old, and the beauty of the family. In her the Glover pallor had a luminous, pearly quality, its thinness an almost ethereal fragility. People not ordinarily generous would give her apples and sweets; once a lady who was staying at the Hall had called her a little angel and bought her a pair of woolly-lined boots; and she could have been useful in little matters like borrowing things or getting another shillingsworth of credit, if only she had been bright. But she wasn't: she was vague and forgetful, careless and clumsy, and there was nothing behind that pretty face, Araminta had learned long ago, nothing that you could talk to and get hold of and make to see sense. Most families had a simple member, and Araminta supposed that the Glovers were lucky to have got off with only one. Sarann, aged six, quite a normal child, if a bit undersized, occupied the other half of this bed.

"You'll hev to push one of 'em a bit into the middle," Mary Glover whispered. But Araminta only drew her shawl closer about her and found a place for her head to lie. She was too tired to be critical and too tired to think; she was asleep almost as soon as she lay down.

Only Mrs. Glover, after she had quenched the little friendly flame of the dip between her wetted thumb and finger, lay awake for a while, thinking. She thought how strange it was that Araminta should have come home on this, the first Saturday night in her memory when there was no food in the house. She thought about the thirteen shillings. She thought how queer it was to have all her children sleeping in the one room again; and then her mind dwelt for a few fleeting seconds on her dead children. She thought of them without longing, for if anything, she was glad that they had died young and not added to the almost intolerable burden; yet they had all been pretty, taking little things, and, in a way, dear to her. She still remembered their names, and sometimes when she had occasion to go past the churchyard she slackened her step and looked over the wall. From that she went on to think about this new, this utterly unwanted child that was coming. Tommy was three, and she had really thought he was the last. For a year he had been able to walk and could be left even in simple Betsy's care, which meant that Mrs. Glover was free to earn a shilling or two where she could. She worked fairly regularly at Mrs. Whistler's, and did occasional jobs in other houses. At the proper seasons she had gone stone-picking, hay-tossing, shocking corn and gleaning. It had made a difference. And now she was fixed again; already feeling ill and tired and heavy and desperately, perpetually hungry. She must face the time when she would be house-bound; for she was too good a mother to leave a new baby to Betsy. It was a very sorry future.

She felt miserable and hungry, and far from sleep. And then she thought about Araminta. She'd laid down every penny of her money; she'd said with such confidence that she'd get fifty shillings a year in her next place. What a comfort the girl was. The thought eased her, and presently she slept.

On Sunday there was fourpennyworth of meat in the potato stew, a gallon loaf on the table, and a threepenny pinch of cheap tea done up in a screw of paper. Betsy and Sarann looked with great eyes at the wonderful sister who was always being held up to them as an example. . . . "When Minta were your age . . ."; little Tommy added her name to his slowly-growing vocabulary. Tom Glover gave no sign of the wound which his pride had received at having failed to provide his family with a Sunday dinner, or of his half-resentful gratitude to Araminta for having done so. On the whole it was a happy day.

On Monday Araminta, after a breakfast of bread and tea, went across the Green to see Mrs. Whistler. She was not particularly anxious to work for that lady whom she knew from experience to be mean in the extreme and more than a bit of a bully. But Mrs. Whistler was one of an immense and thriving family, with ramifications all over the district. She would most likely know of someone, a brother or a sister or a cousin or an aunt, or even some more distant relative who wanted, or in turn knew someone who wanted a good dairymaid.

And Mrs. Whistler, with hardly a second's hesitation, announced that she did know of the very place for Araminta. The widow of her sister's second cousin by marriage, a Mrs. Stancy, of Abbey Farm, Summerfield, had asked her at Baildon Market, only the week before last, if she knew of a good experienced girl, not afraid of work, who would be free at Michaelmas.

"Mind you, Araminta Glover," said Mrs. Whistler, wagging her head solemnly, "that'll be a very different place from any you've bin used to. I tell you that for the start. You'll hev to mind your p's and q's if you're took on *there*. Very particular is my sister's second cousin by marriage, Caroline Stancy. So don't say I didn't warn you. She supply goods to all the quality for miles around, and I hear that folks'll go traipsing over to Summerfield just to look at her dairy and her cows. Very fancy they are. And I should reckon her gals is fancy too. She pay four pound a year. Thass scandalous to my mind. Two pound ten is as much as any gal on earth is worth. But seemingly money's no object to her where her dairy is concerned, and it do seem as though she knew her business." She ran on in this strain for several minutes; she was a very garrulous woman and could repeat herself endlessly. Finally she studied Araminta with her head on one side.

"You've grown a lot. I never reckoned you'd make much of a woman, to tell you the truth. But I should think you'd suit Mrs. Stancy nicely. That is if you can get into your head that thass a different sort of place. Mind you, I never seen it, and maybe thass all just tales. But I hear that most things is done there quite different."

Araminta kept silence, but she wondered in what way the milking of a cow and the churning of butter could be so very different. But even if it were, she would willingly chance her hand at it. Four pounds a year! Incredible wages for a dairymaid. And if other girls could be worth it, so could she. She looked back with justifiable pride on her own steady and rapid rise in the world of labour. Less than eight years ago she had been the lowest and most-put-upon little scullery maid . . . and she was head girl at Uplands before she left.

"Well," said Mrs. Whistler, "I'll send a message about you and let you know what Mrs. Stancy says." Privately she was pleased to be able to recommend what she was sure was a good girl to her remote and well-to-do relative; for, like most people, she enjoyed doing a favour to a social superior, especially when she could do it for nothing.

That settled, she passed on to another topic.

"Is your mum coming to work to-day?"

"Yes. She was having a bit of turn with the cramp just now, but she said to tell you she'd be here . . . unless ma'am you'd have me instead."

Mrs. Whistler knew a bargain when she saw one, but she must know all about it before she committed herself.

"Why . . . what're you up to, Araminta? I reckoned you'd just come home for Sunday and was going back right now."

"I got a bit of a holiday."

"A holiday! Well, what is the world coming to, pray? I never heard of such a thing! Well, in that case, surely you can come. To tell you the truth—and that wouldn't take a blind man long to see it, either—your mum ain't what she was. These last weeks she bin so slow that really I only keep her on outa kindness. What in the world did she think she was doing, having another baby at her time of life? Well, you might as well start right in. There's a tub of clothes waiting."

"I'll just run back and tell mum, then. She'll be glad of the rest."

"I see your dad in the yard just now. He's back then. About time, too."

She did not ask after the injured foot, or even wonder how the big family had managed to support itself for a fortnight on Jackie's two shillings a week. Araminta fairly hated her—but she had promised to name her for one of the best jobs in the world. The tub of dirty linen, when Araminta had finished with it, was snowy white and creaseless. Mrs. Whistler proceeded to find other work for these busy and capable hands, and Araminta's "holiday" passed in a whirl of curtain-washing, carpet-beating, floor-scrubbing, brass-polishing and the remaking of two feather beds. It was hard work, and she missed the good farmhouse food; she missed even more the cheerful company of silly Cissie and Mrs. Pollard; but she was pleasantly conscious that the extra jobs done now would be so much relief to her mother in the future and that the few days' partial rest had done the poor creature good. Before the end of the week she was able to report that she had been taken on at the Abbey Farm and would in future be the mistress of four pounds a year.

She deliberately saved the news until the best moment of the day, after she had finished work and was home, a little ahead of Jackie and Dad, and had made a cup of tea which she and her mother drank with almost ritual joy.

"I never heard tell of a dairymaid getting that much," said Mary Glover. "You sure you heard aright, Minta? Well, thass wonderful, surely. Three pounds a year was reckoned the top price for a best woman in my day, and that was afore wages fell so cruel. You're right a lucky girl."

"That on't make much difference to me," Araminta with a frankness which had no intention to give offence. "I reckon I can manage on ten shillings shoe money the same as I always have."

Mrs. Glover looked at her bright, determined little face and realized that it had grown thinner in these last few days. It did seem hard. She thought of all the ribbons and the lengths of bright gingham and the white cotton stockings that a girl could buy for four pounds a year.

"I'm sorry you're got this family on your back, Minta. That ain't right. You should ought to hev your money like the rest of 'em do. Get pretty things and make the most of yourself. A girl is only young once."

Araminta looked up from the little brown teapot, and with the cheerful mockery which she used so often to combat the melancholy which was ingrained into Mary's soul as the dirt was ingrained in her hands, said:

"If you're thinking I couldn't catch a husband in this old dress, you're wrong. I had an offer."

She shouldn't have said that: not even in fun; not even to cheer Mum and make her take pleasure in her tea. It was a mistake to think about that offer of a white cottage with flowers in the garden, much more a mistake to mention it. But having started she must go on. For her mother was looking at her with sharp interest which lifted the sagging lines of her face.

"Did you, Minta? You never towd me."

"Well, there worn't a lot to tell. A chap arst me . . . wanted to put up the banns so we could marry at Michaelmas. But I said no."

"Why? Wasn't he a good chap?"

"Oh yes, he was all right. But I reckon marrying ain't much in my line."

She gave Mary her lopsided smile and carefully poured out two cups of pale brown liquid, adding a few grains of sugar and a dribble of blue skim milk to each cup. It wasn't tea as she liked it, but it was hot and refreshing.

"I shouldn't like to think of you not getting married at all," Mary Glover said. Araminta longed to ask: Why? What's marriage done for you except make you an old woman before your time? To any other woman she would have rapped out the words, but not to her mother. Nor could she say, here and now, that she didn't intend to marry a labouring man. Oddly enough, Mary said that.

"I only hope that when you do, Minta, he on't be a labouring chap."

"I'll see to that," Araminta said dryly; it was permissible to say it now that it had been said. At the same time she added perversely, "All the same, somebody's got to marry the poor sods. They got feelings the same as anybody else. Though you'd think they hadn't to hear people talk." She thought of how Mrs. Whistler had said, "Time too," instead of saying, "Is his foot better?" The thoughts

54

which had seared her mind ever since she had been old enough to look about her at the world in which she lived and worked, worked like yeast in her mind. She had never voiced one of them. The girls with whom she worked had been too silly to understand and the subject was not one which could be mentioned to an employer, however indulgent. And she knew, as soon as she began putting her thoughts into words now, that she was being silly herself: but she had started thinking about Jan again and it was a relief to speak bitterly—even to her mother—about the state of affairs which had, when it came to the root of the matter, been responsible for the breaking of her heart.

"You'd think labourers was dirt instead of being the most important folks there is," she said, almost violently. "Thass what I often think when I see Mrs. Whistler's piano in the parlour and Dora Whistler's press full of dresses."

"Whass that got to with it?" asked Mrs. Glover, whose mind, never given to abstract thought, was now further lulled by the pleasant cup of tea and the pleasure of Araminta's company.

"Well, thass like this. Look at Minsham. There's Squire up at Mortiboys with more money than he can think what to do with, so he talk about pulling down a good house and building a fancy new one. Where do his money come from? Everybody know where. From his land, and from what the Whistlers and the Stanfords and the Finches and the rest of 'em pay for rent. And where do they get their rent and the money for shiny gigs and nice horses and pianners and silk gowns for Sunday? Out of the fields, don't they? And who work the fields? The labouring chaps that they grutch a extra shilling to, the labouring chaps what can't get married." Carried away by eloquence utterly foreign to her, eloquence which, if her mother had but known it, had its roots in the memory of a moonlight September evening, Araminta drew a thick sharp breath and rushed on. "Who milk this cow?" She shook the little broken jug fiercely. "Who feed this cow and muck her out and sit up time she calve? Jackie do. But do he get the cream she give and the butter? No, he don't. He get a little skim now and then because the Whistlers is good Christian people that'll get grut

55

shiny crowns in Heaven for giving us what their pigs is too full to want. And all the time, if the labouring chaps, if Jackie and Dad and the rest of 'em could all stop work for one week, that'd be a different story. Where'd their fields and their cows be then?"

There was certainly nothing new in the situation thus summed up for Mrs. Glover's shocked ears to hear. She had lived with it all her life, but she had never given it a thought. And now she was frightened.

"Don't you go saying things like that outa this house, Minta. Mrs. Whistler'd never give us another drop did she hear what you been saying. And likely as not we'd all get the sack."

"Yes," said Araminta savagely, "because there'd be another ploughman and cowboy and odd woman crazy mad to hev the work and live in this cottage. There's too many of us, thass all thass the matter with us. We're like poppies. If there wasn't so many the quality'd hev 'em planted in gardens; and if everybody was like me and wouldn't marry labouring chaps and make a lot of little labourers as fast as they could manage, they'd give a good cow-boy why, maybe, a pound a week."

She snatched up her cooling cup and drained it without taking her lips from its edge.

Mrs. Glover, who had been staring at her daughter as though she were some denizen from another world, gathered her wits, which had been quite shattered by this revolutionary aspect of the question of supply and demand and proffered the eternal feminine excuse.

"Thass all very well, Minta. That sound sense I'm bound to say. But time you find the proper chap you'll alter your mind, and then the little 'uns come whether you want 'em or not."

Araminta said slowly, "Don't I know it? Coming away from Uplands was like tearing my heart outa my body. I shall never feel the same again. Why, last time he spoke to me he said about daffodils in the garden. And he get what Dad do, nine shillings a week, time I can get bed and board and four pound a year."

"We ain't starved yet," said Mrs. Glover bravely.

"Taters," said Araminta with succinct brutality, "*is* starving to my mind. Let's say no more about it, Mum. Pass your cup."

After that conversation Araminta was conscious of a slight discomfort in her mother's presence. She wished she had not confessed her feeling for Jan; she wished she had not spoken about the folly of making little labourers; and she was sorry that she had decried the useful, ubiquitous potato upon which Mrs. Glover's family so largely subsisted. All things considered, it was with a feeling of relief and expectancy that she set out at six o'clock on the morning of Michaelmas Day to walk to Summerfield in search of Mrs. Stancy and Abbey Farm and a new life.

Mrs. Whistler had given her lengthy and slightly conflicting directions as to the way, but as soon as Araminta had left the mist-hung Lower Road and gained the main turnpike to Baildon, there was no lack of travellers from whom to inquire the next turning. It was Michaelmas Day and the roads were busy, for during this twenty-four hour space a vast, quiet migration took place throughout the length and breadth of the country. Big farm wagons piled high with household goods, herds of animals being driven, little carts pushed or pulled by their owners, maids and men with all their goods in a bundle, craftsmen bearing the tools of their trade passed or followed one another along the main road. Fortunately the very first person of whom Araminta asked direction had left Summerfield the night before and spent the hours of darkness in a hedge. He explained, with much arm-waving and pointing of the finger, how Araminta could save herself three miles.

"That'll make it but twelve from here to Summerfield Church. Where're you bound for?"

"Abbey Farm."

"Then that'll be a good bit more. Past the church you go and on the left a little way on you'll see two stone posts either side a lane like. Thass your way. I ain't never been there, but I reckon 'tis about another mile."

He had directed her well, and soon after nine o'clock Araminta reached the stone posts, high massive pillars with some weather-worn carving upon their tops. Between them, curving into the distance was a narrow lane, grassy, but worn into three tracks which bore evidence to a considerable amount of wheeled, horse-drawn traffic. For some distance the land on either side was marshy and the lane was almost like a long bridge spanning the damp soggy waste. But about half-way along there was a genuine bridge with two arches made of stone like the pillars at the lane's mouth, and, like them, carved in places with undecipherable figures. After that the lane rose gradually and was hedged on either side by neat low hedges and the marshland gave way to rich green pastures, still unwithered despite the sun of a long hot summer.

By this time the sun had struggled through the mist and was shining warmly, and the sight of a red brick wall a little way along the lane made Araminta remove her red shawl from her head and wrap it tidily round her bundle after wiping her face and hands on the corner of it. She stroked the pleats of her dress—and brushed the dust from her shoes with a tuft of grass. There, now she looked tidy; and she tried to banish a slight nervousness by remembering occasions when Mrs. Pollard had praised her work.

The wall stood at right angles to the lane and would have appeared to end it had not the tracks of wheels and horse hoofs turned off to the left and continued close to the wall itself. Directly facing the lane was a great gateway, with more stone pillars and tall gates of worked iron. Araminta paused for a moment and peered through, catching a hasty glimpse of a big house of timber and red brick, with gables and a terrace and great windows made up of countless little leaded panes. Between the gates and the house stretched a great garden. There were no flowers, only grass and yew trees planted in a formal pattern, and some stone statues and a fountain with a kneeling boy petrified in the action of pouring water over his shoulders. It was not, at first glance, a farmhouse garden, but even her momentary sight of it showed Araminta how ruthlessly its beauty had been utilized. There were hen coops dotted about on the lawn which had been roughly scythed, probably for hay. The stone figures were broken and green with moss. The yews were overgrown and no water poured into the stretched hands of the kneeling boy.

Araminta passed on, not knowing that she had been regarding

the loved and treasured country retreat of the last sad Abbot of Summerfield, who, when the storm-clouds of the Dissolution were threatening had passively awaited their breaking and taken solace from walking in the ecclesiastical shade of his yew trees and from the frozen beauty of the boy's ablutions.

The track turned again, following the rectangle of the red wall, and after a moment's walk ended in another gateway, and ordinary wide farmyard gate giving upon a square yard.

There was nothing homely or reassuring about it, however, and as she moved forward, glancing from left to right, Araminta absorbed the first confirmative evidence of her new employer's "particularness."

The whole yard was as neat as a parlour. The ground was spread with dry yellow gravel, weedless and raked. The back of the big red house formed the right-hand side of the square, and by an open door stood a shiny brown gig with yellow-spoked wheels. A girl with a white cap pulled low, hiding her hair, and a man with one shoulder higher than the other, were busily loading baskets into the back of the gig. On the side opposite the entrance gate was an open cart-shed which might have housed a display of brand new agricultural implements. Carts and wagons and tumbrils, all washed and brightly painted, were ranged in a straight line, all their shafts pointing the same way. The square was closed upon the other side by a range of stone buildings, each one painted to shoulder height with shiny black pitch and whitewashed above. They were all thatched and the reed was as neat as a vain woman's hair. And just as there was none of the mud and muddle of the Uplands yard, there was also none of the sound and bustle. The man and the girl loading the gig worked in silence; the small boy who held the head of the horse might have been dumb; if the stone buildings housed pigs or cows they too were under the spell of quietude. As she moved forward over the raked gravel, Araminta was conscious of the gritting noise of each step and tried to walk more lightly. When she was half-way towards the open back door and the gig another white-capped girl came from the house, carrying from a wide wooden yoke a couple of buckets. She scuttled across and opened a door in one of the stone buildings and disappeared. She had passed within arms' length of Araminta and had certainly looked at her, but without a sign of the interest which would have expected a sight of a stranger in such a remote place to provoke. And when she was close to the gig and halted nervously the crook-backed man turned his head and regarded her in much the same way, without interest, and without a word.

Speechlessness seemed to have seized upon Araminta's throat, too, and she was obliged to clear it before she said shyly, "I'm the new dairymaid. Is Mrs. Stancy about?"

"Aye, she's about," he said mildly. His eyes, a rather faded speedwell blue in colour, dwelt on Araminta for a second, and then looked back at the white-capped girl who came from the house-door with a scrubbed wooden tray upon which rested the plucked and dressed carcases of half a dozen fowls, ready for the oven. The man fitted the tray into a space left by the baskets and then drew over the whole load a neat tarpaulin cover which pulled taut and was secured by cords. But, now that the job was finished, neither he nor the girl made any move towards taking Araminta into the house and the presence of her employer, and in a moment she understood why. From the house-door emerged another figure, not very tall, thickish, but moving with unmistakable dignity. She was neatly, even richly dressed in the fashion of any well-to-do matron about to make a visit to town. But, striking a strangely incongruous note against the little curled plume in her hat and the gold ear-bobs in her hair and the black lace mittens upon her hands, was the big white apron which covered the whole of her black silk skirt and which was so stiff with starch that it crackled as she walked. Both the crook-back and the yellow-haired girl seemed to draw themselves to attention and stand rigidly, and Araminta found herself in the grip of a nervousness hitherto unknown to her.

Mrs. Stancy halted by the side of the gig and Araminta knew that she was being studied. She made a little bob.

"You're the new girl?" she asked in a deep quiet voice which brought to mind the sound of a low note on a violin. "Araminta

Glover; that's right, isn't it? You are smaller than I had been led to think. Nancy!"

"Yes, ma'am."

"Take this key and change the aprons." The mittened hands moved to a bunch of keys which Mrs. Stancy wore on a kind of silver chain contraption at her waist and selected, without apparent hesitation, one of the dozen or so which hung there. Nancy nervously extended a swollen red hand and took the key in her palm. Then, very nimbly, Mrs. Stancy climbed into the gig, took the reins in one hand and the driving-whip in the other and nodded to the boy. He let go the horse's head and jumped to one side. The horse lunged forward, the yellow spokes flashed and Mrs. Stancy was borne out of sight.

A subtle slackening of tension was felt in the yard. The little boy turned a somersault and bolted; the crook-back let out a soft breathy sigh and brushed his forehead with the back of his hand; Nancy drew out an immaculate white handkerchief and blew her nose. Not one of the actions was extraordinary or in the least dramatic, but they were the actions of human beings, and Araminta knew that not one of them would have been performed while Mrs. Stancy was still in the yard. She herself had a feeling as though a heavy weight had rolled over her, and when Nancy, putting away the handkerchief, said curtly, "You come with me," she followed meekly, grateful for being noticed at all.

Inside the doorway was a long flagged passage spotlessly white-washed, and with little panes of glass let into the top of the walls on either side. Half-way along it on the right was a door which Nancy opened, disclosing a largish room lined with cupboards and drawers and furnished with a long solid table and one chair. At the far end of the table laid a little pile of clothing. Nancy sorted it out with her red hands and pushed towards Araminta three white mob-caps, three white handkerchiefs, two print aprons of blue and white stripe, and one of sacking. The three white aprons which had completed the pile Nancy carried with her to one of the cupboards which she unlocked. Lifting down another apron she measured it against Araminta's body, gave a nod of satisfaction, and selected two of similar size. She straightened the pile upon which she placed the large aprons, and the one from which she had taken the smaller ones and then carefully locked the door.

Turning back to Araminta she said in a curious flat voice which lacked all trace of the Essex dialect:

"The three white aprons are for dairy work and you must keep them clean. The caps, too, and the handkerchiefs. Mrs. Stancy is very particular, and if she sees you dirty there'll be trouble. The print aprons are for rough work, and you wear the other when you scrub. Is that clear?" Araminta nodded. "All right, then. Now I'll show you our room and you can put your things away before we start."

She led the way along the passage and up some scrubbed white steps which ended in a long passage similar to the one downstairs. She opened the first door on the side opposite the stair-head and Araminta followed into a square room of which a third was occupied by a kind of low shelf running along the wall. On this shelf were three straw palliasses each made into a bed and covered by a patchwork quilt. There was a chest of drawers with brightly-polished handles, a row of wooden pegs, and a washing-stand. The top of it was covered by a thick white cloth upon which stood a basin and ewer and two brass cans. Under the stand was a wide shallow bath, painted white inside and brown outside. On a rail beside it hung some coarse, brightly-coloured towels.

Compared with many which she had seen and occupied it was a well-furnished room; and it was, like everything else, specklessly clean. But there was no sign of human occupation and for some reason, looking round at it, Araminta knew a curious sinking of the heart. It wasn't natural to be so tidy.

"There's a long drawer and a short one for you," said Nancy, in her dead voice. "And unless you've something like a cloak that can't be put away neatly, Mrs. Stancy doesn't like the pegs to be used. We make our own beds and take turns at doing the room. You wash your neck and ears and up to the elbow every morning in the basin, and take a whole bath on Saturday. That's what the cans are for. I have the first bath, you the second, and Susie the last.

There, now I think I've told you everything. If you'll put on a white apron and a cap, we'll go down. There's a lot to do this morning. You can unpack to-night, but you'd better put your bundle in the drawer out of sight." Her voice took on an even wearier note. "You see, sometimes people come to see Mrs. Stancy's dairy, and then she always shows them our room. Not many places treat the girls so well. And if it happened to be untidy she would be very cross indeed."

"Is she a cross woman?" asked Araminta, pulling the cap over her curls. Nancy was silent for just a second, then she said stiffly:

"Not if you're careful. She's particular."

By this time Araminta had mastered her first shyness and the impact of Mrs. Stancy's personality had worn off a little. As she followed Nancy out of the room once more she compared it unfavourably with the little cluttered room which she had shared with Cissie at Uplands. There the big sagging feather bed had occupied most of the floor space and there had been only a hook on the door for their clothes and no washing apparatus at all. They had done that at the sink in the scullery. But it had somehow been cheerful and intended for sleeping in, not for show.

But when she reached the dairy which opened off the north side of the passage, almost opposite the room with the cupboards and drawers, she was impressed anew. Never, not even at the Manor, had she seen such a dairy. It seemed as big as a church. It had four windows tightly netted against flies and dust. The flags on the floor were so clean that their variegated colours, rose and ochre and primrose and brown shone like jewels. It had a sink in one corner, with a pump over it. And all round it ran a shelf made of slate which here and there widened out into a butter-making slab. Higher up wooden shelves bore the neatly arranged tools of the business. Ranged along one side were scrubbed wooden buckets bound with brass bands which were polished until they shone like gold. And there were three big churns. The milk which was "settling" stood in shallow bowls which were cream on the inside and a pleasant tawny colour outside; the cream which was "ripening" stood in deep jars which matched the pans. There was not a soiled cloth or a dirty utensil in the whole dairy, and despite herself Araminta found herself filled with admiration. It was all very marvellous, and no doubt her own lowness of spirit was due to having risen so early and walked so far and being in strange surroundings and feeling a little hungry. It must be past ten and by this time at Mrs. Pollard's there would be milk or tea to drink and a slice of oatcake and cheese or a slab of cold pudding to sustain one.

"There's your churn," said Nancy, "and there's your cream." She pointed to two jars which stood a little apart, and then, taking up the shallow, perforated "fleeter," began to skim the top from the pans of settled milk. Araminta, who was interested in this girl who was for perhaps two years to be her companion in work, in leisure moved to the far side of the churn so that as she worked she might study Nancy.

She was fairly old, twenty-two or three, tall, thin and pale. Her hair was scraped back and knotted into a tight knob at the edge of her white cap. Her eyes were pale grey and the lids were slightly swollen. Her face was completely without expression. But she was a good worker, Araminta could see that in the first five minutes. Her movements were accurate and careful and rapid. Once, as she stooped to pour the cream she had collected into one of the tall jars which stood on the floor, her skirt belled out at the back and Araminta caught a glimpse of her legs. They were hideously swollen and knotted, and at the sight of them Araminta's mind nodded with sad wisdom. Years ago, at her first place, there had been a maid with legs like that; she was a good worker, too, but her working days had ended prematurely.

She wished Nancy would talk to her. There were so many things she wanted to know. You could avoid so many false steps by finding out things beforehand. But Nancy worked away in silence, and it was not for the newcomer to start a conversation. Perhaps the other girl, the one who crossed the yard with the buckets would be more communicative and more companionable.

Presently the butter thudded, and Araminta, after peeping into the churn, said, "It's come."

"I'm glad of that," said Nancy, "because I'm just ready to make it up. Susie ought to be back now. She'll clean the churn. You take this one now. That's the cream."

No mention of 'levenses, Araminta thought disconsolately. And two churnings straight on top of one another. People that had never swung a churn might not realize what hard work it was, but Nancy must have known and might have given her a moment's respite. However, Nancy seemed not to need a respite herself, she began at once to work on the freshly-made butter, slapping and shaping it with a pair of wooden patters and Araminta, not to be outdone, began the second churning.

Almost immediately the girl Susie came into the dairy, and Araminta, who had found Nancy such poor company, looked up with interest and hope which were instantly dashed. Susie's lack of mental stability was written upon her face; it wore the same expression of vacuity which was beginning to show through Betsy's childish loveliness. But this girl was ugly; her face was thin and yet bumpy, and so pale that it had a greenish tinge. Her eyes were brown and slightly protuberant, so that she wore a perpetually startled air. Her hair which might have done something to redeem and soften her countenance, was a harsh gingery-red in colour, and cut so short that nothing save some spiky ends showed beneath her cap. There was a smear of wet meal on the side of her mouth, and another on the print apron which she wore over her white one.

Araminta's scrutiny had lasted but a very brief moment, and she was removing her gaze with an inward sigh of disappointment when Susie who had borne inspection with such a dull look that she might not even have been conscious of it, suddenly smiled. It was a shy smile and very fleeting, but it was the first sign of warmth and friendliness which Araminta had seen that morning. She returned it heartily and said "Hello."

Susie's over-exposed eyes shot a glance at Nancy and then she said, almost in a whisper, "Hello."

"I'm Araminta. Araminta Glover."

Without turning her head Nancy said, "You set about that churn, Susie." And then, slightly softening the edge in her voice she added, for Araminta's benefit, "Mrs. Stancy doesn't like much talk in the dairy."

"But I hadn't stopped work," Araminta protested. "Do you mean we mustn't talk at all?"

"Of course not. There's things we must say. But if you talk to Susie she'll just stand and forget what she's doing. You see, she's a loony from the Poor Farm. They got too full there last winter and some of the big farmers had to take some on to work. Mrs. Stancy wasn't very pleased about it, I can tell you."

She spoke with as much indifference as though she were discussing one of the churns; but Araminta, shooting a swift glance at Susie from under her eyelids, saw that Susie had heard and quite understood. Her rather loose lower lip was tremulous and the big eyes were moistening.

Quixotic sympathy was not one of Araminta's weaknesses; her own life had been too hard to encourage such a growth. But Susie had smiled, which no one else at Abbey Farm had done, and perhaps for that reason Araminta felt a little wave of anger redden her cheeks. And the dreaded words "Poor Farm" had set her interest instantly alight. The Glovers were always precariously balanced upon the brink of destitution and had indeed lived all their lives under the shadow of the threat of that awful institution, but they had escaped it so far and Araminta was interested to see someone who had experienced all its rumoured and imagined horrors and survived. Maybe that was why Susie looked so simple, for one of the well-established beliefs in the countryside was that the women in charge of the Poor Farm babies knocked them unconscious by a blow from a wooden mallet on the head if they cried overmuch.

Work in the dairy proceeded in silence. Susie cleaned the churn, collected the skimmed milk from the pans Nancy had worked upon, and then washed the pans. When they were wiped and stacked she took a basket of eggs and sorted them, putting big brown ones in one smaller basket, big white ones in another, and any undersized ones of either colour in yet a third. Araminta, watching her covertly, decided that she worked quite quickly and seemed to know what she was doing. And once, when their eyes met, they exchanged hasty smiles again. By the end of the morning Araminta had changed her mind about Susie. She wasn't really simple at all, she was just ugly, and looked dull because there was nothing to look bright about. I'll look dull myself if it's like this always, no running in and out, nobody speaking, and no 'levenses, she thought.

Just after midday a bell rang. Susie and Nancy stopped what they were doing, and Araminta, who had known for about five minutes that her second churnful had turned into butter but had not announced the fact because her arm was aching and she was snatching a short rest, let go the handle which she had been idly turning.

Nancy was on her like a lynx immediately. "You stay till it's come," she said. "Mrs. Nead will save your dinner."

"It has come, just this minute."

Nancy gave her a queer look and lifted the churn lid.

"You're lucky," she said.

Susie had poured water into a bowl and taken a towel from a little heap which lay neatly folded on one of the upper shelves. Nancy washed and wiped her hands. "You next," she said to Araminta, who obediently took her place at the bowl. Susie washed last, and when her hands were in the water Araminta said, "There's some meal on your face, did you know?" Apparently Susie had not known; a sudden rush of colour seemed almost to blacken her face before she thrust it into the water. Nancy, standing by the door in a patient attitude of waiting, seemed to resent the further delay; she looked at Araminta with something very much like hatred. But she only said, and whether it was information or an underhanded rebuke, Araminta could not decide.

"We all go in together unless one of us has a job to finish. It saves disturbance."

Susie hastily dabbed her wet face and rolled the towel between her hands. Then she emptied the bowl and spread the towel along the edge of a shelf. "I'm ready now, Nancy," she said, in a placating voice.

Nancy led the way out of the dairy and into the passage, at the end of which, next to the foot of the stairs, was the kitchen door.

67

After the chill and dimness and church-like atmosphere of the dairy the kitchen struck a bright cheerful note which sent Araminta's spirits soaring. It was an oblong room with a big stove at one end of it. There was a vast dresser bearing many brightly-coloured plates and dishes; there were dazzlingly-polished bits of copper and brassware on a long shelf over the stove. There was a rag rug in brilliant colours, undimmed by dirt, on the scrubbed flagged floor in front of the hearth, and in the very centre of it a great white cat lay curled in slumber. At the end of the kitchen nearest the passage door was an oblong table, set for a meal and spread with a scarlet and white checked cloth; and up near the fire was another table, big, square, scrubbed white and bearing evidence of cooking having been done upon it. A rather wizened little woman in a big white apron and a young girl in a print dress were already in the kitchen, and as soon as the dairymaids had entered by one door another, between the hearth and the window opened, and the crook-back entered followed by a boy of seven-or-eighteen and two smaller ones, one of them the boy who had held the horse.

Nancy moved to the top place at one side of the table, and Araminta, who was by now acquainted with the laws of precedence, took the seat next her. She was a little disappointed to see that Susie did not sit in the third place, but went to the end of the table. The crook-back sat down opposite to Nancy, the boy across the table from Araminta, the two youngsters taking the other places. Mrs. Nead came and stood at the head of the table and the girl in the print dress, after placing a big dish and a pile of wooden bowls before her, slipped into the vacant seat between Araminta and Susie.

Each place was marked by a horn-handled knife and fork and a bone spoon, neatly arranged. In the middle of the table was a wooden bowl larger in size, but similar to those into which Mrs. Nead was dishing food from the big dish, and in it were some small thick slices of brown bread. On either side of it was an even smaller bowl containing salt. It was neat and pleasing to the eye, just as the savour of the food was titillating to the appetite. Araminta, who had breakfasted sketchily at half-past five that morning, awaited her portion with impatience. It smelt of pork; and farmhouse pork was usually good, quite unlike the unpalatable fat squashy stuff which found its way to labourers' tables.

The bowls went from hand to hand quickly, and as soon as hers came to rest before her Araminta, after a glance which showed that this was, disappointingly, spoon food, after all, lifted her spoon and had it poised for the plunge when something told her that she had made a mistake, and that all eyes were on her. Into the silence Mrs. Nead said coldly:

"We say Grace here. This is a Christian household, young woman."

Araminta looked into her bowl, studying its contents intently, this time to cover her confusion. It was a grey, moist mass of boiled peas, pease-pudding they called it, and, after boiled potatoes, it was the cheapest, poorest food. A faint shininess upon the surface of it told that a piece of fat pork had been boiled with it, but there was no sign that any of the meat—so recently despised and now suddenly so desirable—had found its way into Araminta's portion. She was extremely disappointed. Her sensuous nature as well as her young hardworking body derived great pleasure from food; and two years of Mrs. Pollard's generous housekeeping had introduced her to many agreeable dishes. She knew all about pease-pudding. It filled you, it stayed the pangs, nobody could deny that. But it didn't stay by you; it was like eating wind, and often it forced you to get up in the night.

Mrs. Nead laid down her serving-ladle and all along the table heads were bent.

"For what we are about to receive, may the Lord make us truly thankful. Amen."

"Amen," came a mumbled chorus.

Well, it was hot, and it was well-cooked, and there was a faint flavour of pork about it. And the piece of bread, taken from the solemnly passed bowl, though smaller than one might have wished, was dry and solid, and gave you something to bite upon. And perhaps this was just an unlucky day, or perhaps the real meal came at supper time when work was finished and you could take your time and really enjoy your food. One mustn't be disappointed too soon, though it would be a queer thing if, in a house where everything else was so good and solid and well-ordered, the food was going to be bad.

The pease-pudding was eaten in almost complete silence. Once the crook-back addressed Mrs. Nead, saying, "Well, a fine day for Michaelmas. Thass a good thing."

She said "Yes," and the monosyllable disposed of the weather.

Once Mrs. Nead spoke to the girl in the print dress, "Bella, did you move the black pot before you set down?"

Bella said "Yes," through a mouthful of stale bread, and Mrs. Nead looked at her with disapproval.

And once the boy who had held the horse's head let his spoon tip out of the bowl, and a shot fired into the kitchen could hardly have caused more consternation.

"Hev that marked the cloth?" Mrs. Nead demanded.

"No ma'am, no."

"Take a look, Bella."

Bella half rose from her seat on the bench and inspected the tablecloth.

"No ma'am. There ain't no mark."

"Thass lucky for you, Ben," said Mrs. Nead. The boy's face showed that he shared her opinion of his good fortune.

That was the extent of the conversation, and once again Araminta's mind went back to the rather crowded, rather untidy kitchen at Uplands where the two boys who stayed to dinner, Cissie and herself and the master and mistress all sat down together for the midday meal and the atmosphere, if not invariably amicable, was at least lively and free. She glanced at the clock which wagged a polished brass pendulum against the spotless white of the kitchen wall. It was just half-past twelve. Yes, they would be sitting down now, and Mrs. Pollard would be throwing great portions of food on to the plates and perhaps scolding Cissie, and Cissie might be half-crying, but at the same time she would be half-grinning at the boys who would wink and nudge, and after a second or two Mrs. Pollard would say, impatiently, but at the same time kindly, "Don't cry into your dinner, girl, Heaven knows you put enough salt in these potatoes!" It was all so different from the subdued, unfriendly atmosphere of this place and, thinking about it, Araminta's heart sank another stave. At the same time she became aware of a sneaking wonder as to whether she had been a fool. But then she thought of the four pounds a year, and of the certainty that now she had escaped from temptation; and she straightened her thin square shoulders.

Mrs. Nead looked along the table and saw that every bowl was emptied, every crumb of bread consumed. She rose to her feet and said another Grace, differing only in the substitution of the words, "have received" in place of "about to receive." Dinner was over, and Araminta rose from the table wondering if everyone still felt as hungry as she did herself.

She began her afternoon's work by churning for the third time. Nancy went on making up the butter, carefully salting some and setting it apart, and then, taking a set of scales from the shelf she began to pat up meticulous pounds and halves. When the third churnful was made she paused in her work and asked gravely, "Can you make shells and cones? Mrs. Stancy didn't tell me."

"I've never tried. Mrs. Pollard didn't do anything fancy." She did not add that as often as not Mrs. Pollard didn't weigh either; she had a few customers, who all seemed to be friendly and unlikely to care whether their butter was an ounce over or under the weight it was supposed to be; and generally they were lucky, for Mrs. Pollard was very heavy-handed.

"You'd better go on weighing then, and stamping. But I hope you will learn shells at least, or else I shall have to do it all."

"Oh, I'll learn," said Araminta confidently. "I'll watch you."

Nancy's glance said that her art was not to be acquired so easily. Aloud she said, "But you'll have to mind to set the stamps straight. There's nothing Mrs. Stancy hates so much as a crooked pattern. I'd better show you."

From a bowl of cold water in which they were floating she lifted two tools, one smaller than the other, and both the shape of a brick, made of wood and with a pattern hollowed out upon one

71

face. Drawing a pound and a half pound of butter to the edge of the shelf she knotted her brows, sucked in her lips and pressed the patterns home.

"See. They've got to be square." Araminta looked, and once again the admiration which had alternated with her distrust of this new place came uppermost. The stamps were intricate and beautiful. The pound of butter had a square medallion with linked, curling letters A F in the centre of it; and on either side was a posy of flowers, a wild rose, with each petal and stamen quite plainly shown, a poppy and a cornflower. The whole was enclosed in a ridged edging which exactly fitted the piece of butter. The half-pound was similarly enclosed, and had the lettered medallion, slightly smaller in size, and the wreath was a simple, but very pleasing arrangement of marguerite daisies. The two slabs of butter, thus marked, really looked too good to eat. Nancy pushed them back into place.

"Do you think you can do it? Then you can go on weighing and marking, and I'll do the shells."

Susie, who had spent the time after dinner polishing every bit of brasswork in the dairy, fetched a bucket of hot water and proceeded to wipe the shelves and the floor.

Araminta, with an unwonted tremor in her hand, because Nancy had made the thing seem so solemn and important, stamped two pounds of butter. The first she stamped too lightly, and Nancy said, "It must be clearer than that." The next she pressed on too firmly, so that the whole pound flattened out slightly. Nancy sighed. "That's too hard." Desperately anxious now and with a sickening collapse of confidence, Araminta tried again and stood back in triumph. The pattern was clear, perfect. Nancy might have said so, but she turned in silence and took up her patters and a piece of butter about the size of a marble and with a couple of deft twists of the wrist which made the operation look as simple as tying a shoelace, produced a little shell of butter, curved and crinkled, closed and pointed at one end, open like a petal at the other, as sweet and pretty as any little shell ever picked up at a wave's edge. Araminta was fascinated.

72

"That is clever," she said. "You must show me how, Nancy. Did it take you long to learn."

"It's a knack," said Nancy, more graciously than she had yet spoken. "Some people can never do it. I make dozens a week. They go twenty-four to a pound."

The afternoon stretched out endlessly. Araminta weighed and patted and stamped; Nancy produced butter-shells with the silent, relentless efficiency of a machine; Susie scrubbed everything, and then, without being told, fetched in a number of big wicker butter-baskets, some ready-cut oblongs of paper and a pile of snowy butter-muslin. Nancy finished a shell and put her patters into a bowl of water, and then, without a pause, fetched from a shelf near the door a single sheet of paper scrawled all over with words and figures written in a small slanting hand with very black ink. Araminta's sense of inferiority, pricked to life by the matter of the butter stamping, spurred by the sight of the immaculate little shells, now went ramping. Did this particular Mrs. Stancy expect her dairy-maids to *read*? Apparently so, for Nancy, after consulting the list, began to pack pounds and half-pounds and shells of butter into the basket in exact accordance with the instructions upon the paper. Becoming conscious of Araminta's wondering and freshly-admiring eyes upon her, she said, as she covered a completed basket with a piece of the snowy muslin, "Can you read?"

"No."

"Couldn't you learn?"

"I don't know. I never tried."

"I couldn't when I came here. But Mrs. Stancy said if I wanted to be her head girl I must learn. She taught me."

"Was it hard?"

A curious kind of spasm cracked the immobility of Nancy's face. For a moment she looked like a person remembering a past torment. Then she said, "It didn't take long," and turned back to the list.

At that moment Mrs. Nead's grey head appeared round the door.

"Nance, his Reverence has sent up for his stuff and he want two dozen eggs to-day, stead of a dozen."

"Oh dear," said Nancy, turning pale and putting down the list with the air of one upon whom calamity has fallen. "Now I don't know what to do. He always has brown eggs, but do I send him two dozen of them, maybe there won't be enough to go round."

"That's your business," said Mrs. Nead unkindly. "The boy's waiting." She withdrew her head.

Nancy lifted a basket into which she had already packed some butter, including two dozen of her shells and fluttered along to the end of the shelf where the eggs, washed and polished by Susie earlier in the day, stood waiting. She counted and recounted, packed and repacked in such a flurry of agitation that at last Araminta said, with intent at reassurance, "Surely that can't be so important."

"Sh," said Nancy fiercely, changing one egg for another with the frenzied absorption of someone arranging the crown jewels. Finally she drew the muslin over the basket.

"I've sent eighteen brown and six white. I do hope that'll do. I wouldn't make a mistake to-day of all days, when she's out."

She took up the basket, and with a last, dubious look at the eggs on the shelf, as though even at this moment she might try some other arrangement after all, she hurried out of the dairy. Unconsciously Araminta gave a great sigh of relief, and laying down her tools, straightened up to rest her back. As she did so she saw that Susie had left her bucket in the middle of the floor, and was standing quite near her twisting her floorcloth between her hands and smiling in a shy, strained way.

"The meal," she said. "Meal on my face. I et it. Don't tell her, will you?"

"No," said Araminta, with another sinking of the heart. She was soft then, after all. Fancy telling that to a strange girl if she minded.

"What did you say your name was?"

"Araminta Glover."

"Mine's Susie. You on't tell tales on me, will you?"

"No."

"She do, you know." She nodded towards the door. "She's a bumsucker. She'll tell tales about you, too. You watch out. And

74

the woman, Mrs. Nead. But I et it." Her smile stretched suddenly into a grin; then, with the swift movements of ferret she was back in the middle of the floor swabbing away for dear life. The door opened and Nancy was back.

"You finished?" she said to Susie. Her voice was a trifle brisker than usual, and Araminta guessed that she was finding it necessary to cover, by an assertion of authority, her lack of composure over the matter of the eggs. "Cows are in, and Luke's waiting."

"Don't we milk?" Araminta asked as Susie, after a few wild splashes and plunges, emptied the pail, washed her hands, and gathered up a great bunch of milking buckets.

"Yes," said Nancy, without looking up from the list which she had snatched up as soon as she entered and which she now held in one hand while with the other she deftly assembled the items required for the basket she was packing. "But Luke and Susie do it until we've done the day's butter and these orders. If we can't start with them, we're all behind for the rest of the day." She spoke accusingly, as though to-day's lag were entirely Araminta's fault. "Of course, you're new. Were you in a big place before?"

"No—not what you'd call big. There was only two of us, and we didn't work in the dairy all the time. It wasn't like this." She thought of the steady unremitting labour which had gone on, with the single respite of dinner, since ten o'clock that morning, and asked, diffidently, because Nancy might misconstrue her motive, "Is this the busiest day here?"

"Good gracious no. It's always the same. Mrs. Stancy goes to market four days a week, Baildon, Bywater, Fretton and Colchester. And 'sides that, we have customers in lots of big houses. Why, even at Tewsbury Park where they have a great dairy, they buy a pound of butter and twenty-four shells a week because old Lady Dolman, his lordship's mother I mean, won't eat any other." Pride loosed the muzzle of her silence. "They say she can tell in a minute if they give her their own make." She began to pack the last basket, and Araminta thankfully laid down the stampers and leaned her aching back against the edge of the shelf. "Jacob drives as far afield as Wardwyck and Standover," Nancy said. "Everybody knows we make the best butter and sell the freshest eggs in Essex. The Abbey cheese is famous too."

There was, evidently, one subject upon which Nancy could discourse freely and enthusiastically, and Araminta made a note of it. Better to talk about the glories of the Abbey butter than to stand making it in glum silence. She was meditating a sly question or two to see whether Nancy, once talking, could be drawn into more personal gossip, but the other girl, covering the last basket with its muslin cover, said, in her old manner, "Come on. It's time we were in the milking shed."

Araminta had never heard it called that before, and as she crossed the yard by Nancy's side, she wondered what Mrs. Stancy's passion for order and cleanliness had done to cows, which were, at best, messy creatures. And what was a milking shed? In her previous places she had milked in the meadow when the weather was really warm and the cows lying out, otherwise in the darkish, stuffy, smelly cowhouse. But the shed which she now entered was cleaner and more habitable than any cottage on Minsham Green. Even here the floor was flagged and had been scrubbed during the day; not a scrap of straw or a bit of cow-dung defiled it. It hardly even smelled of cows; yet they were there, a double row of them, tethered at even-spaced intervals against mangers which ran along each side of the building. They were twitching their tails and breathing audibly and munching away at the food in the manger after the manner of cows, but for all that they were strange. For one thing they were bigger than ordinary, and they were all exactly alike, marked queerly with great splashes of black and white. Araminta, who had been accustomed to Daisy being red, Buttercup black, and Queenie brindled, wondered how these could be told one from the other.

But she had no time to wonder. Nancy said, "There's your stool, and you start here. Don't mix the buckets because we have to know how much each one gives." Then, with her own stool in one hand and her first bucket in the other, she was suddenly stricken into stone.

"Oh dear," she said, quite brokenly, "we've come out in our white aprons. That's all on account of my talking to you. Now you see what chattering does for you. Susie, run and fetch my print and the new girl's. And hurry, for goodness sake."

Having despatched Susie she passed along between the double lines of cows, and Araminta heard her set down her stool and begin to murmur a mixture of apologies and endearments to one of the cows. Looking across from the place which she dared not leave for an instant, for if she lost it she would never find this particular cow again, Araminta saw that the crook-back was milking the opposite cow, and, with his head pressed sideways against the cow's flank, was regarding her with an expression of friendly interest in his washed-out eyes. She smiled diffidently, and as though he had been waiting for a sign he said quietly, "Seem strange to you, I reckon." Araminta nodded.

"Whass your name?"

"Araminta."

"Mine's Luke. How long you bound for?"

"Two year."

"I been here ten to-day."

"You like it then?"

"That'll do," he said, without enthusiasm. "Where'd you come from?" When Araminta, conscious of another wave of nostalgia, had named her last home, he nodded. "Ah yes, I'n heard of Pollard. What'd you come here for?"

"The money," said Araminta, pleased that there was a reason which was so simple and so acceptable.

Luke turned his head away for a second, and Araminta, developing a sense which up to now she had not much needed—a spy sense—looked and saw that Nancy had left her cow and was standing not far away. At that moment Susie dashed in breathless with the two print aprons. Araminta donned hers and sat down to her cow. In a minute or two she looked up and saw that Nancy was likewise busy and that the crook-back had turned his face again.

"She tell you about the money?" he asked, managing, by a jerk of his head, to indicate Nancy.

"No," said Araminta, raising her voice above the hissing of the milk into the bucket.

"Well, look out then. The Missus say four pound, but less you're wonderful clever you don't get that much. She keep a book, and every time you break anything that go down against you. And there's fines too. If she'd catched you and her milking in dairy aprons that'd be fourpence off most like. And do you break a egg thass twopence. That mount up, you know."

"Thank you for telling me," Araminta said with another sickening decline of spirit.

Luke stood up.

"I stop milking and start to measure now," he said in a different, louder voice, which anyone might hear. "Them that yield good gets extry supper. Had y'ever heard of that afore, new girl? Thass the rule at the Abbey Farm, more work, more grub, less work, less grub."

He spoke in a jocular way as though he were rather stupid and rather amused; but Araminta, who could still see his face, saw that it was serious, and yes—and sorry, too. And she realized that he was warning her again.

As each cow was milked Luke studied the bucket, and Araminta, looking into one, too, saw that the inside was marked with a series of grooved circles. By one cow, which Susie had just finished milking, Luke paused and clicked his tongue.

"That won't do, 'Fanta. You'll be on short commons if thass the best you can manage. Take warning by your maid here. She missed her breakfust this morning, you know."

So that was why Susie had eaten the hens' meal.

A dreadful darkening of the spirit came down upon Araminta. It had been gathering all day, in the neat unhomely bedroom, during the silent meal, at the moment when Susie gabbled out her words about tale-bearing, when Luke turned his head away and fell silent under Nancy's eye. Now it fell completely and she admitted that she had come to a strange and crazy place, full of rules which seemed made to catch you, and full of fears. Everybody seemed frightened. That was it; and though she had tried to fight the feeling she was frightened too.

Milking her last cow, and feeling flustered and fumble-fingered because she was last and Nancy and Susie were already carrying the buckets away and Luke was adding the extra portions to some mangers and turning other cows out through a big double door at the far end of the shed, Araminta began to think about Mrs. Stancy. It must be that everybody was scared of her. And yet, except that she wore an apron when she was dressed 'up she was ordinary enough. With that thought Araminta's stout little heart gave a leap of real panic; for, with her fingers weakening on the soft teats and the stream of milk failing suddenly, she realized, for the first time that day, that she had not the slightest idea of what Mrs. Stancy looked like. Her figure, yes; but not her face. She had been overcome by something, shyness, nervousness she would have said a moment ago, but now she suspected that it was fear. She had not been able to look her new mistress in the face at all.

And so, before she had really encountered her, Mrs. Stancy, a stout faceless figure, with particular ideas and a passion for rules, had frightened this latest recruit to her service.

Long ago, as a child, often hungry, often cold, often tired to point of tears, Araminta had discovered that a certain modicum of comfort could be obtained by the simple rule of thinking about something else. She had once, as a young child, had a vivid and powerful imagination, but, since most of the things she imagined were terrifying and there was nothing in her circumstances to encourage or purge the growth, she lost it gradually, and the "something else" to which she so often turned her thoughts was usually something quite dull and practical. So, picking stones in a biting wind on Mr. Whistler's Forty Acre Field, she would think about the shapes of them, and by seeing in this one a horse's head and this a pig's foot, would keep herself from brooding upon her frozen hands and empty stomach.

So now, since the habit had grown with her, she began to think about a cup of tea, replacing the faceless Mrs. Stancy in her mind by the vision of a steaming cup. Surely soon there must be a cup of tea. Why, even her mother, drudging round doing the roughest work in Mrs. Whistler's kitchen never failed to get a cup of some sort, even if it were only brewed from leaves left in the pot after Mrs. Whistler had drunk her fill.

And as she carried the last buckets across the yard her hopes seemed near fulfilment. For there was a light already in the kitchen, and through its window, which looked upon the yard, she could see Mrs. Nead pouring water into a brown teapot. Apart from the tea the kitchen looked remarkably cosy; the stove was glowing, and there were candles in brass sticks on the mantelshelf and table. How daft she had been to despair so soon. The day's work was nearly done. The milk would be to set up and then they would all go to that cosy, cave-like kitchen and drink tea, and get warm, and talk together as people did everywhere else in the world.

In the dairy, Nancy and Susie were straining the milk by pouring it out of the buckets into the settling pans through a slackly-stretched piece of muslin over the mouth of the bowl. They both seemed to be relieved to see her.

Nancy said with asperity, "You'll have to be quicker. Come now and hold this muslin, this idiot has let it slip once," but somehow her manner showed that she hoped better things of Araminta.

"I can go and do the hens then," said Susie, looking pleased. And Araminta wondered whether she was pleased to get out of Nancy's sight or at the prospect of gulping another mouthful of meal.

When the milk was strained, since Nancy showed no signs of knowing that the tea was made, Araminta said innocently, "Mrs. Nead was making the tea when I came across the yard."

"What's that got to do with us?" asked Nancy. "We get our supper at eight."

"Don't we get *no* tea?"

"I told you, we get supper at eight."

"Do we get tea then?"

"No."

"Don't we get no tea never?"

There was still enough light in the dairy for Araminta to see a definitely harassed look cross Nancy's face.

"We get it at breakfast. And during the day sometimes Mrs. Stancy has give me a cup."

"How often?"

"Oh, how you keep on! Don't keep saying 'Tea, tea, tea' like that. We've got the cheeses to turn. And then there's the plucking to do for to-morrow. We shall be lucky if we're ready for supper by eight. Have a drink of water if you're all that thirsty."

"I ain't thirsty for water. I want a cup of tea, thass all."

"If you say that word again I shall tell Mrs. Stancy you're a tormenting creature, and then you'll see."

"You want one, too," said Araminta softly. Nancy looked at her with sheer hatred, and pointing to one of a trio of large vats at the extreme end of the dairy, said, "Go and break those curds and keep quiet. I suppose you know about cheese."

"Yes," said Araminta meekly. She was puzzled by Nancy and afraid that she had made an enemy. Any other girl would have said yes, I do, I long for a cup of tea; and the lack of it would have made a common grievance.

Nancy fetched and lighted a big lamp while Araminta rolled her sleeves above the elbow and plunged her hands into the vat, breaking and crumbling the curds until they were as fine as meal. Susie came back, caught Araminta's eye and rubbed the back of her hand across her mouth with a conspiratorial grin. She began at once to scour and scald the milking buckets, the stampers and the patters. Nancy, after waiting for a few minutes to see that the lamp burned clearly and needed no adjusting, mounted a stool and began turning the cheeses which were ripening in the great rack which extended across a quarter of the dairy's ceiling.

They were all busily engaged when, from outside in the passage, a low clear voice made itself heard through the silence.

"All right, Luke. Now tell the new girl I want her to come and help put the goods away."

"Thass you," said Susie, unnecessarily. Araminta had already withdrawn her hands and was wiping them when Luke put his head around the dairy door. Dragging up the tattered remnants of her old confidence as one might pull a torn garment into some semblance of order, Araminta stepped into the passage which was now lighted by a hanging lantern. Luke pointed to the door of the room from which, earlier in this endless day, Nancy had issued the aprons. Araminta walked in and closed the door carefully behind her.

There was now a big lamp burning clearly in the centre of the long scrubbed table. On the doorward side of it a number of packages and parcels were laid out. At the far end were two silver candlesticks, each flowering with three pointed flames, and between them was a big silver tray, set for tea. Behind the tray, her face brightly lighted from the combined candle and lamp light, was Mrs. Stancy, sitting in the room's single chair.

As Araminta entered she was lifting her hat from her head. Slowly she ran the brim of it through her fingers, touched the curled feather with a lingering touch, and then laid the hat away in the middle of the space between the lamp and the tray. Then she looked up and said kindly, with a slight smile, "So you're Araminta. Let me look at you."

Araminta lifted her head and drew a deep breath and felt fear eased within her. It was all right, she assured herself. The faceless ogre had never existed. Instead there was a pleasant-looking, quite handsome woman of between forty-five and fifty, a little tired from a day's marketing and about to refresh herself with a cup of tea. Indeed, after that first smiling glance she removed her gaze from Araminta and lifted the big silver teapot and gave her full attention to pouring a fragrant amber stream into a delicate china cup painted with roses; so that Araminta, still a little puzzled by her blindness in the morning, could stare her fill, unobserved.

Once upon a time Mrs. Stancy must have been very handsome indeed; even now her skin was good, very pale and soft-looking like well-rolled pastry, and although there were folds in it, between the thick black brows and on either side the full pale mouth, it had not sagged or wrinkled. And the smile had shown that she still had her teeth which alone was remarkable in any woman over forty. Her hair reminded Araminta of the big cows, it had been black and was now about half black and half perfectly white, not grey anywhere, but seeming to be streaked evenly. It was parted in the centre of her smooth white brow and then plaited; the plaits wound all over the back of the head, apparently without beginning or end, and the outer edge of the first one on her crown stood up a little, making a kind of halo. The whole thing might have been a head-dress made of wood and painted, for although she had just removed her hat, not a single hair was ruffled or separate from the rest.

Mrs. Stancy added a meticulously measured dribble of cream to the cup, lifted it to her lips and drank for a long moment. Then she looked at Araminta.

Everything else, the skin, the plaited hair, the firm cheeks and the rounded chin were meaningless, mere features assembled to be a frame for a pair of remarkable eyes. They were clear yellow in colour, as clear and as yellow as tea, and round the yellow was drawn a fine black line. They were completely expressionless. Even when, at the end of a long moment, Mrs. Stancy smiled again and said, "Well, you look quite a promising girl, Araminta," the quality of her stare did not alter in the least. The yellow eyes just went on boring and boring into Araminta's until her first feeling of surprise at their colour, and her following surprise at their changelessness had given way to a feeling of acutest discomfort. She felt her cheeks growing hot, and her own eyelids fluttered, and a nerve near the corner of her mouth began to twitch. And then, with sickening force, all the doubts which had been in her mind all day, became certainties. And then her confidence collapsed completely and the things upon which she had prided herself, her industry and efficiency, her physical endurance, her honesty over other people's possessions, all the things which had hitherto marked Araminta Glover off from the ordinary run of the mill were suddenly as nothing. Even her action in running away from temptation, her proud determination not to go the way of Agnes and the rest, seemed silly and senseless.

And then at last she could not think at all; she could only stare into those dreadful yellow eyes and plead soundlessly, let me go, let me go.

With a little gesture of satisfaction Mrs. Stancy looked down at her tray and began to refill her cup. "Yes," she said slowly, "I was a little doubtful. I never engage a girl without seeing her first, but

Mrs. Whistler spoke so highly of you that I broke my rule for once. Now, tell me, how have you been getting on to-day? I expect everything seems very strange."

"It does, rather," said Araminta, hearing her own voice small and thin, and rather surprised that she could speak at all.

"Let me see, you were at Uplands with a Mrs.—Mrs. Pollard, weren't you? Quite a small place. Were you happy there?"

"Yes." Oh, how happy!

"But you changed and came to Abbey Farm. Why?"

"The money is better." The old answer, coming easily now; only what had Luke said about the money?

"Ah!" Mrs. Stancy sipped from her cup. "Do you know, Araminta, I ask every girl that, and I think you are the first to give me a frank answer. I value that. Thank you. Now I can be equally frank with you. Yes, the money is better. I pay more and I expect more. I have no doubt that you have given satisfaction in your former places, that you can milk and churn, make butter and cheese, tend fowls, scrub and scour. But so can dozens of girls whom I would never employ. And I want you to begin here as though you knew nothing. Only in that way can you attain the standard I desire. What do you think of Nancy?"

"She's——she's very clever," said Araminta, startled by the suddenness of the question.

"She is improving. She is starting her fourth year and she is beginning to give satisfaction. But I think, you know, that if you really *tried* Araminta, if you gave your whole heart to your work, you could be as good as, perhaps better than, Nancy. Bear that in mind."

As she spoke the last words she lifted a small silver cover from the tray and from the plate beneath it took a thin strip of perfectly browned toast, dripping with butter. Araminta, to whom the sight of the pouring tea had been torture, now found her mouth filled with water and was obliged to swallow hastily. Mrs. Stancy bit the toast, which made a faint crunching sound, and when she had chewed for a second or two, said suddenly:

"Of course your standards of personal cleanliness are deplorable.

I noticed your ankles this morning. Certainly you had just had a long walk. But have you done anything about them since?"

"I been working all the time."

"Have been." Mrs. Stancy made the correction almost absent-mindedly. "I see. Well, you must take a thorough bath this evening. Preferably before supper. Mrs. Nead will give you some hot water." She ran her glance over Araminta again, from head to foot. "Otherwise you are quite neat, except for your hair. You must do something about that. If you can't confine it tidily, like Nancy's, you must cut it shorter. Yes, I should advise cutting it."

Araminta's heart fell again. Like most people, she tended to admire a type of looks to which she could never attain, and had thought Cissie, at Uplands, with her pink and white cheeks, little pursed mouth and plumply blurred contours, the absolute perfection of beauty. She was quite blind to the good bone formation of her own face and thought it at once too wide and too thin and too brown. But she did like her own hair, and had, as soon as her adolescent vanity wakened, taken some pains to keep it clean and tidy. One of the first things she had ever bought was a harsh cheap comb. And her hair was pretty, a light bright brown, with sun-bleached streaks in it which almost matched the dark honey colour of her skin. It was not very long, and grew straight down from a parting in the very centre of her crown, making a fringe on her forehead and curling into tendrils over her ears and her nape. The thought of cutting it into wispy rat-bitten strands like Susie's was extremely distasteful. But she made no protest; life had taught her the folly of opposing the wishes of those who paid wages. She simply determined to comb it all upwards and hide it under her cap.

"Well, that's settled then," said Mrs. Stancy, pushing her chair a trifle back from the table and diving for her keys. "Now you can help to put the things away. Unlock this tall cupboard. Now that blue package is sugar. Empty it into the brown jar with a lid, there on the left. The white package is rice—that goes into the blue jar. Put the block salt into the box at the bottom of the cupboard—no, no, not on top of a block already started, below. The next is tea; that red canister, unlock it, here is the key. Be careful. . . ."

Accompanied by a constant stream of directions and admonishments Araminta worked away for about five-and-twenty minutes, performing such diverse physical feats as dragging a heavy bale of new sacking into its appointed place at the bottom of one cupboard, lifting four stones of washing soda to the top of another, and sorting five tiny packages of spices into the minute compartments of a spice chest. At the end of it her nerves were jangling, and tiny points of perspiration shone on her forehead and upper lip, though the October evening was chill in the storeroom, and Mrs. Stancy, who had removed nothing save her hat and her mittens, once or twice chafed her big white hands together to warm them. At last everything was sorted and stored and there remained nothing visible of the day's marketing except some pieces of wrapping-paper which Araminta, who was already absorbing something of the Abbey Farm's worship of the fetish of tidiness, had the sense to fold small and pile neatly, instead of crumpling them together as she would have done had she been putting away Mrs. Pollard's shopping.

Then Mrs. Stancy said, "There, that's done. Now perhaps you would like a cup of tea, eh?"

Araminta thought of Nancy's words, and she thought too that the tea would be cooled, it would have lost the sterling virtue of "pulling you together," which was the chief charm of hot tea, however weak. Still, it would be better than nothing.

Mrs. Stancy, with elaborate care, rinsed out her own cup with hot water from the silver jug, held it to drain for a moment over the slop basin, and then lifted the teapot. She was not blind to the avidity on Araminta's face.

"I'm sorry," she said, "there's none left. But it would hardly have been worth drinking. Carry the tray to the kitchen and ask Mrs. Nead for your bath water."

She stood up, and shielding each candle-flame with her hand, blew them out, one by one, making quite a ritual of even so simple an action. Araminta, with a little core of hatred forming and hardening in her heart, because there was enough hot water still to have made quite a tolerable cup of tea, lifted the tray and followed her mistress along the passage. At the dairy door Mrs. Stancy paused. Araminta passed on into the kitchen and set the tray on the dresser. The kitchen was very hot and full of the pleasant, toothsome savour of freshly-baked bread just removed from the great brick oven. Mrs. Nead was busy at the square table, putting finishing, fancy touches to the crust of a pie. The girl Bella was polishing the steel knives and forks with a scrap of moistened rag and some powdered bath-brick.

"Mrs. Stancy said you'd give me some hot water," said Araminta, a trifle timidly.

"All right. . . . Wait time I just finish this." Mrs. Nead took a strip of pastry and began to fashion a rose. "Bella, empty that teapot right away, and rinse it."

Araminta watched while Bella took the teapot and emptied the tea-leaves and quite half a pint of tea into a bucket near a door. A wavering thin column of steam arose as she did so.

"Don't stand gawping," said Mrs. Nead. "Go fetch your can. Take a candle." She pressed the rose into place in the centre of the pie and at the same time jerked her head towards a row of candle-sticks which stood on a shelf beyond the dresser.

Araminta took one, lighted the candle, and by its light climbed the stairs and fetched down the largest of the brass cans. Upstairs again she dragged out the shallow bath, poured in the hot water and added cold, and then shiveringly stripped off her clothes. Carefully and painstakingly she set about taking the first whole bath of her life. And all the time her mind was grappling with the mystery of Mrs. Stancy. Why had she said that the tea was finished? Was it possible that she was just a little crazy, with her rules and her odd changes of manner and her peculiar eyes? It was not until she was again dressed and engaged in running the comb through the damp tendrils of her threatened hair that another possible explanation presented itself. Could it be that Mrs. Stancy had seen her watching the tea and had made and then withdrawn the offer of a cup out of a desire to torment her? Araminta pushed the thought away. It was silly. What had Mrs. Stancy to gain by making a new girl feel badly? But the desire to torment did explain an otherwise reasonless action. Araminta ceased combing her hair, and a long shudder made its cold way down her spine. If she had hit on the right reason; if, in addition to its rules and its silence and its horrible lack of little cheering things like tea, this place had a deliberately cruel mistress, it was a poor lookout for a person who had two years, all but a day, to go.

This Caroline Stancy, upon whose temper and disposition so many people's happiness, beside Araminta's depended, mystified almost everyone who came into contact with her. She could not even—though she was a woman of some education—have explained her actions and her motives. And she lived and died before the era of the psychologists who could see a guilt complex in a neurotic passion for cleanliness, an inferiority complex in that deliberate wearing of a white apron as a badge of pride, and a power complex in the thwarting of à young maid's desire for a cup of tea. But Mrs. Stancy knew, and she was the only person who did know, for she kept her secrets well, what had gone wrong in a life which had once brimmed with promise.

She was the eldest child and only daughter of a moderately prosperous solicitor in the town of Bury St. Edmund's, across the Suffolk border. When she was six years old her mother had died, leaving two babies, both boys, one aged a year and a half, the other only two months. Caroline had been an exceptionally lovely little girl with her black fringe and her yellow eyes set off by a wild-rose pallor. Her father had seemed to transfer the affection which he had felt for his wife to his daughter and had never thwarted her wishes. His favouritism and her few years seniority had given her an authority over her brothers, Stephen and Charles, which was later to bear bitter fruit. Both she and her father had been certain that she would make an unusually good match; she was beautiful and talented, a fluent conversationalist, a gifted pianist, and an excellent housekeeper. Between them, through pride and ambition, they had ruined every chance of an ordinary happy marriage for her, and when her father died she was twenty-seven and still unmarried. But she was, and for a short time remained, undisputed mistress of the big, rather shabby house on the Abbey Hill. Charles, lately taken into partnership, and Stephen, in his last year at Cambridge, still appeared to regard her as head of the house; and if, at times, she was conscious of a vague dissatisfaction, she assuaged it by reflecting that her position was better than would have been the case had she married any one of the suitors who had presented themselves.

When her father's estate was settled it was found that he had left little save the business and the house—both of which passed naturally to Charles, and the first real shock of Caroline's life came when Charles refused to buy her an expensive new gown.

"I'm sorry, Caro," he said. "Funds just won't allow. And I can't make you the allowance father did. For one thing, I'm thinking of getting married."

Presently, the young wife was installed, and the inevitable struggle began. At first it had seemed an easy thing to gain ascendancy over the shy incompetent little creature, for Charles, like most brothers, had married beneath him and his bride was for the first few weeks overawed by her new home and by her beautiful, domineering sister-in-law. But by the time Stephen returned for his long vacation, Caroline had a long list of injuries and insults, of slights and complaints to reel off to him, certain that she would find in him a staunch ally. But Charles was financing his young brother, not without some self-sacrifice, and Stephen, who had suffered especially from Caroline's domination, was unsympathetic, if not unhelpful.

"It's his house, my dear, and his wife and what you don't like you must lump. The best thing you could do, you know, would be to get married yourself. You'd still stand a chance with an oldish man."

Amongst Charles' clients there was an Essex man named Reginald Stancy. His forbears had farmed well and prosperously at the Abbey Farm, Summerfield, for something over two hundred years. They had acquired other property and made careful matrimonial alliances and reached eventually the position of small Squires. In his youth Reginald Stancy would have been a welcome match even to the proud father on Abbey Hill. But he had lived dissolutely and idly and was incurably litigious. He had quarrelled with every lawyer in Essex, and had eventually carried his business over the border. At some time during the summer after old Stancy's death he came to Bury St. Edmund's to inspect Charles and decide whether the young man was capable of filling his father's shoes. It seems likely that Stephen had dropped a word in Charles' ear and that the brothers had plotted together. For Stancy was not lodged at "The Angel," but offered the hospitality of the Abbey Hill house, and Caroline, in a gown which she thought outdated, but which dazzled everyone else, was allowed to take the credit for the excellent dinner and the considerable efforts which had been made for the guest's comfort. The young wife remained demurely in the background.

Reginald Stancy was fifty-three years of age and his looks were going, although a certain seedy elegance remained to him and his manners, when he exerted himself, were gracious and insinuating. But free favours no longer came his way easily, and, although almost completely without money sense, he was beginning to realize that he could no longer afford to purchase the kind of women he preferred. His latest mistress, a big strapping Essex girl, a maid at the Abbey, was becoming truculent and extortionate. It occurred to him once or twice during his visit that he could do worse than marry this handsome, agreeable woman, who accepted every trivial, conventional courtesy so graciously. Before he left he had invited the younger brother, who seemed to be at a loose end, down to Essex for a "bit of rough shooting," and Stephen returned with stories of the glories of the Abbey which only needed a mistress to make it a "right proper place." In the autumn, Reginald Stancy spent another night in Bury, and in the morning took Miss Caroline for a drive in his gig. It was a smart turnout, for he was a judge of horseflesh anywhere but on the racecourse, and she was gratified by the curious and admiring glances cast upon them by the towns-folk whom she professed to despise. From that moment she threw herself heartily into the business. Within three months they were married, and Caroline, with Charles' blessing, an elaborate trousseau and a hardly-spared hundred pounds as a marriage portion, crossed over into Essex to live in a house which she had never seen with a man she scarcely knew and did not much like.

But she was grateful to him and perfectly prepared to make him a model wife, to run his home, consider his interests, and bear his children quickly before she was too old.

At that time she was ordinary enough, proud, spoilt, and despite the lessons of the last six months, still accustomed to having her own way. What happened to change her nobody ever knew. If she were disappointed by the house, lovely yet dilapidated, or by the discovery that Reginald Stancy was all-but ruined financially; or if she were shocked to find that the dirty, truculent girl in the intolerably filthy kitchen had been her husband's mistress, she never spoke, either of the disappointment or the shock. There was no one to whom to speak. Friendless she had come into Essex, and friendless, largely by choice, she remained. There was no female friend to listen to, and then to report in glutinous whispers, the account of marital experiences with an unloved, unlovable male creature who was growing impotent and was furious and cruel in his impotence. She told no one of the time when she had cleaned the kitchen with her own cherished white hands; or cried, "If I must be a common farmer's wife I'll be the best farmer's wife in six counties!" because it was galling to have refused a personable young farmer and then after all do no better, but rather worse for yourself. Even in her own mind she tried not to remember how she had scrimped and saved and cheated, a penny here and a penny there, in order to put by a little store against the day which must surely come, the day when Stancy's stupidity and drunkenness and incurable passion for going to law would bring ruin so complete that even the farm itself would be lost. For months she lived in dread of that day; for even she, who had once despised a mere farm, had come to see that this was an excellent one of its kind, and to regard it as the one anchor against the inevitable storm. And then there came a day—which was another of those days about which, later on, she must *not* think—when she realized that the storm was not, perhaps, so inevitable after all. That was the day when Reginald Stancy first spoke of raising money by mortgaging the Abbey. She

91

knew then that his position was desperate, for hitherto, either from blind instinct or from some remaining vestige of good sense he had clung through all vicissitudes to his home.

He had done things to her about which it was impossible to speak or think, but now he had threatened the very roof over her head. In wild night thoughts she could see herself returning to the cold hospitality of brother's house, or finding a squalid lodging and some kind of work by which she could support herself and this foolish, drooling creature whom she had once looked upon as a saviour. It was not to be borne. Caroline Stancy must not be pushed too far.

Stancy's death interested a good many people who knew or had known him, but it shocked no one, surprised no one. It was easy enough to believe that after a bout of hard drinking he had fallen in a fit, been helped to bed by his wife and died before the doctor could be fetched from Baildon to bleed him. Some people were a little sorry for the widow, who must be left poorly off, others held that his death could only be a happy release for her. Many farmers began to take stock of their resources—swollen by the corn prices of the war—wondering whether they could manage to buy the Abbey now that it had at last, after remaining so long in the possession of one family, come to the market. It was unanimously assumed that the widow, who did not come of farming stock and who had retained her "foreignness," would sell out and return to her own place and people.

But the Abbey was not sold. Some outlying fields of arable land, four cottages and some timber were disposed of; a few pressing and indisputable debts were paid. And then Caroline Stancy began to put into action certain plans of her own. She began modestly, with four cows of the famous Collings Brothers breed, and a stall in Baildon market-place. She was thirty years old then, in the prime of her life, tireless, indefatigable, ruthless. Twenty years later, when Araminta Glover went to work in the now-famous dairy, she had built up a business and a reputation unique to herself. Her butter, her cream and her cheeses, her fowls and her eggs were sought after, as Nancy had said, as far afield as Wardwyke and Standover.

Nor did the business end there. The experiments of Coke and the Collings had wakened the more progressive farmers and many petty Squires to the importance of breed in cattle. Mrs. Stancy, interested by an account of Dutch dairy-farming in an agricultural journal, had, quite early in her career, imported two Friesland cows and a bull. Now she was doing a thriving trade in livestock. People cognisant of such matters would speak with respect of the "Stancy Strain." Three of her calves, two heifers and a little blunt bull had even crossed the salt seas to America. The long-drawn out war had served her well, too, for it had increased the value of home produce and forced up prices, and although she willingly poured money back into the farm itself, she spent little upon herself, kept all the details of the business under her own control, and economized, almost with ferocity, in the matter of labour.

Her story might have been a simple and even cheerful chronicle of success wrested from adversity, but for those dark passages about which nobody knew; and but for the fact that, side by side with the growth of her wealth and her activity, another grisly, unnameable thing had spread its tentacles. She had longed for power and for security, now they were abundantly hers; but they were no longer sufficient. Somewhere, somehow, the ordinary young woman had become warped and twisted until almost every normal impulse within the woman of fifty was utterly corrupt.

Mean mistresses were common as gooseberries in June, strict ones plentiful as September blackberries, but Araminta would have gone a long way to find another of whom she could, over the matter of a cup of tea, think with deadly accuracy, "She done it to torment me," and still be pitiably short of the truth.

Araminta completed her toilet by tucking every strand of hair well away out of sight under her cap. Then she went downstairs. The dairy was lighted, perfectly clean, scrupulously tidy, but unoccupied. She stood in it, feeling lonely and depressed for a few moments, waiting to see if Nancy or Susie would come. Presently she walked into the kitchen. At Uplands she would have known that, with the dairy work so obviously finished for the day she would either help Mrs. Pollard with the supper, or be free to follow her own devices. But here, somehow, she felt that she ought to be busy and was not sure what she should be busy about. Bella was alone in the kitchen, setting the table for supper.

Bella was ordinary enough, with a little, lightly-freckled snub nose. Araminta had noticed her during the dinner spell, and thought it possible that, given a chance, she might strike up a friendship with this girl who was neither so solemn and superior as Nancy, nor so plainly dull as Susie. So, finding her now alone, she made her approach a friendly one, smiling as she said, "I don't quite know what I oughta be at."

Bella did not return the smile. Instead, after a glance towards a door which opened out of the inner side of the kitchen, half hidden by the big dresser, she said primly, "You shouldn't ought to be here. I can tell you that. Supper ain't till eight." Araminta looked at the clock. It still lacked a quarter to the hour.

"Would you know what I should be doing?" she asked, still placatingly.

"Nance and Susie's plucking."

"Oh. Where?"

"In the plucking-shed."

"Where's that?"

"Outside. The door on the right."

"Thanks," said Araminta and moved away. Ordinarily she would have said, half-laughing, half-rebuking, "You're a chatty one, ain't you?" or "Ain't you ever been new in a place?" But somehow to-night there was no spirit in her. She hardly resented the girl's manner. It was all part of the place. She left the kitchen reluctantly. She would have liked to stay; at least it was warm and bright, and she could smell the cooking. It would have been nice to stay and chat and watch the clock's hand move on to the moment when her stomach would have something other than the peas-pudding to gnaw on. One again she was visited by a memory of the Uplands kitchen at this hour.

The plucking-shed was small, and cold and very businesslike. There was a bench along the wall, a high "skep" for the reception of feathers, a bucket for the entrails, a basket of freshly-killed fowls and a tray upon which the denuded, disembowelled bodies were placed at the end of the plucking. Nancy and Susie sat side by side on the bench, plucking away for dear life at the carcasses which they held between their knees. Well, at least it would be something to sit down for ten minutes, Araminta thought, taking her place beside them.

Susie, with violent, would-be secret grimaces, indicated her own sacking apron and drew Araminta's attention to the fact that she was wearing a white one.

"Susie, stop making those faces," said Nancy sharply, "You get on my nerves. The way you twitch is bad enough. Don't make it worse."

"But that'll be sixpence in the book do she pluck in her white," said Susie, instantly giving the whole thing away.

"That'll hurt you a lot," said Nancy nastily. "Mind your business and get on, do. What with one thing and another, it'll be midnight before we're done to-night."

"Here," said Susie, lifting a corner of her own voluminous apron and stretching it over Araminta's knee. "That'll do, on't it Nance?" She spoke almost beseechingly. "You on't tell on her this once, will you?"

"Mind your own business," said Nancy, not pausing in her work. It occurred to Araminta that Nancy wanted her to lose sixpence. She said meekly, "Thass such a short time. That was quarter to before I came out of the kitchen."

"So that's where you were." Nancy did lift her head then, and gave Araminta a look which was dull and yet spiteful. "No wonder we're all behind."

"I didn't stay in there. Mrs. Stancy sent me to hev a bath and when I came down I went to the kitchen to ask what I should do."

"I should think you might have guessed. Or did chickens pluck theirselves at your last place?"

A sharp retort rose to Araminta's lips, but she held it back. She'd had a lesson about losing her temper. And for two years she had to work with and under this girl. It wouldn't do to make an enemy

95

of her the first day. But why, she wondered, as she began to tear out the feathers rapidly, why should Nancy be so hateful? She must know that on the first day you were bound to make mistakes and be a little slower and more awkward than usual. Araminta did not know that, while she was bathing and pondering the puzzle of Mrs. Stancy and the tea Mrs. Stancy had been in the dairy, carefully inspecting the butter which she had churned and stamped, and had praised it, not because she wanted to give it its due, but in order to annoy and humiliate Nancy and to set her against her new work-fellow. Girls worked better when they got on badly; they kept a sharper look out for mistakes, they vied with one another and so increased the output, and they didn't chatter and giggle and combine against their mistress. Also, quite apart from all these practical considerations, Caroline Stancy could no more have resisted a sly taunt at Nancy than she could have flown. It was quite pleasant to see that stolid face quiver under the impact of a few carefully-chosen words. "This new girl certainly looks very promising. I can't tell her work from yours, Nancy. And this is her first day." And, "If Araminta handles everything as well as she handled the stores you'll have no reason to think you're overworked any more, Nancy. Do you remember breaking the sugar jar lid the first time you put things away?"

Each venom-tipped word found its mark and implanted poison. Nancy, who despite her apparent indifference had been impressed by Araminta's energy and dexterity and relieved to think that she would now obtain adequate help in her overburdened life, became a prey to jealousy and fear for her own prestige. And now, looking back at her first quarter at the Abbey and remembering how at its end she had drawn only five miserable shillings, she was quite willing, almost anxious, that the new girl who was so very marvellous, should suffer as she had suffered. Araminta guessed, quite rightly, that the lapse over the aprons would be reported; only Susie, whose simple mind could never fully understand how the whole atmosphere of a place could be poisoned from above, hoped that Nancy's spite could be averted by an appeal to her better nature.

Soon the bell rang for supper; Araminta and Susie rose eagerly; but Nancy stopped work with a sigh of weary impatience. She was too tired to feel hungry, at least for anything which the Abbey table offered, and would rather have worked on and then gone straight to bed. But a rule was a rule, as she presently pointed out to the new girl, thus salving her own weariness and discontent. For when they turned in at the dairy door, instead of proceeding straight to the kitchen, Susie, seeing Araminta's look of astonishment, said, "We wash now."

"Not me," said Araminta, "why, I just had a bath and I hadn't pulled more than a few feathers. I'm as clean as a pin."

"You'll wash just the same," Nancy snapped. "That's a rule, and I wish you'd quit arguing. I reckon I'm extra tired to-night on account of explaining everything to you. If you're all that clever, you shouldn't want telling things twice."

"I never said I was clever."

Nancy folded her lips tightly and washed her own hands as though she hated them. Araminta wetted hers and dried them on the towel, and then, as Susie took her place at the sink, pulled a face behind Nancy's back. The silly creature giggled and spluttered and Araminta sighed . . . you couldn't act naturally with either one of them.

Supper, to her intense disappointment, consisted of a stodgy dollop of oatmeal porridge. At Uplands this had been a breakfast dish, eaten with creamy milk and a generous sprinkling of brown sugar. Good enough for anybody; good enough for Mr. Pollard himself. But there was no milk, no sugar on this table. The oatmeal was slightly salted in the cooking and was eaten as it was, accompanied by another small thick chunk of dry brown bread. There was water to drink.

There was no sign of the beautiful pie which Mrs. Nead had been decorating earlier in the evening; and the lovely new bread had been put away, to wait, Araminta thought crossly, until it was as dry and stale as that in the wooden bowl; but the scent of it still hung about the kitchen, mocking the appetite.

The meal was over in less than ten minutes. Nancy rose as soon as Mrs. Nead had said Grace and was making for the passage door when the hunchback called, "Nancy, d'you mind if I speak to Susie for a minnit. I want to tell her about Sheba."

"Tell her quickly then. We're busy."

Luke stood close to Susie and began to say, "You milked Sheba s'afternoon, din't you, Sue?" Araminta heard no more; she followed Nancy into the passage. Susie, trotting, joined them by the door of the plucking-shed. There was a look of fatuous pleasure on her face.

They worked in silence until the basket of fowls was emptied and the big wooden dish piled with plucked bodies. Then Nancy straightened her back and yawned.

"I'll go and ask about the trussing," she said. "Maybe, as we're so late to-night, Mrs. Stancy would rather we left it till before breakfast. You two clear up while I'm gone."

As soon as she had closed the door, Susie's hand plunged into her pocket and came out clasped about a lump of cheese, quite a large lump, about eight ounces of it. She broke it in halves between her rough red hands and extended one half to Araminta, at the same instant cramming the end of her own piece into her mouth. Araminta's mouth watered, but she hesitated for a moment. Susie was so unreliable; she might have stolen the cheese, and it wouldn't do to get wrong on the very first day for the sake of a few tasty mouthfuls of food.

"Go on, eat it quick afore she get back. Thass all right, Luke give it to me time he was saying about Sheba."

"Luke? The one with the bad back?"

Susie nodded. "He often give me stuff. Give you some, too, if he reckon you're all right. But you marn't let Nancy know. I dunno how I'd manage without Luke." She stuffed her mouth again and chewed vigorously. "The Missus hold it agin me, you see, acause the Poor Farm made her take me and pay them two pounds a year."

Araminta saw the reason for Mrs. Stancy's grievance. You could get a good sensible girl for that money.

"So she take it out on me," said Susie, biting again. "I don't reckon I've had me three meals above twice since I bin here. Partly thass Nancy. I bet she's in there now saying how I towd you about

98

the apron, and so on. That'll be me breakfast gone agin. Three days running. Yesterday I spotted the cloth, and to-day I bruk a egg. She can't dock me money acause the overseer take that, so she dock me grub, see? Thass why Luke gimme the cheese."

A completely novel feeling moved in Araminta's breast. All her life she had been the underdog, with the underdog's policy of snatch and run. Now, for the first time, she was face to face with someone who was worse off than herself, somebody who hadn't even the incentive to earn money. She looked at the piece of cheese from which she had bitten a semi-circle as soon as Susie had told her of its origin. It was good cheese; it had the substance and flavour for which she had craved, but she held it out, saying gruffly, "Here, you'd best eat this yourself in case of what Nancy is saying and you lose your breakfast to-morrow."

Susie hesitated for only a second. Then she took the cheese and began cramming it into her mouth. Nancy would be back at any moment now.

But they had tidied the plucking-shed and carried the tray of birds into the dairy, where, Susie said, the trussing would be done when it was done, and still Nancy had not returned.

"Who was here before me?" Araminta asked, leaning back against the dairy shelf and preparing to spend the time of waiting in satisfying her curiosity.

"A girl," said Susie simply. And then, as though guessing that this answer would not satisfy her listener, she twitched her face grotesquely in the effort to remember. "Maggie were her name. She worn't here long, though. She din't come till arter Christmas, and she left afore Michaelmas. She was lucky. Her dad garden for the doctor and he took her away."

"Who, the doctor or her dad?"

"They got together."

"And who was here before Maggie?"

"Old woman called Grace." A brighter expression came over the simpleton's face. "Ah, right a nice old woman she were, pore old dear. She took and died." The big red hands moved gropingly over the front of the sacking apron. Susie's body twisted round until she was facing the door. She even had the good sense to lower her voice. "Reckon that were Nancy's doing as much as anything. Old Grace were that clever. She'd make anything you liked to name outa butter. Just with a little old knife she did it. She were making a grut cow for the Christmas Show in the market and then she took ill. Corf, you never heard the like of it, bark like a dog she would, hour arter hour. Then she took to her bed and told Nance she were dying and Nance gotta finish the cow, see?" With one of her incomprehensible lapses Susie dropped her voice as though the story were completed there, fully told, easily understood. Araminta wondered whether she had heard Nancy's step in the passage. But after waiting a moment, in which nothing happened, she said:

"Yes, I see so far. But what happened?"

"She died at it."

"At work? Why?"

"Well, Nance couldn't do it. She knew she couldn't. So she told Mrs. Stancy old Grace were foxing."

"Pretending to be ill?"

"Thass right. I heard her. And the missus fetched her down, with a push and a shove. That were a cold old day, too. They stood over her, just there where you stand now, to see she din't stop and there she dropped down dead. Cow was done all but the tail to it, and Nance put that on arterwards. Then Nance were put to head girl, and a bad old day for me that was. Missus give her tea at times. I bet thass what they're doing now. Swallering tea and talking about us."

"I could do with a cup myself," Araminta said. "Is the food always like to-day's?"

"Mostly. Breakfast is best; thass why she make you lose your breakfast do you do anything wrong. I told you, din't I, I mostly lose mine."

"You'll have to be more careful, Susie. You go at things in such a splutter," Araminta said, quite kindly.

"Do I'm careful, they say I dawdle," Susie said solemnly. "And do I'm quick, I break things. Thass all the same."

She spoke resignedly and grinned as she spoke. It occurred to Araminta that, except that she was ugly, which would make it all the harder for her, she was very much like Betsy. And unless something happened, something like a miracle, Betsy would have much this kind of life once she went out to work. Work was hard enough if you were bright and had all your wits about you; if you were slow and simple and prone to make mistakes, it must be dreadful.

Just then Nancy returned. She walked to the tray of fowls and after a look at it stood for a second with her eyes closed as though the one glance had sickened her to the heart. Then she rallied and said crossly, "Come on, come on. They've got to be done to-night." She reached a ball of thin white twine and a handful of skewers from the shelf overhead. Susie, after a look of blank bewilderment, remembered her part in this performance and got a taper and a candle.

Nancy *had* had a cup of tea. She had also had the perverted pleasure of seeing the date and the offence "not wearing sacking apron," and the sum of sixpence, entered against Araminta's name in the book. Susie was to lose her breakfast for "playing and chattering and wasting time." These things, together with the tea, had made Nancy feel superior and privileged, Mrs. Stancy's confidential servant. Then, by an adroit move, "I'd like the fowls finished to-night, Nancy," Mrs. Stancy had cancelled out all Nancy's pleasure, reducing her at once to a bone-weary, overworked slave with another hour's toil between her and her bed. Mrs. Stancy had had twenty years' experience in handling girls.

It was just on half-past eleven when they went upstairs, blind and dumb with weariness. Nancy mumbled, "Luke'll call us at six" as she tumbled into bed, Araminta was too tired to acknowledge the information with anything more lucid than a grunt. Susie seemed to have been asleep for the last hour.

For a few seconds everything she had seen and done and heard and thought whirled together in a dizzy dance around Araminta's remaining speck of consciousness, and then she slept. At six o'clock there was a heavy hammering on the door and Luke's mild voice called "Time to get up, girls. Thass a fine morning." They rose, washed, dressed, made their beds and tidied the room, and were in the milking-shed by twenty minutes past the hour, still drowsy and heavy-eyed and loath to make the effort required for speech. At half-past seven they breakfasted—all except Susie—and Araminta learned why the forfeiture of breakfast was a punishment to dread. There was tea for breakfast, scalding hot and strong, and a slice of fried bacon and two slices of bread. After the meal she felt completely renewed, wide awake, and ready to face the day. When breakfast was over the day's milk was strained and set up, the buckets washed; then the gig was loaded, and Mrs. Stancy, in a fresh white apron, drove away.

Back in the dairy, starting the day's churning, Araminta realized that she had now been through the whole round of twenty-four hours at the Abbey Farm, and, rested by her night's sleep and refreshed by her breakfast, she could spare a little energy for thought. This was to begin with, a bad place; not only on account of the hard work and the meagre food. Her second place had been as general help to the wife of a poor struggling farmer whose few acres had been wrested from the unrewarding heathland beyond Sible Havers; there had been five young children in the family, and Araminta and the farmer's wife had toiled from morning to night on very poor diet indeed, because every egg, every pint of milk that could possibly be spared and all but the offal after a pig-killing had to be snatched away and taken to market. But there hadn't been a *spirit* of meanness in that humble place, and Araminta, though often hungry and always overworked, had been tolerably happy and had stayed two years, though she had been free to leave at the end of the first. Here she was, tied for two years, and already liked it so little that she would have left at once had that been possible. There was such a gloom, such a sourness about the whole place, and about all the people except Susie—and Luke; and Susie was simple, and Luke would cross her path very seldom. She thought again of the happy, cheerful bustling place she had left, and wondered at the sick folly which had made her leave it. The feelings which had seemed so powerful then, and the danger which had seemed so inescapable that she must flee from it, seemed utterly remote, seemed trivial and foolish now. Why hadn't she been able to deal with Jan as she had done with other troublesome menfolk, given him a piece of her mind and, if necessary, a box on the ear and sent him to the right-about? Fool, fool, fool that I was, she thought, setting the heavy churn in motion. Yet, after a few turns of the handle, because she was trained by life to make the best of things, she was thinking about the wages paid in this strange and gloomy place. Three pounds ten instead of thirty shillings she would send home this year; and the extra fifty shillings would make up for the time her mother would lose over the new baby. That was something to rejoice over. And *she* wasn't having a baby (which God knew she might have done), and she wasn't simple like Susie, or swollen-legged like Nancy. She'd got a lot to be thankful for. Her indomitable spirit rose steadily and presently, without knowing it, she was humming a tune and turning the churn to its rhythm. Nancy looked at her sourly. She had seen others start off like that. They were not the ones who lasted.

The first week seemed interminable. Friday was the busiest day, for on Saturday Mrs. Stancy went to Colchester market, which was more important than the ones at Baildon, Bywater and Fretton; and besides, early on Saturday morning Jacob, the biggest of the boys, drove off in a light farm cart to deliver his share of the week's private orders. It was usually one o'clock on Friday night before all the big and little baskets and all the trays were packed. But Saturday itself brought a little relief from the dairy work. There was no market on Sunday or Monday, so there was no churning and no plucking to be done. Saturday was devoted to a frenzied bout of cleaning and polishing. The bedroom and the stairs and the passages and the dairy and the storeroom and the plucking-shed were scrubbed and polished from top to bottom. Every apron and cap which had been worn through the week must be washed, starched and ironed; all the bits of butter-muslin and all the cloths used throughout the week had to be boiled and ironed and sorted back into their proper places; and in the evening, after Mrs. Stancy's return from market, every one of the baskets and trays was scrubbed with hot water and strong soap, rinsed with cold, and stood on end to dry. But despite the work, Araminta liked Saturday; it was a change from the monotony of churning and patting-up and marking the interminable pounds of butter, and it meant running hither and thither and a chance to exchange a word now and then with Luke or one of the boys who were raking and weeding the gravel or putting touches of whitewash on any marks which sullied the white walls; and, above all, it measured the passing of the week. With each Saturday's cleaning, and after the first two or three they seemed to come round quite quickly, she could reckon another week gone, and subtract one from the total of a hundred and four.

Sunday was a different day too, and might have been enjoyable. In the morning everyone except Mrs. Nead, who was making the dinner and Luke who stayed with the cows, walked the three miles to Summerfield Church for the morning service. It was the only time in the week when the girls got out of the house, and would have been a treat but for the fact that Mrs. Stancy, dressed very grandly and without her apron for once, always walked with them. Before they set out she inspected them to see that they were clean and tidy, then the three boys walked on ahead, followed by Araminta, Bella and Susie; Nancy always walked with Mrs. Stancy and carried her prayerbook. At the church door they waited, Mrs. Stancy took the book from Nancy and walked ahead then, her boys and girls followed her and trooped into the pew just in front. So her eye was upon them all the time. Both the Rector and his sister, who was married and lived across the Square from the Church, bought Mrs. Stancy's produce, and had a high opinion of everything connected with the Abbey; and when at times local gossip hinted, as it was bound to do, that Mrs. Stancy was a bad mistress, there were, besides the Rector and his sister, several pious church-goers who argued that such stories were fabrications of jealousy and spite. Only a thoroughly good woman would bring her entire staff, all neat and clean and well-behaved, into the public eye once a week.

Sunday dinner was good, the best in the week, stewed or roast meat, followed by pudding or pie. And after the six miles of walking and sitting through the long service appetites were keen. Milking took place as usual in the afternoon, and when that was done there was a little space, the only one in the whole week, which the girls had to themselves. There was usually some mending to do. At six everyone, except Luke who went to chapel on Sunday evenings with unvarying regularity, met in the kitchen. Mrs. Stancy seated herself on a chair to the side, and Mrs. Nead and Nancy took turns to stumble through a chapter of the Bible. They could both read after a fashion, but it was a slow and painful process. The Lord's Prayer was then repeated, Mrs. Stancy wished everyone good night, and went away.

Supper was served informally; it was always currant cake and a glass of very sour cider. That over, the day was ended and everybody was in bed by eight o'clock.

In a life so monotonous, the slightest break in the routine seemed enormous. There were two for Araminta before Christmas. The first was pleasant. One morning, not a market day, Mrs. Stancy looked in at the dairy door and said graciously, "Araminta, there's a carter from Mr. Whistler's in the yard. He asked to speak to you. Go out to him."

It was quite exciting to see Ted Somers who lived on the Green and often walked home with Dad, doing all the talking while Dad said "Ugh" and "Aye" and "Thass so." She gave him the benefit of her dimples, though ordinarily she thought him a poor sort of fellow, spending his money in "The Evening Star" when he should have been working at his patch of garden.

"Y'mum heard I was coming this way and arst me to look you up, Minta. She said to arst how you was faring and to tell you that she's nicely herself and able to get to work most days."

"Oh, thank you, Tom. Thass nice to hear that, and to see somebody from home."

"How'd'yer like it here, Minta? Fine sort of place that seem. Summat different to our yard at Whistler's."

"Yes, thass a nice place," Araminta said guardedly. "You tell Mum I'm getting on all right, won't you?"

"You look sorta peaked though," the carter said, peering into her face. "I seen you time you was home at Michaelmas and I thought to myself, she hev turned out a bonny mawther. Now I ain't so sure. You look sorta different."

You go home and tell Mum that and she'll worry a bit, Araminta thought. She put on her best smile again.

"You always was a rude chap, Tom. Can't you see thass my cap? I got all my hair in it to keep it outa the way. Why, you put a cap like this on Lizzie White and she'd look peaked too."

Lizzie White was the buxom, red-cheeked siren who drew Tom's custom to "The Evening Star" night after night. His broad brown face reddened a little.

"And you always had a edge to your tongue, Minta," he retorted, without malice. "So thass it. Then I'll tell your mum you looked bonny and bobbish for all your cap. Is that right?"

"Thass right. And tell her she'll be hearing from me at Christmas." Oh, it was almost worth changing a good place for a bad one to think of the whole sovereign that would carry the season's greetings into the cottage.

"I'll tell her," Tom promised. He waited a few moments and then shuffled his feet and said, "Well," and Araminta who had been wondering what to ask, what to say next, said, "Well," too.

"Well," said Tom again. "I dessay I shall see you another time, do I get over this way agin."

"I hope so, Tom. And thanks for the messages." Belatedly she remembered that she had other relatives besides her mother.

"Rest of my folks all right?"

"Aye. They're fine. Yer sister Betsy got a job I'm told, minding Mrs. Clem Barber's bebby; but she got a-playing with some more of 'em on the Green, time the bebby fell into the pond. They drug it out all green and black with weed and mud and nigh choking, and Mrs. Clem give Betsy a hiding. Sixpence a week she were to hev had; yer Mum worn't half mad, too."

Only a short time ago Araminta would have snorted with scorn; but now, almost despite herself, she was getting fond of Susie and was beginning to see that being short of wits was a real affliction, almost worse than being short of a limb; and Susie did try, so perhaps Betsy, who was so like her in many ways, tried too. So she said tolerantly:

"You tell Mum not to let Betsy mind brats or anything else people value much. She oughta start stone-picking or scaring birds, like I did. She couldn't do much harm then, even if she din't do much good."

"I'll tell her that, do I think of it. And you're fine and bobbish and she'll hear from you Christmas. Is that right?"

"Thass right, Tom. Well . . ."

"Well . . . I reckon I should git back. Thass a long road."

"And I got plenty to do, Tom. Good-bye, and thanks again."

"You're welcome, Minta. Good-bye."

She turned to re-enter the house, and as she did so she felt, rather than heard, a slight movement overhead. She looked up sharply and saw the edge of a black sleeve and a big white hand near the catch of the window directly above the passage door. She lowered, her eyes hastily, stricken by a feeling of shame which she did not understand and which was utterly new in her experience—shame for another person. To think of Mrs. Stancy bothering to climb those stairs and walk to the end of the upper passage and open the window and stand there just in order to listen to a conversation between a dairymaid and a carter. It was contemptible. Well, thank God, she had guarded her tongue, not from fear of eavesdropping but out of thought for her mother's feelings. So no harm was done. But her opinion of Mrs. Stancy dropped a little further, and with it some of the awe which the woman had inspired.

However, that was quickly restored. On the very next Monday, when, since it was not a market day, the sense of the mistress' imminence was heavy and tense in the dairy, Araminta, who had heard the door open, but had not turned her head, suddenly felt her cap whisked from her head. All the golden-brown curls which had been simply pushed up to the crown of her head and been confined only by the edge of the cap, tumbled down over her forehead, her ears and her neck, transforming her from a thin, hard-faced little creature into the pretty girl whom Jan Honeywood had loved. Her face went hot and her heart began to beat hard and irregularly behind her collar bone.

"I thought I advised you to cut your hair." Mrs. Stancy's voice was not angry at all. Confused by the discovery of her little subterfuge and surprised because of her mistress' mild manner, Araminta blurted out the truth without thinking.

"I reckoned I'd look right ugly without my hair, ma'am. So I tucked it well away."

"That," said Mrs. Stancy gently, "is hardly the point. Tidy yourself now and come to my room after supper." She held out the cap, and Araminta, by this time sensing the threat behind the soft manner, dragged it on with a sense of foreboding.

"Arguing'll be your downfall, as I've said before," commented Nancy, who had watched the little episode with pleasure. The curliness and thickness of Araminta's hair when she combed it night and morning had irritated the older girl, whose own thin straight locks had to be brushed back with a damp brush and pulled so tightly from her forehead and twisted so fiercely into such a small knob that even when it was released it still looked nothing.

"D'you reckon she mean to cut it herself? Or should I do it before I go?" Araminta asked, overlooking Nancy's enmity because she was in real need of guidance. Nancy shrugged.

"How should I know?" she asked, turning back to her butter.

"She cut mine," said Susie, eagerly.

"That don't say much for her as a barber," said Araminta with a quirk of her mouth. But for once Susie's ready silly smile was wanting.

"Do she do it, you stand stock still. Do you move only a mite, them scissors'll jab your skull. I had a sore place for weeks."

In the face of this advice Araminta decided to hack off her hair herself, and would have done so but for the fact that there was never a second all that day during which she could get away to her room and use the scissors. At supper the hair was still on her head, and as soon as the meal was eaten, Mrs. Nead looked along the table and said, "Araminta, you're wanted in the room."

Araminta went through the baize-covered door through which she had so often seen Bella carry delectable dishes. Behind it there was a square lobby, unfurnished, with another flight of stairs, which, she knew, led to the room where the boys slept. Mrs. Stancy's room was through the door to the right, Susie had told her that. She knocked and a voice called, "Come in."

It was a large room on the front of the house, and its tall, many-paned window looked out on to the lawns and the yew trees and the boy in the fountain and the chickens which Susie attended. Araminta wondered whether it had occurred to Susie that when she was feeding and cleaning her birds, and taking mouthfuls of their meal she was practically under Mrs. Stancy's eye. She would mention it as soon as she got out of this.

On the far side of the room was an arched alcove, not shut off from the room in any way, and in it stood a big bed, hung with velvet curtains and with a kind of velvet-covered platform to help one to climb into it. Under the window stood a great desk with little piles of papers neatly arranged and weighted down; in the middle of the room was a small solid table and one chair; near the fire was another chair, and opposite the desk was a chest of drawers; but the room was so large that it still seemed underfurnished, and despite the velvet hangings and the thick rugs on the highly-polished floor and the bright fire in the grate, it was chilly and somehow cheerless. There was nothing except a small brass clock on the wide marble overmantel, and the papers on the desk to show that the room was used at all. There was not a flower, nor an ornament, not a cushion nor a picture; just the plain solid pieces of furniture—and Mrs. Stancy standing just as solidly, with her back to the fire, midway between the hearth and the table.

"It is six weeks since you came here, Araminta; and I am sorry to see that you have not yet adapted yourself. You seemed an intelligent girl. Has it not dawned on you that a suggestion from me is tantamount to an order?"

"Tantamount" was new to Araminta; but she guessed that Mrs. Stancy was talking about her hair. She said meekly, "I'm sorry, ma'am."

"Take off your cap. Yes, yes, I see the reason for your vanity. It *is* beautiful hair; your best feature. You have cared for it, too, haven't you?"

"I've tried," said Araminta. Was the hair to be reprieved at the last moment?

"Well, we'll see if it can be confined like Nancy's. Hers was terribly untidy when she first came here."

Mrs. Stancy turned and walked to one of the cupboards which were set almost invisibly in the panelled wall on either side of the fireplace. She took out a comb and a pair of scissors.

"Sit down, Araminta."

The cupboard had been left open, and from her seat Araminta could see its interior, many shelves and a row of pigeon-holes, all scrupulously neat with piles of papers tied with string, several big boxes, and some meticulously-folded linen. She tried to keep her attention on the cupboard, guessing at the contents of the boxes, while Mrs. Stancy's hands, amazingly heavy and violent, combed the hair back from her forehead and tugged the curls towards the back of her neck. The comb had sharp teeth and seemed to rake at her scalp and the tugging was so painful that it felt as though the woman were trying to pull her hair out by the roots.

"No. It's no good, it isn't long enough to dress so. It will have to be cut. Take off your bodice."

Mrs. Stancy went to the cupboard and took out two clean towels. One she spread on the floor. "Stand on that. And put this one round your shoulders."

Now her touch was light and rapid, and the scissors were sharp. One by one Araminta's curls fell on to the white towel, springing together as they fell, so that they seemed closer and thicker than they had done when on her head; and against the whiteness they look brighter too, less brown, more golden. Once the cold scissors touched the back of her bare neck and she shuddered. Mrs. Stancy paused and looked round at her face, "You silly vain girl, surely you're not *crying* over your hair?" What was it about her voice, then? She sounded hopeful. Did she want to bring tears? If only she knew what Araminta had given up without so much as a snivel?

She thought suddenly of the moment when she had thrown the ivy spray out of the window.

The scissors crunched on. There, it must be nearly over. She could feel by the lightness and coolness that the hair was shorn close above her brow and over both ears. And then, all at once there was a sharp pain in her ear and something warm and wet trickled down the side of her neck.

"There," said Mrs. Stancy, "now I've cut you. You silly girl, you jerked your head." Araminta knew that was a lie; she had been standing like stone. Besides the hair had all gone from her ears minutes ago. Mrs. Stancy had cut her deliberately. She felt cold and sick and faint; not from pain, for she had borne sharper pangs without blenching, and not from the thought of blood, for she was not squeamish; she could skin a rabbit or wring the neck of a fowl, and she had been at home when Tommy was born; but there was something about the deliberate infliction of a wound which was terrible. She remembered what Susie had said about the scissors being jabbed into her skull and all the half-formed fears which she had felt and smothered and felt again during the last six weeks rushed upon her overwhelmingly. She put an unsteady hand out to rest upon the edge of the table.

Mrs. Stancy went to the window; a third of its lower half opened outwards like a casement, and she flung it as wide as it would go. The cold air of the November night streamed in, laving over Araminta's bare arms and neck like water.

"That'll keep you from fainting," Mrs. Stancy said, "if you feel like fainting over such a small thing." She moved away to the cupboard and took from a small brown box a little square of white linen and a blue bottle. When she turned back to Araminta the girl could see that there was a dusky, dark look about her pale cheeks and her eyes were very brightly yellow.

Usually so rapid and deft, the big white hands seemed to move slowly about the staunching of the little wound. Below the line of her collar Araminta's neck was as white as a lady's, the scarlet trickle of blood upon it made a sharp contrast. Mrs. Stancy stared at it so long, so entrancedly, while her hands shook the bottle and fumbled with the bit of linen, that at last Araminta turned her head inquiringly. Instantly the linen, soaked in some cold, pungently-scented lotion was laid on her ear, and she almost jumped out of the chair from the pain of it. It was a hundred times worse than the cut itself. That's just the sort of ointment she would keep, Araminta thought wryly. There rushed through her mind a memory of the simple remedies of Uplands: rose-water and honey for cuts, so nice you were tempted to lick it off; sweet oil of almonds for burns; liquorice and horehound and honey for coughs; pure goose grease for chilblains. What would you get for coughs or chilblains here?

The skin of her neck and arms was standing in goose-pimples; even her shorn scalp felt cold. And Mrs. Stancy was standing behind her, staring with those glassy yellow eyes. She wanted to scream.

"There," said the smooth voice at last. "Dress yourself now. You must shake the hair into the kitchen fire and put both the towels with your washing. Does your hair grow quickly?"

"No," said Araminta between her chattering teeth. "It never was cut before, and thass all I've ever grown."

"Cutting may stimulate its growth. When it reaches the edge of your cap I'll cut it again."

Be damned if you do, Araminta thought, buttoning her bodice so quickly that she muddled the buttons and buttonholes. She crammed the cap on to her head. It was too big now, she would have to tighten the string.

"Good night, Araminta," said Mrs. Stancy pleasantly.

"Good night, ma'am."

Before she shook the towel over the fire she picked out two of the thickest, most curly strands and tucked them into the front of her bodice. She would keep them for ever, so if her hair failed to grow, she would always have something to show to back up her claim to having had pretty hair once. When she went to bed she wrapped them in a screw of paper and laid them in her drawer. Then she turned and slowly took off her cap before the little mirror that hung over the wash-bowl.

"Oh," said Susie. "Oh, thass a shame, Araminta. Thass as bad as mine."

It was true; the rough unevenly hacked ends stuck out at all angles and looked lustreless and brittle. She turned away after one glance and, ignoring Susie's oozing sympathy and Nancy's cold superior stare, began to undress for bed. She looked a proper guy, and no mistake. Not that it mattered. There was nobody here to care what she looked like. Suddenly she thought of Jan with a fiery violent longing which she had not felt for six weeks. He had liked her hair; had run his big hand so gently over her curls. How angry he would be if he could see her now. Not that his anger would make any difference. He was a man and he was big and strong, but he would be as powerless against Mrs. Stancy as Araminta herself. Those who paid wages could do what they liked; those who worked for them had to bear things as best they could. Hopping into bed she grinned at Susie and said:

"Well, we do make a nice pair now."

"Did she cane you for keeping it on so long?" Susie asked.

"Don't talk so daft, Susie," Nancy said, releasing the end of her thin pigtail from between her teeth where she had been holding it what time she smoothed out the piece of ribbon with which she tied it at night. "Missus only canes you and the boys because you're the ones talking is wasted on."

"She caned you time you was learning your letters. Owd Grace said so," retorted Susie, who was enjoying one of the recklessly mad moods which alternated with her meek submissiveness.

"That's a lie," said Nancy, quite violently. "And I've had enough of your cheek, Susie Miller. I shall tell Mrs. Stancy to-morrow that you've been gossiping and telling lies and cheeking me. Then we shall see who gets caned."

Her vehemence betrayed her, Araminta thought. She remembered the curious look on the stolid face when the reading lessons were first referred to.

"I ain't a liar," Susie said recklessly; asking for trouble and certain to get it. "I ain't a liar, Araminta. Nancy had the cane, Nancy had the cane, Nancy had . . ." She was making a chant of it.

"Shut your silly face and get into bed," snapped Araminta, losing patience. "What if she did? I nearly had my lug cut off to-night.

We should stick together, us three, and not make life worse, squabbling amongst ourselves." She raised her head from the pillow and turned her face towards Nancy. "Don't go and make any trouble for her, Nancy. She didn't mean no harm; only that we was all in it together and she was sorry for you."

"I don't want her sorrow, thank you," said Nancy. "Nor her cheek. I'm head here now, and I'm relied upon. And I can read and write, don't you forget that."

During the next evening Susie was sent for to "the room," and when she returned her greenish face was swollen and blubbered with tears. As soon as she could do so unobserved by Nancy she held out her hands for Araminta's inspection. Three livid red stripes ran across each clean, calloused palm. It was inadvisable to speak a word either of sympathy or cheer, and the former was very difficult to convey by gesture. So Araminta pulled a funny face and pointed to the lobe of her own ear and grinned. Susie took heart and managed a smile.

November sank down into December. The weather turned very cold, though remaining open, without much frost, so that never once before Christmas did Mrs. Stancy fail to go to market on the appointed days. But all day and every day the bitter east wind swept in from the sea, howling around the house, lashing the leafless trees and piercing human beings to the bones. Now Mrs. Stancy wore a great black cape lined through, bordered and collared, with rich brown fur; a hood lined with the same fur covered her head; and at the last moment when the gig was loaded Bella ran out with a scorching hot brick, wrapped in flannel, to place under her mistress' feet which were already cosily esconced in fur-lined boots. But indoors Mrs. Stancy made no concessions to the cold; the bedroom where the girls rose in the dark bitter mornings had no means of heating; the dairy was as cold as the tomb, and never once did she suggest that before going to bed they should warm their chilly bodies through before the kitchen fire. From the moment when she rose in the candlelight to cross the windswept yard to the milking-shed, until the moment when she crept into bed again, Araminta was conscious of the cold. She tried to warm herself by working extra hard, but dairy work, even in warm weather, is concerned with cold things, cold water, slate slabs and stone floors. She sacrificed her shawl at last, hacking it into a queer-shaped underbodice which she wore day and night. Nancy, who had no family, and whose wages were all her own, had a drawerful of flannel underclothes; and even poor Susie had a red flannel petticoat, a pair of grey woollen drawers, and a pair of thick stockings; because two hundred years ago a charitable Lady of the Manor had bequeathed a certain sum of money with which the Parish Overseers were for ever to purchase "sturdy warm winter cloathing for six industrious poor girls." But even with their extra clothing, Nancy and Susie seemed to be as cold as Araminta, and it was after Susie had forced upon her the loan of the petticoat one day that Araminta decided to cut up her shawl; for even with the petticoat she was still cold, and it didn't seem fair to Susie either to borrow her garment or make her feel selfish to wear it; besides, after the first hour the petticoat had seemed to lose its virtue, or else the wind found a way through it. It wasn't petticoats you wanted, Araminta decided, so much as a fire, or the hope of a good warm through, and a scalding cup of tea every hour or so. At Uplands the dairy had been cold enough, but every now and then you could go into the kitchen; and in the evenings she and Cissie had sat by a fire so hot that the very candles had wilted and lurched; and there had been hot drinks and apples and walnuts and jokes and laughter. She had never gone to bed cold there. .

Here the only comfort against the cold was provided by Luke the hunchback, who, amongst his mixing of draughts and drenches and pills and lotions for sick animals, found time to produce a brittle kind of toffee, very sweet and toothsome, flavoured with hot substances, ginger and peppermint. Even Nancy would accept a piece of this confection if it were offered to her by Luke, and would eat it while she was milking; but when she found that Araminta and Susie kept a supply of it in their apron pockets she said they could not eat it in the dairy because it stank.

Araminta, who on her first day had with her suspicion of Mrs.

Stancy's "tormenting" tendencies come at least to the edge of probing the secret of her mistress' personality, was, at Christmas, as far from understanding Luke as ever. As she knew him better—though the rules and the timetable of the place prohibited any real friendship springing up—she wondered about him more and more. He was such a kind little man, and so independent, and so obviously opposed to almost everything that Mrs. Stancy stood for that it was puzzling to think that he chose to work for her. He was unmarried, a free man, and so skilled in his handling of cows that he could have found work, and a welcome, in a dozen places. People came from miles around to ask his advice about sick beasts; the little harness-room where he lived was always full of medicines; the battered old saucepan on the tiny fire, his herbs and drugs laid out on the shelf amongst his Sunday clothes, his clean linen, his pipe and his tobacco.

Mrs. Stancy valued him highly; she paid him nine pounds a year, which was a vast sum for a man living in; and she bullied him less than anybody. If he were busy with his pills and his plasters he missed a meal when he liked; he attended his own chapel; and he lived in the harness-room so that his comings and goings were unobserved. Yet in many ways he seemed to conform willingly to the rules of the place, and his kindnesses were always done furtively. He spent a good deal of money on food, which he shared with the boys and with Susie and Araminta. He bought Susie a pair of heavy shoes for the winter after Lady Pettergull's Charity had failed to provide them. And just before Christmas, when Araminta, blue and shivering, walked into the milking-shed one morning, he asked, as soon as they were seated, "Hevn't you got a shawl?"

"Yes," she said, with a quirk of her mouth, and opening the front of her print bodice, she showed him the garment she had cobbled. Next morning he handed her her stool, and under its seat, held in place by his gnarled brown hand was a new shawl, folded small, red, like the old one, but thick and woolly with all its virtues unimpaired by time and hard wear. She started to thank him, but he said "Shush," and glanced towards Nancy's end of the shed.

He seemed to regard the head dairymaid with an odd mixture of distrust, contempt and pity; and one day, when Susie was in a sensible mood and Nancy was making butter shells for a special order so that they were in the plucking-shed alone, Araminta mentioned the matter.

"Thass acause she tell tales; and acause of what she did about old Grace. Did I ever tell you about that?"

"Yes, you did. Did Luke like Nancy before that?"

"He liked her better. I told him about the cow . . . just like I did you, and he said fools and children allust spoke the truth. That were Luke went and got the doctor; but that weren't no good, acause she were dead afore I told him. Since that he don't hev no truck with Nance."

"He gives her sweets in the morning."

"Ah, sometimes he do. He say he's sorry for her. He said why once . . . something about her soul."

"Her soul? Are you sure, Susie?"

"Yes . . . one time when Maggie was here and Nance made us both cry just afore afternoon milking. Luke say, never you mind, girls, he say, she's the one I be sorry for . . . and then something about her soul. I misremember what. They was long words."

That was the worst of Susie; even at her most sensible, she wasn't really a companion. She forgot so easily, or drifted off on to another subject just when she had aroused your interest. Araminta would dearly have loved to hear what Luke had had to say about Nancy's soul. It might have thrown some light upon the girl's queer character. For it was queer. You'd have thought, to see her and be with her, that Mrs. Stancy was really kind to her, or paid her double. She never stood up for herself, never complained, never sided with the other girls, always with the mistress. Yet she was dead scared of her; and, save for an occasional cup of tea drunk hastily during a visit to "the room," and the unexciting pleasure of carrying Mrs. Stancy's prayerbook on Sunday morning, she had no privileges that Araminta could ever see. Like Luke, Nancy was a mystery.

Christmas loomed ahead; everybody wanted eggs for puddings and cakes; the special cheeses which had been ripening for this season were taken down from the racks and inspected and weighed and wrapped. Besides the chickens there were sixty prime turkeys to be plucked and dressed. And all to be done in the darkest, shortest days. Jacob and Luke helped with the plucking, and after one spell in the cold shed Luke rigged up a brazier, which, together with the heat of the five bodies pressed together around the baskets of feathers and birds, warmed Araminta thoroughly; and Luke, although he directly addressed the girls very seldom, in case Nancy should say time was wasted in chattering, spoke often and cheerily to Jacob, talking of old Christmas customs and the merrymaking he had enjoyed as a boy. For four evenings in the week before Christmas they worked until after midnight, and although Araminta, with secret pride, stood up to the labour unflagging, even deriving pleasure from the warmth and the company, Susie fainted three times, and had to be revived by slapping and the application of burnt feathers to her nose; and on the night before Christmas Eve Nancy herself broke down and had a short, violent fit of hysteria in which she tried to tear off a turkey's head and scratched Luke's face when he restrained her.

But by Christmas Eve everything was ready. At about half-past ten in the morning, Nancy went into "the room" and returned presently with some of her complacency restored. As she said, "Mrs. Stancy wants you now, Araminta," she rather ostentatiously took out her handkerchief and tied a golden sovereign and two florins into its corner before replacing it in her pocket. So, thought Araminta, she either earns more than I do, or else she's had a present.

Mrs. Stancy was already dressed for driving. Her gloves and her purse lay on the table beside a small open book. On the book itself were sixteen shillings.

"Come in Araminta. I always make Christmas Eve pay day. I see that you have forfeited four shillings during the quarter. I expect you remember for what the deductions were made—or shall I remind you? I like to have these things perfectly clear."

"I . . . I didn't know I'd done anything," Araminta said with a sinking heart; she had so wanted to send the full sum home, a whole round substantial sovereign—so different from sixteen shillings. And what *had* she done, after all, except live hard and sleep hard and work till she was almost blind?

"Then let us see. Yes, in October . . . plucking in your white apron, sixpence. In November . . . being disobedient about your hair, a shilling. November again, chattering with Susie and inciting her to be rude to Nancy, sixpence. On the last day of November . . . having an untidy drawer, sixpence. Mrs. Nead reported that she found sticky sweetmeats in paper and some disgusting bits of hair amongst your caps when she made her round. And the last item, December . . . here it is, eighteen-pence, in part payment for the milk pan you broke . . . you remember that?" Her voice was quiet, so pleasant, in fact, that she might have been reeling off a series of good deeds for which Araminta was about to receive a reward. Araminta's heart felt scalded. Four shillings must mean so little to this woman; and it would have meant so much to her mum, just at Christmas-time, too. She said rashly:

"I told you ma'am, I told you at the time that my hands were so cold I couldn't help dropping the pan. I didn't think you'd hold that against me."

Mrs. Stancy studied her deliberately. "You know, Araminta, I'm inclined to think Nancy is right about you. You *have* a tendency to argue. You should try to curb it. Take your wages and remember they have to last until Easter. Don't spend the money foolishly."

That was nearly funny; it only missed being so by the matter of four shillings. If she had been receiving her full money, Araminta would have enjoyed a wry inward laugh over the thought of spending it foolishly.

She took up the money and drew a breath to steady herself.

"Would you mind, ma'am, if I spoke to Luke for a minute, now. He's going through Minsham with some of the turkeys and he said he'd leave my money with my mother for me."

"Very obliging of him," said Mrs. Stancy, closing the book. "Yes, you may go out and find him, but don't waste a lot of time."

Luke was struggling into his top coat which had been airing

before the fire in the little harness-room. He seldom went out except on foot and the coat was too heavy to walk in. Taken down from its nail to-day for the first time since last winter it had a musty smell.

"Well," he said, as Araminta entered, "how much did she dock you?"

"Four mortal shillings, Luke, and all for such silly little things."

"Oh, thass not so bad," he said kindly. "Thass better than most do their first quarter. Leave you sixteen, eh? Well, thass better than you did at your last place, I reckon."

"So it is," said Araminta, who had been too sore and disappointed to make comparisons. "All the same, I did want to send the lot. Now mum'll think I spent some on myself."

"And that'd matter, would it?"

"Yes. She'll think I'm going to the bad in my old age." She smiled; her anger eased a little.

"There's youngsters in your fam'ly maybe?" Luke asked.

Araminta nodded.

"Then I'll take along a poke of my sweeties, eh? And is there a message for your mum?"

"Yes. Tell her I wish 'em all a Happy Christmas, and I hope Mr. Whistler give her a bit of beef this year; and tell her I would of send the pound, only . . ."—how much could she say without making her mother think this a very strict place?—"only I had to pay for a milk pan I broke. Tell her that, Luke. She'll wonder what sorta pan that could be to be worth such a mortal lot, china with a gilt edge I should reckon." She smiled again.

"See you here, Araminta," the hunchback said abruptly. "I were going to buy you a little geegaw to mark the day when I come back through Baildon`s'afternoon. Would you ruther I made up your money or brung you back something pretty. Thass for you to say. That don't make no manner of difference to me."

"Oh Luke, you weren't going to give four shillings for me a present, surely. Thass a lot of money."

"Come on, make up your mind. I got to be off."

"Oh Luke. . . . Oh, make it up then. Thank you, thank you. I don't know what to say to thank you. Oh, Luke, you are the kindest, nicest . . ."

"Get along girl, you'll be losing sixpence for gossiping in another minute. Four shillings is nowt to me."

January came in with sleet and snow. For the rest of her life Araminta could provoke a shiver by remembering that terrible month. There were days when Mrs. Stancy could not go to market, and roamed round the house like a caged beast, finding fault with everything. A heavy cold, starting with Jacob, went through the house, and Araminta learned—but without astonishment—that at the Abbey a cold was not a matter for sympathy. You were not sent to bed with an extra blanket and a hot brick wrapped in flannel, given a comforting hot posset and some pleasant-tasting concoction to ease your throat. Here you were regarded as unclean, told not to snuffle, to be careful to use your handkerchief, and the only dose administered was one of some fierce opening medicine which made your stomach as uncomfortable as your thick aching head.

But January passed, and somehow everyone survived and the work went on as usual, until suddenly, in the middle of February, the wind changed overnight. A spell of warm wet weather came to comfort the tormented land. A bird began to sing, confident and urgent, in one of the garden trees, and there came a morning when Susie came in from her work with the fowls carrying three half-open snowdrop buds. The sight of them in her big red hand drew all three girls together as nothing had ever done before. The three white-capped heads bent over the flowery trophy, and behind the white bibs of their starched aprons three hearts lifted with the promise of spring. Light mornings and evenings, an end to coughs and chilblains, a less avid craving for a warm chimney corner and a comforting cup of tea.

And then, with the utmost perversity, in this spell of warmer weather, in this time of fleeting sunshine and hopeful birdsong, Araminta was specially afflicted; her chilblains broke. She had had them all the winter, and had shared with Susie and Nancy the nightly application of a scarifying ointment of pig's fat and mustard which Mrs. Stancy provided and insisted upon having used. Up to the end of February, the mixture, though extremely painful when applied, had proved effectual, and now, when the other girls' hands were returning to normal size and shape, Araminta's broke over-night and became stiff, swollen lumps of disgusting, skinless flesh.

Mrs. Stancy professed the utmost horror of them.

"It's the worst affliction a dairymaid can have, apart from eczema," she said unkindly. "If I had known that you were prone to have them so severely I should never have engaged you. I suppose Mrs. Whistler didn't think to mention them."

Araminta pressed her lips together. All dairymaids had chilblains, it went with the trade, everybody knew that. She said mildly:

"I never had them break before."

"I can't have you in the dairy," Mrs. Stancy said, ignoring the fact that Araminta had spoken. "It's particularly annoying to-day, because I have someone coming to see the dairy. I wouldn't for worlds have a visitor think that such hands had touched even the outside of a churn. You must find some work out of doors. Go and find Luke. He has just opened a mangold hale. You can go on with that, and he can come back and see that the boys have the cows ready for inspection."

It was irritating to be spoken to as though you had deliberately chosen to have this happen to your hands; but it was pleasant to be out. The wind from the west was damp and warm, and over the sky, which was the colour of a hedge-wren's egg, great white clouds were drifting, so that the fields and the meadows were patched with sunlight and shadow. In the neglected shrubbery a great sheet of aconites lay like gold and above in the tallest trees the rooks were noisy and busy. On a morning like this it was far nicer out than in; and if Mrs. Stancy thought, as her manner had sug-gested, that being sent to work in the fields was a penalty, she was wrong.

Luke had already opened the mangold hale at one end. The quiet old brown horse attached to the tumbril in which the roots were to be carted back to the yard was nosing in the hedgerow between the field and the lane.

"Hallo," Luke said. "Want me?"

"Yes . . . you're to go back and see that the boys make the cows pretty. There's going to be a visitor."

"I know. Young Mr. Loveless—Sir Edward's nephew—come to see a model dairy. I seen to the cows. I can't stop this job on account of *him*."

"I got to cart the mangolds. On account of my chilblains breaking."

"Thass a rum cure for chilblains," said Luke, straightening his back as far as it would straighten. "My, they do look bad, Araminta. Do you get muck in them they'll fester."

"Maybe thass what she was counting on," Araminta said.

"You'd best hev my gloves," he began drawing them off. "They'll be a bit big, but they'll keep your hands from the dirt."

They were very nice gloves, knitted in double stitch and the palms were lined with bits of old soft leather. Inside they were warm and a little damp. Very comfortable, thought Araminta, wriggling her stiff fingers.

"Did you make these, Luke?" She knew that he did his own mending.

"No, I dint," Luke said. A peculiar look, almost of confusion, came into his mild blue eyes. "They was give me by a friend."

"A woman?" Araminta asked. Somehow you never thought about the hunchback as a man; but perhaps, somewhere there was a woman who did.

"Aye."

"She must be right fond of you, Luke."

"Maybe she is."

"Then whyn't you marry her and get your legs under your own table. I would. Lord, I wouldn't stay here for a day if I was as free and as clever as you, Luke. You could get a job anywhere."

A queer, far-seeing look came into his eyes.

"I got a job to do here, Araminta."

"I know. But you could get a nicer place."

"Maybe. But this is where I must bide."

"Why?"

"Because I'm waiting for something; and doing what I can while I wait."

She stared at him, mystified. What was he waiting for? And what did he do at the Abbey that he could not do equally well elsewhere?

"What're you waiting for, Luke. Tell me."

"Ah," he said, turning and taking his jacket from the shaft of the tumbril. "There's a question I can't answer yet, My dear. But one day I shall know. The mills of God grind slowly, but they grind exceeding small."

"Why, thass out of the Bible, Luke," said Araminta, who had a good memory for words.

"Aye. And very true it is. Well, do I stay here there'll be botheration. You can leave the gloves at the milking-shed door time you bring in the load."

He smiled and ambled away, rather insect-like with his spindly legs, curved back and out-thrust head. Araminta, with the fork already in her hand, looked after him with puzzled affection. He was very nice, quite the nicest person at the Abbey; but he was a little queer, too. Why should so kind a person choose to stay in this place where every kindness must be done secretly? Yet how much less bearable life would be without him. And what was he waiting for? For Mrs. Stancy to die? That was a daft idea. She was little older than he, and oh, far, far stronger and tougher. And look at the way she cared for herself. Most likely she would outlive them all.

Not me, Araminta thought, recanting instantly; I've stood the worst of the winter, and summer is coming; at Michaelmas I shall have done half my time; and what I can do once I can do twice, and then my time'll be up. I'll be out of here like a shot out of a gun, and I'll get a good job in a proper place, surely. Two years at a place like this, with everything so fussy, ought to count for a lot when you look for another job.

She widened the opening in the clods and dragged aside the inner lining of straw which had protected the roots from the frost. Then she pulled the brown horse's head out of the hedgerow and backed the tumbril close to the clamp. Using her hands she began dragging out the mangolds, three or four at a time and throwing them into the cart. The work and the fresh air set her winter-staled blood coursing. Every time she lifted her head she could see the great clouds sailing across the pale blue and their shadows moving across the sunny fields and meadows. Far away, towards the end of the lane, a clump of elms, thick with buds, took on a dark rose colour. Araminta's volatile spirits rushed upwards. She began to sing and to work to the rhythm of her singing, stoop, grab, straighten, turn, swing and throw; stoop, grab, straighten, turn, swing and throw. The song she sang was a little plaintive and more than a little bawdy; all about a lass who had loved a soldier who had marched away to the wars and never come back, though he had left a pledge behind him. Araminta, remembering that Wednesday evening when she had dug the cobbler's potatoes, sang with real feeling, but none the less lustily for that. Behind her the field was brown from its recent ploughing, and against the sombre colour of it the scarlet of her shawl, which she had pushed from her hair and knotted loosely on her breast, the soft buff of her sacking apron, the bright golden-brown of her short close curls, the fading tan and the gathering carnation of her face made a picture which fell upon the eye as a symphony might fall upon the ear.

It was so that Francis Loveless first saw her.

She had been so engrossed with her work and her singing that she had not heard the soft thud of hoofs on the grass track of the lane just over the hedge, and his clear "Good morning" took her by surprise. She straightened herself, and with four mangolds balanced between her gloved hands, turned towards the hedge.

She saw a young gentleman, hatless, wearing a plain blue coat with silver buttons which winked in the sunshine, mounted upon a tall grey horse. He was not a handsome young man; he had inherited the heavy Follesmark features without the plumpness and rosy colour which gave Sir Edward's face its cherubic charm; but the face was saved from a plainness by a pair of clear grey eyes and a mouth which, even to Araminta's inexperienced glance, betokened an unusual sweetness of character. Below it his chin was stubborn.

"Good morning, sir," said Araminta, with a little bob and a smile that showed all her dimples.

"It's a lovely morning," he said, letting his eyes rest with satisfaction upon the little rustic picture, the opened hale, the placid brown horse, the slender young work-girl in her red shawl.

"Yes," said Araminta. "Spring is coming."

"I expect you can tell me whether I'm right for Abbey Farm."

"Yes," she extended an arm in a gesture he thought free and beautiful. Between the loose cuff of Luke's big glove and the sleeve of the print dress which she had rolled back lest she should "mucky" it, he caught a glimpse of a slim brown arm, smooth and honey-coloured. "You'll see it at the next turn. But nobody uses the front gate. Follow the wall and you'll come to the back."

She was careful of her speech, drawing upon years of conscious and unconscious observation.

"Thank you," he said. "Do you work there?"

"Yes. In the dairy mostly."

"It's the dairy I've come to see. I'm going to make some alterations in my own; and I've heard such a lot about the Abbey that I asked Mrs. Stancy if she would kindly allow me to look round."

Araminta was silent; thinking that he would go away pleased, go away thinking maybe that she and Nancy and Susie were lucky to work in such a clean, shining, well-run place, never guessing that all the shining brasswork, all the spotless white walls, the snowy muslin and the starched aprons had meant hours and hours of extra work when your legs and arms were aching and your eyes scarcely able to stay open. She had seen people shown round the place before this, and heard their ecstatic praises.

Something, some link already forged between them, enabled him to gauge, faintly, the quality of her silence.

He asked, with something of Sir Edward's bluntness:

"Is it a nice place to work in?"

"It's nice to look at." He'd be shown the table where the work-people ate, with the cloth so clean; but he wouldn't be told of the fines for putting a spot on it; he'd see the bedroom with its washing arrangements, and the polished chest of drawers, but he wouldn't know that she couldn't even keep her two curls in the drawer that was supposed to be there for her use. And like a hot needle the thought ran through her mind that now, by her silence, she was playing Mrs. Stancy's game, taking part in the deception. But what could she say? What dare she say?

"Thass so nice to look at," she said slowly, "that my hands'd spoil the picture. Thass why I'm carting mangolds." She shook her right hand and the loose glove fell to the ground. A thread or two of grey wool clung to the edges of the raw red cracks. The young man seemed to flinch. Araminta saw that with satisfaction; not guessing that she had, with a single gesture destroyed a poet's vision of a singing girl working in a brown field, brought the girl close, made her human and pitiable.

"I don't think that, with hands like that, you should be working at all," he said.

Suppose he went and said so. Gentlemen with good coats and good horses didn't mind what they said, she knew that, they were so used to speaking their minds.

"For the love of God," she said, quite desperately, "don't you go and say that to *her!* I can't tell you what trouble I'd get into."

He was silent for so long that Araminta was afraid she had given offence. The quality were very peculiar; they'd talk as friendly as friendly one moment and then step back across the gulf that had been there all the time; she'd been too frank, too oncoming. She should have said, "Yes, it's nice to work in," and left it at that.

"Please sir," she was beginning, forcing a conciliatory smile and turning it towards him. Then she saw that he was dismounting. He led the grey horse to the side of the lane, and then, dropping the bridle, came himself and stepped over the low, tidy hedge which divided the field from the lane.

"Look," he said, in a way that was at once friendly, confidential and urgent. "You could help me a great deal if you would tell me all about working in a dairy. I have a reason for being interested in these things . . . I'll explain as we go along. I suppose you've got to get this job finished. Let me help."

"No, no, sir, you'll mucky yourself, and if Mrs. Stancy saw you . . ."

"I think I could explain to her." He delved into the hale and brought out two mangolds which he threw towards the tumbril. One reached its goal, the other overshot it and landed on the brown horse's broad back. The animal looked round in startled reproach. Araminta and Francis laughed.

"Now listen," he said, his face serious again. "I'm going to make an experiment at my place. My father died last September, and I came into the property and now I'm going to do something that I've had in mind for a long time. I'm going to turn the Home Farm into a kind of model farm. I've been all round my village, into all the cottages. They're shocking and disgusting, and I'm going to pull them all down. I'm going to build new ones, with gardens and wash-houses and three or four bedrooms. D'you know I found as many as eight people of all ages sleeping in one room? Then I intend to turn the Home Farm into a kind of . . ."—he fumbled for an easy word and failed to find it—"communal farm. The men in the new cottages will work at the farm just as they do now, but at the end of the year, after I've worked out a certain amount of interest on the money I've spent on it, I shall divide the profits between them, taking into account what sort of workmen they are and how much responsibility they have shouldered. Have I made that clear?"

Araminta nodded as she threw four roots into the tumbril.

"Thass a wonderful plan," she said.

"Yes," he said, with ill-concealed pride, "I think well of it, too. Only, the thing is this. I want it to be a success, because if it isn't I shall be a laughing-stock. Not that I mind that, personally. But if a rather . . . a rather revolutionary idea fails, its failure sets *all* progress back for a long time. So, since I'd heard a great deal about the success of the Abbey Dairy, I thought I might try to install one on something the same lines. I thought it would be rather pleasant if the men's wives and daughters could run the dairy and have the profits of that between *them*. I've often thought that financially women had rather a bad time. Especially married women."

Araminta looked at him with a stunned expression. Her very thought, her reason for coming here, and she had thought that she alone had cherished such ideas.

"I could tell you a lot about *that*," she said solemnly.

"Well then, you see I wanted to know how to make a dairy *pay;* not for myself exactly, but for my scheme. So I thought I would visit the Abbey and see if I could find out why exactly Lady Dolman must have Abbey butter, for example. But my uncle—he's Sir Edward Follesmark, and I dare say you've heard of him—says that Mrs. Stancy is the worst slave-driver outside the Sugar Islands, and I don't want to buy a successful dairy at the price of the people who work in it. If you, who must know all about it, could explain to me what to aim at and what to avoid, I should be extremely grateful."

He remembered that he was supposed to be helping, and threw into the tumbril the two mangolds which he had been holding throughout his long speech.

"But thass so simple," Araminta said. "People buy the Abbey stuff because it is so good. You wouldn't believe how clean and particular we are about everything. Even the hens' food is measured out, and all of the best. If Mrs. Stancy took care of the girls like she do of the fowls and the animals, it'd be a lovely place to work in."

"Is she very strict? I've wondered about discipline, both concerning the farm and the dairy. I rather thought—and hoped—that if the people knew that they were working for themselves that question would solve itself. What do you think?"

"It wouldn't," said Araminta, thinking of Cissie who was bone idle and of Susie who was dim-witted. "Some would work and some would play. I've always been reckoned a good worker in all my places; I don't mind a mistress being strict; in fact, thass fairer on them that *will* work. But Mrs. Stancy is downright cruel."

"So my uncle says. But at the same time, and there's no harm in my saying this to you, because I have said the same to his face, he has such very *peculiar* ideas. He himself has a houseful of servants, but he never has a really good meal, and often his bed isn't made until the evening because the whole household is so slack. It doesn't matter, he doesn't mind at all. But I couldn't hope to make my community farm a success if it were run like Uncle Edward's place. Tell me, where does strictness stop and cruelty start?"

The conversation was on the verge of taking Araminta out of her depths, especially as throughout its course, she must give a certain perfunctory attention to the mangolds. But she plunged in boldly.

"That was strict of her to cut my hair; but that was cruel to slash into my ear and not let me keep even two curls in my very own drawer. And lots of the rules about washing are strict, but they do make us clean, and the dairy is that much better; but thass cruel not to let us ever see a fire, or have a bit of fun, and the food is only just enough to keep us alive and not very tasty except on Sunday. And thass cruel to cane Susie and make her miss her breakfast, because she *is* simple, you've only to look at her to see that." She felt that she was wandering from the point. "You could have a good dairy, sir, and one that would pay, without making everybody miserable. Only perhaps you wouldn't do it so cheap."

"That wouldn't matter," he said thoughtfully, "if the extra outlay made people happy. Besides, it would be *their* money."

"Thass a funny thing," said Araminta, remembering her one serious conversation with her mother, "but thass a thought I've had in my mind for quite a time. I never thought I'd find anybody, least of all a gentleman, who thought the same way."

"Well," he said, with a smile, "maybe we're both wrong. We shall see. I suppose I had better go along now and keep my appointment. I hope your hands will soon be better. By the way, what is your name? Mine's Francis Loveless."

"I'm Araminta Glover."

' Araminta. That's a charming name. It suits you. It's aromatic." He dusted his hands on a fine linen handkerchief. "Thank you very much for all you have told me. I shall think of you often when I'm planning the dairy."

"I only wish I could work in it, sir."

"When are you free?"

"Not till Michaelmas twelvemonth."

"Well, if you're in the same mind, send me word. My home's at Arbrey Ash, just over the border in Suffolk. I'd very much like to have you helping in the plan."

He smiled, stepped over the hedge and mounted nimbly. From the saddle he smiled again and called "Good-bye."

"Good-bye, sir," said Araminta, turning back to her work with a joyful heart. There, she'd fixed herself up with a job further ahead than anyone had ever been known to do. She began to throw the mangolds into the tumbril, counting March, April, May . . . twenty months to wait, and then she was going to take part in an experiment.

Francis Loveless, throughout his visit to the Abbey and his ride back to Sir Edward's house at Sible Havers, found himself recurrently thinking about Araminta's hands. This annoyed, but did not surprise him. For at least twelve of his twenty-two years he had known himself to be morbidly sensitive to pain in other people. At school he had learned to conceal any sign of this sensitiveness because obvious squeamishness was regarded as unmanly and likely to have unfortunate results; but it was still there, and he was not surprised that, all day long, there should hang at the back of his mind, a vision of two rather small hands, hideously swollen and cracked and raw. He imagined what it would feel like to wash them. This, and similar thoughts annoyed him, because there was something wrong, almost perversely wrong in the hands thus occupying his mind to the exclusion of their owner. The girl—even her name was right—Araminta, had been such a delight to the eye; the fact that she had been alone, engaged upon manual work, and singing, that she had been frank of manner, peculiarly sweet of smile and unusually intelligent to talk to, were all so right; part of that poetic aspect of the world so exemplified by his favourite poet,

Wordsworth. If Wordsworth had chanced upon a singing girl in a field he would have given her a lyric immortality, red shawl and all. Francis Loveless could only remember that her hands were swollen and sore.

It was to ease this fidgeting memory that, after the five o'clock dinner he found his way into the huge, hopelessly cluttered kitchen of his uncle's house. Sir Edward's cook and housekeeper, a stout woman known as Mrs. Liza, had been his friend from his early days, and it was only with a slight feeling of embarrassment that he brought out his question.

"Mrs. Liza, what is the best thing for chilblains, after they've broken?"

"You ain't got broken chilblains, Mr. Francis, I should hope."

"No, no. It's not for myself I'm asking. It's somebody I know. What would you advise?"

"Well, in a manner of speaking, once they're broke thass too late to do much. But real goose fat is the best thing. Very comforting."

"Is there any about?"

"There might be. We did hev a goose some time back, and I don't reckon Jenny's turned the larder out lately. I'll hev a look."

She rose ponderously and trundled into the vast, overcrowded larder, where after some grunting and hard breathing, she found at the very back of the most crowded shelf, a pan of soft yellow-white fat.

"There's enough here for the whole army," she said, setting it down. "How much did you want, Mr. Francis?"

"Oh, just a little potful."

She rooted about on the shelves of the dresser, scooped something out of a pot, gave it a perfunctory rub on the corner of her apron, and then filled it with grease. While she was doing so he looked round the kitchen with a certain distaste. It was a curious thing, he thought, but working people, unless carefully overlooked, had a strong tendency to live in squalor. Their cottages, he knew, made squalor inevitable, being small and dark and overcrowded;

but surely this big airy kitchen, with every convenience to hand, oughtn't to look like this. He began to wonder what his new cottages would look like at the end of a year.

"There you are. I hope it'll work on whoever it is," said Mrs. Liza, beaming kindly. That was another thing he had noticed—the untidy, the muddlers, were very often kindhearted and amiable. Was cleanliness really such a virtue?

Once the little pot was wrapped and addressed and despatched his mental vision of the chilblained hands faded and its place was taken by the memory of Araminta herself. It was odd, he thought, throughout the next day or two, how vividly and constantly she haunted him. He seemed still to hear her singing voice, strong and vibrant, not very tuneful, but unusually rhythmical; and again and again the picture of her shape and colouring, the swing and sway of her body as she worked, the slim brown arm outstretched as she pointed the way, the queer lopsided smile which moved the dimples in her cheeks, came between him and the things upon which his actual sight rested. And every memory of her stirred him in a way which was new, bewildering, and a little alarming.

He had never been in love and was, though not precisely ashamed of the fact, rather acutely aware of it. Privately he had come to regard his complete indifference to women as women as part of his Follesmark heritage. Edward Follesmark, his favourite relative, was that unique thing, a happy bachelor who was neither soured nor furtively lecherous; Uncle William, who had fitted out a ship to fight against the French and now that the war was ended had disappeared somewhere into the South Pacific, he knew less about, but certainly he was unmarried too; Aunt Grace, the most eccentric of an eccentric family, had joined the Bethlehem Sisters as soon as she had gained control of her considerable fortune, and after six years' work in the riverside slums of London had gone to Virginia to help found a new settlement there. Of all the family, only his mother had married, and, by doing so, had perhaps proved that the others had been wise in their choice of celibacy.

At Eton, where the older boys had boasted, perhaps untruthfully, of their triumphs with chambermaids and milliners; and at Cambridge, where more credible amatory exploits took place under his eyes, he had felt queer and apart and had endeavoured, not without success, to cover his difference by a vast assumed cynicism; but the truth was that he had never, until he had looked over the hedge into the mangold field to see who was singing so lustily, met any woman who had made the slightest appeal to his senses. The two women whom he liked best in the world were his mother and his cousin, Evelyn Hersey. His mother was untidy, vague, charitable, and clever; Evelyn was pretty in a pale, suppressed way, utterly good, incomparably kind. They got on extremely well together, and for about two years he had known that it would please his mother if he married Evelyn; and he had held it in the back of his mind as the only alternative to bachelordom. A house needed a mistress—you had only to stay at Sible Havers to realize that, and Evelyn was intelligent to talk to and pleasant to look at and capable of taking at least an academic interest in his schemes for revolutionizing his village. But he had known, in the secret places of his mind, that such a marriage would be a poor shadowy thing. The idea of going to bed with Evelyn, or with any other woman he had ever known was embarrassing and slightly repulsive. And yet, when Araminta had flashed that smile at him and said "Good-bye, sir" across a handful of mangolds, he could have kissed her.

By the end of three days his memories and his imaginings were inextricably mixed. Could any human creature be as bright, as vital, as pretty, as brave, as the phantom which had taken possession of his mind? "That was strict of her to cut my hair; but that was cruel to slash my ear. . . ." Was there really a dairymaid in all the land capable of making so shrewd, so impersonal an analysis of character? And the way that brown hair tumbled over her brow and the surprisingly white nape of her neck. And the thrust of those small breasts, half seen behind the knot of the red shawl.

On the fourth day he mounted the grey horse again and rode to the Abbey.

It was Monday and Mrs. Stancy was at home. She received him

graciously. Almost alone of the surrounding gentry, Sir Edward Follesmark had cold-shouldered her. Even when, a few years ago, through bad management all his own cows had been dry at the same time, he had eschewed her produce, buying instead from a filthy little farm of ten acres whose owner was Methodist into the bargain. Mrs. Stancy, not being a fool, knew perfectly well why; Sir Edward was a crank, always agitating about labourers' wages, and deploring the game laws and poking his nose into things which didn't concern him so that he could draw up a lot of nonsensical Radical papers for his friend Whitmore, who was the most dangerous revolutionary Member of Parliament. All the same, Sir Edward was not to be despised; his charm and his family connections, his incongruous passion for gaming, and his wealth, gave him the entry of almost every house of consequence in the district; she would have preferred his patronage to his enmity. She had been flattered by Mr. Loveless' visit, and pleased by the interest he had taken in her business and all that appertained to it; she hoped he would carry a favourable report to his uncle. His second visit, ostensibly to order some livestock for next year, when he hoped to start a new herd of his own at Arbrey Ash, was incense to her vanity. It also showed that, for a Follesmark, he had sound good sense.

He refused the glass of wine and the biscuit which she offered.

"Perhaps afterwards," he said, with the smile which lightened his heavy face.

They discussed business for a few moments. She was pleased by her own ability to discuss calving, bulling, and breeding generally as frankly and calmly as a man. How could she guess that behind her listener's polite, even engrossed attention were the questions— why did you slash Araminta's ear? Is she safe with you?

The order for three young heifers and a bull was taken; the price, amazingly heavy, was agreed upon. Then he said, with a mental grimace at his own duplicity, "Mrs. Stancy, you are experienced, I am only beginning. I should value your advice. Good cows and good buildings are wasted without good workers. I wonder if you could tell me how to choose a good dairymaid. And how many to how many cows? Tell me about your own staff. D'you mind?"

Surely now she would say—come and see them at work; four days ago you looked at the dairy, now come and look at the dairymaids. Then he would see Araminta again without betraying his interest.

An awareness of danger sprang into Caroline Stancy's mind. She was not uninformed of the fact that Sir Edward Follesmark had called her a slave-driver. Was this a trick? Were her girls' wages and hours of work to be brought up by that pernicious man Whitmore in one of his Parliamentary harangues?

"Well," she said, fixing her yellow stare upon Francis, "If you want good work you must be prepared to pay for it. Most people think that two pounds or fifty shillings is sufficient to buy a year's work. I don't make that error. I give my girls four pounds. At the moment I am unfortunately placed, because the Poor Farm overseers, in their wisdom, chose to plant upon me a half-witted girl, for whom they have the audacity to demand two pounds a year. She is worth about five shillings, but I suppose we must all accept a certain responsibility for these poor creatures. She does her best. For the rest I have the girl you saw the other morning, an excellent, if rather plodding worker, whom I chose from amongst about twenty applicants for the job three years ago, and another who was, I think, out of the dairy when you inspected it. A very promising girl in a way. But you, Mr. Loveless, would want a bigger staff, naturally. You see, I do a great deal of the work myself; and besides, I have a cowman who has entire charge of the cows and assists with the milking."

"I see; thank you. And the two girls whom you chose . . . for what qualities did you look?"

"Oh," said Mrs. Stancy with a gesture of her large white hands. "That kind of thing is so difficult to explain. Usually I interview them. I look at their hands, their hair, their clothes. I drop something intentionally, and observe how willingly, how nimbly, how quickly they retrieve it. That was how I chose Nancy. She was clean, and I liked her general demeanour. Araminta . . ."

He leaned forward, and then, to cover this involuntary betrayal of interest, said as casually as he could, "That's the one who wasn't in the dairy?"

"Yes. I thought she looked pale and sent her out for some air. Well, her case refutes all rules. I took her unseen and untried on the recommendation of a distant connection of mine who knew her and her family very well. I was exceedingly busy and no suitable girl had offered herself. But I have not been disappointed. Actually, Araminta is quite as good as Nancy now, and she will be better. She has a natural aptitude and considerable intelligence. I intend, when I have time, to teach her to read and write; I have already taught the rudiments of both arts to Nancy."

There, she thought, carry that back to your uncle with his tinpot ideas about village schools; that'll surprise him. She took her visitor's silence as astonishment. Rising, she said, "Would you care to see them at work, sir?"

"Indeed, yes. I'm afraid that on my former visit I was admiring your dairy to the exclusion of everything else."

To his own ears his voice sounded breathless. He was going to see her again. Now he would know.

Nancy was making up the next day's orders; Susie was polishing the bands on the buckets and the churns; Araminta was making butter shells, at which she was by this time adept. She had cast him a glance of startled recognition and then turned back to her work to hide her confusion. Surely to goodness, she thought, as her heart began to race tumultuously, he wouldn't be so soft, so daft, so utterly, utterly ignorant of all the rules as to mention the fact that, at Michaelmas twelvemonth, she was going to work in *his* dairy. All mistresses, even the kindest, hated the thought that you were planning to leave *them;* they liked to think that theirs was the only place in the world, and when they were dissatisfied and gave *you* the sack they always acted as though, by being unsatisfactory, you had got yourself turned out of heaven. If he now said so little as one daft word, Mrs. Stancy would lead her a fine old life for the next twenty months. She could hardly draw breath for agitation and suspense. And then she thought of the goose-grease, which had, most fortunately, reached her unbeknown either to the missus or Nancy. Susie had been doing the hens when a boy on horseback had paused by the front gate and shouted, "Do Miss Araminta Glover live here?" Susie had had sense enough to smuggle the little parcel in. Would Mr. Loveless now expect to be thanked for it? If so, he'd be disappointed, because she daren't speak. Rather he should think her ungrateful for what was, really, a most unusual piece of kindness, than have Mrs. Stancy pounce on her the minute he'd gone, with what did he send you? and why? when did you tell him about your hands, pray? and so on. And, damn it, the stuff had done her so much good that in four days her hands were almost healed. It was bitter not to be able to turn and smile and say thank you, sir. Now perhaps he would think she was ungrateful and not give her a job.

In her agitation she bungled a shell and had to start from the beginning to remake it. Nancy saw, and gave her a down-the-nose look. Nobody else noticed. Mrs. Stancy was saying something about the shells being very easy to make; going twenty-four to the pound; and being just a little speciality of the dairy. Mr. Loveless simply stared and said nothing.

He said nothing. He was enjoying a first upsurge of passionate feeling.

Her arms, this afternoon, were bare to the elbows; he could see the play of the muscles beneath the smooth, honey-brown skin. There was no shawl to-day to obscure the line of slim square shoulders, the print dress hugged the slender back, tapering into the little waist which the white starched apron strings encircled. He stared at her, thinking, with a voluptuousness of which, a week ago, he would have deemed himself incapable, this is the body which is the complement of my own; the body which shall be as close, as dear to me as my own. And through the excitement of the thought he was conscious of awe. He was in the presence of something holy. And he thought, if she had not been singing, if the hedge had been higher, if I had been diverted from my visit by Uncle Edward's opinion of Mrs. Stancy, I should never have known. . . .

"Yes," he said, "yes, I see," aware suddenly that Mrs. Stancy was making a bid for his attention.

"Now would you like to look at the cows whose calves, all being well, will start your herd?"

"Yes," he said, and followed her blindly out of the dairy.

"Now," said Mrs. Stancy briskly, as soon as the dairy door was closed, "perhaps you see what I mean by natural aptitude. The girl who was making the shells has it to a marked degree. It's difficult to define, but a person who has it is constitutionally incapable of tying a shoe-string insecurely. You'll learn what to look out for. Forgive the question, sir, but are you intending to make your dairy merely a hobby or a source of profit?"

"In a way, both," he said, with a slight smile. "It's to be an experiment."

"So was mine, twenty years ago," she said with a slight, deprecating movement of her white hands, as though to say, look at it now. . . . Aloud she continued, "Then take my advice and don't overstaff the place. Too many girls get in one another's way, and waste time in little feuds and gossiping. I know some people consider that my dairy is understaffed, but I assure you that if you get young, strong girls and organize them properly, their capacity for work is greater than some sentimentalists believe."

He knew that Uncle Edward was the sentimentalist she had in mind; and Araminta, who had opened a new world to him, was one of the young strong girls about whom this woman spoke as though they were machines.

"Perhaps I should envy your detachment," he said coldly, "for myself I cannot help but remember that dairymaids grow old, like everyone else; and youth, surely, has other functions than an inexhaustible capacity for labour."

Mrs. Stancy recoiled. A foaming-mouthed Radical after all; and she had liked him. She said smoothly:

"You are quite right, of course. Actually the *best* worker I ever employed was an old woman. I cannot describe the sense of real loss I experienced when she died. Unfortunately old workers know their value, and are intensely stubborn. This old woman rose from her bed, against all orders and advice, to complete a piece of work upon which she was engaged. She died at it. There was a malicious suggestion that I had not done my duty by her. So, if I were you, sir, I should stick to the young. They change their jobs as they change their clothes, they get married and leave you . . . but they seldom become the subjects of a coroner's inquest. As my poor faithful old Grace did."

Her voice dropped on a note of reminiscent melancholy. But it was all wasted. Sir Edward would never hear Mrs. Stancy's own version of that tragic little story. She had said, "They get married . . ." and immediately Francis had realized that, perhaps, somewhere, there was another man who had seen in Araminta the one, the perfect woman. That must be thought about too.

He felt—though he was usually a self-contained, even secretive person—the lover's uncontrollable impulse to talk about his state. On that evening, Sir Edward's library was cosy in the lamplight, a place for confidences.

"Uncle Edward, have you never been in love?"

"Now that," said Edward Follesmark, "is a question which usually signifies that the questioner is suffering from that form of brain sickness. Is it so in this case?"

"I was looking," said Francis mendaciously, "at the fine cluster of cobwebs hanging from the cornice over your head, and thinking that if this house had a mistress it would be somewhat better kept. And that made me wonder why you never married."

Sir Edward stirred in his chair like a buffalo wallowing in mud. The movement scattered the ash from his cigar over his stomach and chest, but he ignored it.

"To tell you the truth, my boy, I must confess that, though I like women well enough, I never saw one whose—shall we say—favours, seemed to offer adequate compensation for the loss of freedom, which the purchase of them would entail."

"What a cold-blooded statement," said Francis with a laugh which robbed the words of reproach.

"It is," agreed Sir Edward easily. "True, all the same. What's a cobweb? It doesn't intrude upon my consciousness; Jenny will remove it whenever I ask her to do so. And to-morrow, or to-night, even if I so fancy, I can get up and ride off to Lincolnshire, or Cumberland, or wherever I've a mind to without asking myself whether I'm leaving a woman lonely; I can tell any man I know that he's a self-seeking rogue without wondering whether his wife will thereupon cease to visit mine and therefore jeopardize the social nonsense that women set such store by; I can gamble away my money or give it away without thinking that I am robbing my wife and children. . . . God knows, Francis, that I have no wish to paint celibacy in too bright colours, but for a chap like me it was the only thing. I realized that before I was twenty. William and Grace, God bless 'em, are just the same. Now Meg was different. I know many people think she's queer, like the rest of us; but there's a strong streak of the normal in your mother, my boy. I'm glad of it. You wouldn't be here to-night if there weren't."

"Suppose . . . Uncle Edward," said Francis, pursuing his own trend, "you *had* met a woman who *did* make the compensations seem adequate, the *one* woman you could have married. Would you have married her, whoever she was?"

There was a long silence. A log on the hearth cracked and spluttered; the wind which was rising, threatening an end to the fine weather, sighed round the old house.

"I think," said Edward Follesmark at last, "that you'd get more satisfaction, if instead of asking all these fatuous questions, you told me exactly what is on your mind. Are you fancying that you're in love with the blacksmith's daughter?"

"It isn't fancy," Francis said, relieved.

"It never is," said Sir Edward with a smile which was at once rueful and indulgent. "Who is she? How long have you known her?"

Deliberately forcing himself to be sparing of words, Francis told him.

"You've said no word? Given no sign? Good, good. It's a difficult position, my boy, and if you'll take the advice of a cold-blooded old cynic like me, you'll take your time about it. For the girl's sake you've got to be sure of your own mind before you take any step at all."

"But I am certain . . . peculiarly certain, Uncle Edward. Until this week I was like you. I'd never seen a woman who moved me one iota. Now I have. And I'll never see another. I know that in a way that I couldn't explain."

How many times, Sir Edward wondered, had he heard the same sentiment expressed in almost the same words. So many young men, revolting from the conservative ideas of their fathers had confided in him, even asked his assistance, mistakenly thinking that because his politics were revolutionary his class consciousness was in abeyance. Young Fawcett had fallen in love with his sister's governess; that dissipated young rake, Weatherby, had completely lost his heart to a girl from "The Ship" at Bywater; Whitmore's son, whom Sir Edward loved as dearly as though he had been his own, had wooed, most romantically, the daughter of one of his father's tenant farmers. The girl's father in that case, had been the most violent opposer of the match and had on one occasion peppered the young gentleman with shot. A little twinkle shone in Sir Edward's eye as he remembered the comic episode; but below the twinkle there was the easy, philosophic pity of man who had always been heart-whole, for the poor silly young cubs who had said, in these words or those, I can't live without her; she is the one woman for me.

And now it was Francis, Meg's only son, a sound, thoughtful, enlightened young man, anxious to make an ass of himself over one of Madam Stancy's poor little slaveys. She's either the toughest female in creation, or she hasn't been there long, or Madam has altered her ways, reflected Sir Edward, following his own particular bent of thought; a couple of months in the Abbey dairy would have rubbed the charm off Helen of Troy, I should have thought.

"I know what you're thinking," said Francis into the silence. "In a minute you'll say it . . . that it's a passing infatuation which time alone will cure."

But that was the kind of thing Sir Edward never said.

"No," he said. "You're wrong. I was merely thinking that Meg would take this hard."

"Mother? No, you're wrong there. Mother is liberal-minded. Why, one of the first things I remember is playing with the village children while Mother visited the cottages. She's probably the only person who wouldn't be even surprised."

"Lay you ten to one she will be," said Sir Edward, almost automatically. "You must remember, my boy, that Meg—if and when she sees the young woman—won't be looking at her with the eye of love. She'll be thinking of her as the future mistress of Arbrey Ash. Have you thought about that?"

"All that kind of thing is beside the question. I'm a little surprised at you, Uncle Edward, for bringing it up."

"And disappointed," said Sir Edward, impenitent. "You're not the first. But it doesn't follow you know, that just because I believe that the labourer is worthy of his hire and that the fellow who sets a man-trap in a game preserve ought to fall into it himself, that I also favour marriages out of one's class. I don't. I'll tell you why if you care to listen. . . ."

"Go on."

"They're so seldom successful. The one who marries above—shall we say *its* own station, though it's generally *her*—has considerable adjustments to make, seldom makes them successfully and loses something in the process; the one who marries below its station gladly makes allowances for little lapses at first, but later on, when the inevitable strains and stresses are felt, is very prone to lay the blame on the other's faulty upbringing. I could quote you several instances which explain exactly what I mean. Moreover, the tendency to marry beneath them, which so many young men evince, has, to my mind, a particular danger. They are usually—saving your presence—misled into thinking that lack of restraint in behaviour is a sign of vitality. The young women of their own kind are trained—nonsensically maybe—to conform to a certain pattern, for even the budding Messalina is pressed and slapped into the approved virginal mould. The poorer wenches escape this moulding as a compensation for their many disadvantages, and the young man finds them refreshingly natural after his sisters and their friends and the little misses Mamma trots out before him. Ha, he cries, here is nature unadorned, here is a creature full of vital and primitive impulses—he even, God help him, thinks that the wench will make love as vigorously as she sweeps floors. If he is headstrong enough he marries her, and what happens? One of two things. The lass adjusts herself, becoming in the process just another lady; or she doesn't, in which case she may make love as she sweeps floors, usually pretty indiscriminatingly, and her natural manners, outside the bedchamber, embarrass him considerably. I expect old Hamilton married Emma because she was so natural."

"I think that's one of the most cynical speeches I ever heard—even at Cambridge."

"Because you recognize at least a grain of truth in it. I'll lay any money that your Araminta's naturalness has been to the forefront of your thoughts . . . eh?" He paused and smiled. "Well, that's very natural, too. And very common, Francis. I should think there's hardly a man living who hasn't at some time or another (and I'm not now speaking of the specially lascivious) thrilled to some untutored little female with bare ankles. Remember that. It helps."

"Araminta has great dignity."

"And you are a little old for the complaint. Well, well, that makes a difference. You may be the exceptional case. Anyhow, advice I know, is odious, and, except in the legal sense, utterly worthless; but if I were you, I should take a little time, just to test the integrity of my feelings; and I should speak to Meg before I said anything to the girl."

"Naturally, I should do so."

He spoke stiffly, with what he hoped sounded like dignity; but Sir Edward's ears were keener to detect the sound of hurt disappointment over a confidence which would for ever be considered misplaced, and the sudden deflation of spirit which the stiff voice betrayed. The wily old man smiled to himself. So often he had proved the value of a detached, dispassionate understatement. Opposition made the young dogs angry and hot in their anger.

His method set them thinking. This young love was like the pig's bladder which little boys kicked in the lanes. Stamp on it, dash it to the ground and it became the more resilient, bounced into higher folly; but take a little pin and apply it here and there. . . .

Francis was aware of the pinpricks; Uncle Edward had succeeded in making this lovely new passion sound commonplace, ordinary as a bout of measles, and more easily explained. Cynical old devil, he thought, of the uncle who had, until this evening, been his adviser and friend, his beau-ideal of everything a gentleman should be. He was far from guessing that Uncle Edward was simply applying tactics which had proved successful in other cases. Uncle Edward wanted him to go back to Arbrey Ash and forget all about Araminta Glover; for Edward Follesmark, automatically on the side of the under-dog, was thinking of the girl's happiness; and, in his wisdom, he did not consider that this would be increased by hopes which might never fructify; or which, if they did, might turn to ashes. Unless this Araminta were a phœnix amongst milk-maids, she would suffer in the process of becoming lady of the manor, and be, in the end, less happy than she would be married to one of her own kind.

Margaret Loveless' reception of the news justified her son's confidence in her . . . or so it seemed to him.

He returned to his home towards the end of the last week in February without seeing Araminta again. He was suffering from a certain confusion in his mind. Deep down, at rock bottom, he was positive that he loved her; that he would marry her and live happily ever after. But, ruffling the surface of this confidence, as the spring wind ruffles a field of young wheat, making it glitter now green, now blue, were the doubts which Edward Follesmark 's talk, and his own common sense had engendered. Suppose this were a common stage of development, late in his case, and therefore more severe than most; suppose when he got back to his own place and people he realized that his feelings were less sure than he had imagined; suppose that by the end of six weeks he had outgrown this passion. Then it would be a never-ceasing source of satisfaction to realize that he had gone away without having disturbed Araminta by so much as a glance. On the other hand, he did not want to repeat the abortive visit to the dairy, much as he craved another sight of the girl. For one thing, it would look peculiar; for another, next time he did go he wanted to see her alone, take her hand, and say things which there would be no withdrawing.

So he rode back to Arbrey Ash, and for something more than a fortnight went about trying over in his mind the sentence which was to take his mother into his confidence. He was depressed by his own vacillation; the thing was so easy to say. Mother, I have seen the woman whom I want to marry. I'm glad of that, my boy. Who is she? A girl who works in a dairy near Uncle Edward's place. . . . So simple, why should it be so embarrassing, so difficult to say? Because of that work in the dairy? Yes, you might as well face it. Say, well Mother, it's Evelyn, you must have known that for years; or, well Mother, it's Clovis Dunne; perhaps that surprises you, but I realized suddenly. . . . Yes, those things would be easy to say. Why? Why? Love should be beyond these petty considerations. And Mother, of all people, who loved the poor and spent her life in dull, undramatic work and projects for their comfort, would certainly understand. Remember how the tears had come into her eyes when he laid before the schemes for the new cottages and the communal farm. "I have begged your father, Francis, to spend just a little money on the cottages. He would never listen, but now my pleas are answered by his son. Bless you."

It was a March evening, the cold blustering wind seeming to mock the lingering daylight, and they were sitting on either side the fire when he told her.

"Mother, there's been something on my mind ever since I came back from Sible Havers. It's time I told you. I've fallen in love."

Her plain thin face, in which the heavy Follesmark features looked disproportionately large, shone with the curiosity and interest which comes to every woman at the mere mention of the word of love.

"Well," she said vivaciously, "fancy keeping it from me all this time! Who is she? Wait, don't tell me. I can guess. This is one of my psychic moments, darling. It's little Phœbe Carraway."

Phœbe Carraway—yes, he remembered her; curls like a spaniel's ears, and eyes like a spaniel's too. Why, he could have been left with her in the middle of a desert for fifty years and never known the quickening of a pulse.

"No, my dear. It isn't Phœbe, or anyone of whom you've ever heard. It's a girl called Araminta Glover. She's a dairymaid in Mrs. Stancy's famous dairy."

There, it was out. Thank God for that. And either his own relief, or the firelight-shot dusk concealed Meg Loveless' involuntary recoil. She was in control of herself in an instant.

"What is she like. Tell me about her, darling."

He allowed himself to speak freely, certain of his hearer's sympathy. He spoke as any man speaks of his first love. He described, in detail, the two times when Araminta had blessed his sight.

"And is that all, Francis? Am I to believe that you said nothing to her at all."

"Nothing. I might have done, perhaps. But Uncle Edward said that I should first be sure of my feelings: and I should tell you."

Bless you Edward; your head, as well as your heart, is the best I've ever known.

"And now you are sure? Of your feelings, I mean."

"Positive. It's nearly a month since I saw her, and I feel the same."

Bless the dear boy, he spoke as though a month were an infinity of time.

She said nothing about the incongruity of a dairymaid taking her place as head of the household at Arbrey Ash; nothing about being dazzled by a pretty face or a forthcoming manner. Thank God for that, too; she'd never been able to follow her own ideas very far, but at heart it was obvious that Mother was more truly liberal-minded than Uncle Edward.

"I would like to see her, Francis. I'd like to see her just as you describe her, so natural . . . singing in the natural gaiety of her heart as she performs menial toil. That would indeed be an experience. Do you think you could show her to me, just as you saw her . . . without any risk of her looking upon me as a potential mother-in-law. So cramping darling, such a dreadfully legal sound to it, isn't there?"

"In her sweet innocence, Mother, she suggested that she would like to work in the dairy. I could show her to you just as you suggest . . . she would think you were inspecting her with a view to employing her."

"Wouldn't that be an exciting situation?"

"When could we go? Mother, I long to show her to you . . . and to see her again."

"Let me think." Meg Loveless put her hand to one of the pins which held her brindled hair precariously on top of her head, put it into place, patted back a stray strand. "Not this week, I'm sorry to say. I've waited nearly thirty years to have those windows put into the servants' bedrooms. Now you've given me my way I do want to see them put in."

"Of course, darling. There's no hurry for a week."

There's no hurry for a week. No hurry; but didn't you yourself, Francis Loveless, while you were deferring from day to day the announcement which has been so calmly, so sympathetically accepted, notice how quickly the days fly and the weeks mount up.

"Darling, I promised Lady Fennel that I'd go to Mary's birthday party. That's on Wednesday, and really I am too old to dart about like a swallow. I can't go to Sible Havers on Monday and back on Tuesday . . . and after Wednesday there won't be time before Sunday because that is the new Rector's first day and I've asked him and his wife to dinner on Saturday. I did want to make them feel at home."

"Francis, shall I write to Edward and suggest visiting him next week? I shall be absolutely free."

"Mother, they're laying the new cottages' foundations next week. I thought I'd told you."

"Of course. I'd forgotten. Of course you must be here for that. Well, next week, perhaps. A week won't make much difference."

A week won't make much difference; but now something peculiar was happening to all time. March was gone, and April going; the new cottages were rising; the men who were picked to occupy them were already working in the plots of garden behind, working with an avidity which proved how deeply the desire for a patch of ground of their own was rooted in their hearts. And plans for the new dairy, the milking-shed and the cowhouses were on paper, ready to be translated into actual buildings of wood and stone, glass and tiles as soon as the cottages reached the thatching stage. And Meg Loveless, seeming to burst from the shell which had hitherto shut her in from much social activity, was busier and gayer than she had ever been in her life; even entertaining, Francis noticed, many of the surrounding gentry who had seemed to be rather his father's friends than hers. In the old days she had entertained unwillingly, under protest; now the house seemed always to be full of people. Then Uncle Edward went to the Isle of Ely to draw up a report upon the fenland which, in the heyday of arable farming during the war, had been reclaimed, and was now being allowed to revert to waste, with consequent unemployment and misery amongst the poor who had laboured on the hard-won acres. Meg was willing to go to Sible Havers during her brother's absence, but it seemed such a pity to miss his company for the sake of a fortnight. And then, when Edward was back, Evelyn must come from Haverhill for her annual visit at Arbrey Ash.

There was no need for Meg Loveless to explain to Francis that poor Evelyn must neither be disappointed of nor delayed in her visit. Sympathy for Evelyn had been, after his love for his mother, the strongest emotion in Francis' heart until that bright February morning. Evelyn was a Loveless, an orphan, who had been brought up by Great-aunt Fanny Loveless, a bad-tempered, painted old harridan who lived in a great grey house in Haverhill. Evelyn spent her time dancing attendance on the fearsome old lady, soothing her evil humour, playing cards with her on her "good" days and devising petty economies for the further increase of the vast fortune Great-uncle Loveless had left. Once, long ago, Meg Loveless in the kindness of her heart had suggested adopting Evelyn, but her husband had vetoed the idea, as he did most of her proposals. It would be a cruel kindness to take the girl away from the place where her fortune, if not her happiness, was assured, he said: Fanny, by the simple course of nature, could not live more than another ten years, and then Evelyn would find herself still a young woman and the heiress to an enviable fortune. Meg had thought, and even said, that she thought the money would be hard-earned; but she could see the force of her husband's argument, especially regarding Fanny's age, she was already well over seventy. Now Evelyn was twenty-three, and Fanny was ninety, senile as well as arbitrary, pitiable as well as detestable, and Meg Loveless, whose pity for the little curly-haired orphan girl had changed and strengthened into sincere liking for the gentle, self-controlled, unselfish woman she had become, had often thought that, for a sober, idealist young man like Francis, Evelyn would make a perfect wife. And now that Francis had become conscious of women in *that* way . . . and Evelyn was pretty, especially at Arbrey Ash where she could be gay and happy . . . perhaps. Anyway, it was worth trying, and she would order Evelyn a new dress, those Fanny chose were always so dowdy and old-fashioned.

"You see, darling, it's the one holiday Evelyn gets in the year, the only change, and she does so look forward to it. And Fanny has another attendant all arranged for the first fortnight in May. If we postpone it she'll probably get crotchety and refuse to let Evelyn come at all. Besides, Evey would so enjoy to see all your improvements. . . ."

"Yes, I do see, Mother. But this is the last time we put off our visit. Even if you've asked the King to your strawberry tea, we're going to Sible Havers on the fifteenth."

"The strawberry tea won't be until next month."

"That's what I was thinking."

She wondered for a moment whether he had seen through all her little subterfuges for the gaining of time, and she thought disconsolately that they had all been wasted. She had given him eight weeks in which to forget, to regain his senses; she had asked every pretty girl within the wide range of her acquaintance to visit at the house; but he was still set on this visit. Now, if Evelyn, even in a new dress, failed to divert his attention, she must go to Essex and see what it was about this dairymaid that was so attractive.

If anything the fortnight of Evelyn's gentle, sympathetic company confirmed him in his obstinate conviction that Araminta was the only woman he could marry. Evelyn was sweet; she was pretty and intelligent, enthusiastic about his schemes; he still liked her immensely, as much as he could ever like any woman. But he never wondered what she would be like stripped of the pretty blue dress, never dreamed of parting those softly folded lips with kisses, never waked in the night hungry for her presence.

On the fourteenth of May Evelyn's rigidly-measured holiday was over, and on the fifteenth, feeling a little as though her well-sprung, richly upholstered carriage were a French tumbril on its way to the guillotine, Meg Loveless set out for Sible Havers.

It was Saturday, the great cleaning day at the Abbey, and Mrs. Stancy was at Colchester market, a fact for which Araminta was presently more than usually thankful. Mrs. Nead poked her head into the dairy about half an hour before dinner-time and announced that a lady and gentleman had come to see the place and the cows. Nancy, flustered as she always was by any slight deviation from the iron daily routine, was none the less excited at the prospect of showing visitors round. As she gave Araminta and Susie a stern glance and an admonition not to waste time in her absence, there played around her mind a half-formed dream that to-day she would make such a favourable impression that the visitors would leave word for Mrs. Stancy, saying how well she had done the honours of the place, what a bright, intelligent, earnest girl she was. Just one such tribute from the outside world would establish her, she thought for ever, within the good opinion of the mistress whom she dreaded, and adored, and admired and distrusted with every fibre of her warped little soul.

But neither young Mr. Loveless, whom Nancy recognized, nor the lady whom she judged to be his mother, seemed to really care about the carefully-bred, uniform black and white cows, or the cleanliness of the cowhouses or the innovation of having a separate milking-shed. When Nancy said, "The dairy is being cleaned at the moment and we're not churning to-day, unfortunately," and began to lead the way to the dairy, hoping that Araminta and Susie had really made efforts to set everything in place, the lady said in her rather hoarse raspy voice, "I think I've seen enough, thank you. But we would like a word with Araminta Glover."

"With Araminta?" repeated Nancy, startled.

"Yes." The lady's smile softened the firmness of her voice. "With Araminta, if you please."

Araminta had worked very hard in Nancy's absence, hustling the piles of muslin and all the straining cloths through the final rinsing and racing them out to the line. Susie, fired by the example of the person she liked best in the world, had put an extra polish on all the brasswork. The dairy looked immaculate when Nancy, with a very sour face, re-entered it.

"They want a word with *you*. Goodness knows what for."

"Who are they?" Araminta asked, hastily swallowing the last small chunk of the tiny green apple she was eating. Susie snatched off the small sour fruit almost as soon as they were formed on every visit to her hens. And although they were so hard and so full of acid that eating them was a dubious pleasure, they had a crispness and a certain firmness of texture very pleasant to a palate cloyed by an almost unvarying diet of dry, or mushy farinaceous food.

"It's that Mr. Loveless who came before, twice; and his mother. He'd seen everything, and she wasn't interested. It was a waste of time taking them round. Susie, there's a swidge on this floor. How many times must I tell you, you slovenly little beast, to wring the floor-cloth dry last time you wipe it."

Araminta's heart swooped down into her shoes. Now, of course, the fat would be in the fire. Picking her out like that and making her conspicuous. Nancy, for one, would never rest until she had found out what quality visitors meant by asking to see *her*, and what could she say except the truth. But not now, not yet; some excuse might offer itself, particularly if they didn't come into the dairy.

"I can't think what they want with me," she said brazenly, wiping her hands. "Are they coming in here, or where are they?"

"I asked them into the storeroom and got an extra chair in."

The unsleeping serpent of self-distrust reared its head in Nancy's mind. "I should think that was right, wasn't it?" she asked the air. "It didn't seem proper to use Mrs. Stancy's room with her not there and the lady made it pretty plain it was you she wanted to talk to, not me or Susie."

"Oh yes, you did right," said Araminta over her shoulder.

The lady sat in the chair which Mrs. Stancy used during her visits to the storeroom. She was a queer-looking person, Araminta decided, after a first nervous glance. Her grey hair was very untidy, straggling down under her hat, and every part of her clothing looked as though she had dipped into a wardrobe blindfold and put on the first thing that came to hand. Nothing matched, and nothing fitted, and for a warm May day she seemed to wear a good many superfluous wraps and scarves. She was drawing her gloves through her hands uneasily, and her long thin fingers glittered with rings. Araminta could not know it, but Meg Loveless had taken unusual pains with her toilet that morning, the rings and the scarves and the brooches which held them together were all fussy little fortifications against the nervousness which she would not admit.

The young gentleman was perched against the edge of the long table; but when Araminta entered he jumped up straight and went through the gesture—without actually doing anything—of ushering her into the room.

"This is Araminta," he said. "Araminta, this is my mother."

His nervousness was obvious, even to Araminta. All of a twitch, she thought to herself; and wondered why. Vaguely, at the back of her mind, a possible theory formed itself. Perhaps, after all, it wasn't his dairy, and he had overreached himself in engaging her without consulting his mother, who had now come to take stock for herself. In that case, better make an impression on the old lady. She made her bob and put on a smile which spoke of sweet temper and willingness to serve and anxiety to please, and which had little in common with the wide, lopsided flash of teeth and dimples which Francis had remembered with something akin to nostalgia. Mrs. Loveless acknowledged with a smile which emphasized the many wrinkles beneath her eyes.

"Sit down, child. I want to talk to you." What a queer voice, as though her throat was sore and she didn't want to hurt it by talking.

Araminta looked from the one vacant chair to Mr. Loveless.

"You sit there, Araminta," he said; and he pulled it nearer to his mother's, and then, instead of going back to perch on the edge of the table, stood just behind, a little to the side. Yes, it was what she had thought; he was ranging himself beside her, and now he and she had to prove to this odd-looking mother of his that he hadn't been wrong to engage her on sight. Araminta squared her shoulders and prepared to give a good account of herself.

Meg Loveless looked at her, screwing up her short-sighted eyes which were responsible for so many of the lines in her face. So this was the girl Francis wanted to marry. She was visited by a sudden vision of Francis as a child, as a baby, a little relaxed body pressed against her breast, reaching up with a fat little hand to pat her chin; as a toddler, such a careful little boy, taking so few risks and yet so incredibly brave when anything hurt him; as a schoolboy, growing serious and a little pedantic, always taking her side in the many arguments which she had with his father; as a young man, gravely shouldering his responsibilities and showing that all the Radical Follesmark ideas had taken root in his mind. And now he wanted to marry this little dairymaid. Why? She screwed her eyes more fiercely as though merely by their agency she could wring out of Araminta the secret of this strange, this dreadful attraction. Pretty? In a way, yes; probably better without that eclipsing cap; but an odd face, young in contour and colouring, but with a kind of hammered look, such a wary—was wary the word?—yes, such a wary eye and such a grimly determined mouth. How old?

She broke the silence just before it became embarrassing, just as Francis had cleared his throat to speak.

"I believe there was some suggestion of your coming to work at Arbrey Ash."

"Yes, ma'am."

"How old are you, Araminta?"

"I was eighteen in April, ma'am."

And they'd been hard years to give her that look in the time. Despite herself, Meg Loveless felt a stab of pity. No, she thought, I can't do anything about it, I can't ask any of the questions I'd planned; I'm sorry for poor people, I do what I can to make their lives more tolerable, I've brought up my son to do the same; but this is an unbearable situation; I don't want to talk to her, I don't even want to look at her; God, I think I shall be hysterical in a moment.

"If you wouldn't mind, Araminta," said the quiet, easy voice behind her, "we'd like to know a little about you, where you live, about your family, what work you have had before."

His nervousness was gone, Araminta noticed; did that mean that he could tell from the lady's manner that she had made a good impression?

Over her head Francis looked at his mother; these were the questions which, during the ride from Sible Havers to Summerfield, she had said that she would ask. "By hearing about her life, Francis— and there's every excuse under the circumstances to ask these questions—we shall hear what her attitude to life is and learn a great deal about her." Mother had sounded so confident then; but now something had happened to her; he'd never before known her at a loss for a word.

"Well," said Araminta, "there isn't much to tell. I come from Minsham, we live on the Green there, and my dad and my mum, when she's well enough, work for Mr. Whistler at Beckwater Farm. Jackie, he work there to, and then there's Betsy, and Sarann, and Tommy, and the new baby mum had at Easter. They call him George, for the King."

"Quite a big family," said Mrs. Loveless.

It was a peculiarity of the quality to approve of big families, God knew why; but if it mattered in a dairymaid, well, they should know that there were plenty of Glovers.

"There's a quantity of us dead, too. There'd have been fifteen—no, sixteen, if we'd all lived."

Behind her young Mr. Loveless seemed to catch his breath.

"I started work when I was ten; scullery maid at the big house, Mr. Helmar's; then, when I knew a bit I went to a place on the far side of Wyck. I was the only one there, and there was five children in the family. That was hard work, but I learnt a mortal lot, doing everything you see, butter and all. That was a hard place, but I liked it all right, only I didn't grow, and one time when I went home my mum crazed me to leave a-before I was all wasted away. So then I did a short time in a proper dairy, and after that I was two years with Mrs. Pollard at Uplands. I finished up head girl there. Here I'm only second, but that's because Nancy is older and was here first. Mrs. Stancy said the other day my work was as good as hers."

"You never had time for school," Mrs. Loveless said, quite kindly. "Can you read at all?"

"No ma'am. But Mrs. Stancy learnt Nancy, and I was in hopes she'd learn me, too." That was an absolute lie; much as she hankered for the knowledge, she dreaded its source, and had been relieved as week followed week without bringing suggestions of lessons.

"Do you learn quickly, Araminta?" If this thing actually happened; if it weren't all a mad, impossible dream, what a lot of things there would be for her to learn.

"I'm quick at most things, ma'am."

"You seem to have confidence, Araminta; and that is a help in most undertakings. Are you healthy?"

"Times I get a cold in bad weather, but I can mostly work it off. And I do get the chilblains." She shot a glance, almost conspiratorial, at Francis, and spread her hands in front of her in a gesture of unconscious grace. Nice hands, Meg Loveless noted, red and roughened, but quite small and shapely, with long, capable fingers. "They never lost me a working day till this winter, and, to tell you the truth, I blame that on the mustard, ma'am." She saw their looks of bewilderment, and explained, "The mustard in the ointment we hatta use. I never had them break before."

"That's all right, Araminta," he said from behind her. "If you . . . if we . . . I mean that at Arbrey Ash the chilblains won't bother you unduly, I'm sure. Well, Mother?"

Mrs. Loveless picked up the gloves which she had dropped on the table, and with them in one hand began with the other to push away the straggling strands of hair and rearrange her wraps. Without looking at Araminta she said slowly, "There was one more thing, Araminta, are you betrothed . . . you know what I mean, walking out, engaged to be married, or in love with anyone at all?" A crucial question; if the little thing said "Yes," then one could point out to Francis that it would be definitely unfair, taking advantage of his position, to ruin some poor yokel's life by snatching away his girl.

"No, I am not," said Araminta, with great firmness. It was very nice of the lady to so mix up the questions that the truth and the lie were evenly balanced. And was it a lie, even? Mostly, nowadays, when she thought of Jan, it was with resentment because he had driven her out of a comfortable job . . . but there were other times, too. "No," she said, even more firmly, "I hevn't seen the man I could marry yet, ma'am; and I ai . . I'm not likely to. I gotta earn my living and do something for my family, you see."

"Well," he said, "I think that's all, Araminta, thank you very much." Yes, he was looking at her as though he was pleased with her. Mrs. Loveless stood up; Araminta jumped to her feet, and with another bob asked, "Shall I send Nancy out to you again?" Much depended upon the answer. If they said yes, she was going to explain the position and beg them to concoct a reason for their interest in her. If they said no, she would save the explanation and fob Nancy off with some tale.

"No, no. We can find our way out, thank you. Good-bye, Araminta."

"Good-bye, ma'am; good-bye, sir." She gave him her special smile.

"I shall see you again, Araminta," he said. That was nice of him; it was his way of telling her that it was all right, she was accepted. Then he added, softly, "Sooner than you think."

Her smile faded. Oh God, she thought, surely they knew everything they wanted to know about her now; surely they wouldn't want to come nosing round, putting her in an awkward corner like this any more. Did anybody ever hear of so much fuss being made over hiring a girl to slap butter. Even Mrs. Stancy . . .

It was all right; they were safely into the yard, climbing into their carriage. Araminta stood in the passage, ready to block any hasty rushing out on Nancy's part—it's all right, Nancy, I asked if they wanted to see you again, and they didn't. As the carriage moved away the young gentleman turned and, looking towards the open door, gave her a steadfast, sweet, reassuring smile. Her heart soared. It was all right, the job was hers; now, if only they could keep away for the rest of her time at the Abbey. . . .

The dinner-bell had sounded during the interview, and Araminta went straight to the kitchen without washing her hands. Nancy put down her spoon and half rose.

"Thass all right," said Araminta. "They said they could let themselves out."

"And what did they want with you?"

Araminta spooned up a mouthful of the cooling potato stew.

"Seems Mrs. Loveless know my dad and mum," she said through

the mush. "She wanted to see how I was getting on so she could tell them next time she went to Minsham."

The carriage wheels were set a little wider than those of the gig and the wagons which had worn the tracks in the lane, so they ran on the grass and made hardly a sound. Francis and his mother rode in silence until the turnpike was reached, and the wheels, resuming their gritty rumbling, enabled them to talk without risk of being heard by Stevens upon his high seat in front. For Francis the little interval was tedious; he longed to begin to talk; Meg Loveless wished that the carriage could go on rolling silently for ever; what could she say which would not either encourage him in his mad scheme, or alienate him perhaps irreconcilably? And suddenly it seemed to her that all her life had been leading up to this one moment, that everything she had ever done or said or thought had been steps in a path towards this inevitable decision. As a young girl she had run around with brother Edward, saying things about Liberty, Equality, Fraternity; she had been reading Voltaire and Rousseau when other young misses were working pretty pious samplers; as a bride she had tried to persuade her husband into the Radical fold, arguing, and then quarrelling with him about the state of his cottages, his labourers' wages, his servants' bedrooms, his keepers' strict enforcement of the Game Laws. Walter's ideas had been so diametrically opposed to hers that it had not been, really, a very happy marriage, though she had loved him very deeply to begin with, and very gratefully, for despite her slight eccentricities of manner and apparel, she had wanted to get married, and she knew that she was plain. Then, disappointed in her husband's conversion, she had, as a mother with an only son, reared him in the Follesmark tradition from his earliest years. . . . "They're human beings, darling, you must always remember that." . . . "Let Tommy ride on your pony, darling. He loves to ride, just as you do, but you see his father can't afford to buy him one; yours can, so you must be willing to share." Quite early she had taken him with her upon her errands of mercy amongst the villagers; unwillingly she had bowed to her husband's dictate over the matter of sending him to Eton; she distrusted a school which had played a part in forging Walter's stubborn Toryism. She had been glad when he returned, still sweet and unspoiled, with scholarly leanings which led him to choose three years at Cambridge rather than a return home and the immediate assumption of the rôle of Squire's son; and when he chose, at that seat of learning, to make an especial friend of a farmer's son, who through ability and the interest of his village parson, had reached the University, she had been delighted. Francis would never say, as his father did, that all farmers were sly, prosperous clodhoppers without a thought outside their bellies and screwing down their rents. But now, when what might seem to be the logical conclusion was reached, when Francis had chosen his wife from amongst the people for whom she professed so much admiration, in whose welfare she took so keen an interest, it was a different matter. She was not a humbug, everything she had ever said or done had had behind it a genuine enthusiasm, a fervent conviction; and, now that she found herself shrinking from the final test she despised herself. The old war-cry, Liberty, Equality, Fraternity, rang often in her mind; you couldn't evade it, the word was Equality, and that being so, how could you draw a line when it came to the question of choosing a wife. None the less, Meg Loveless knew perfectly well, and to her cost, that if Araminta had been hungry she would have fed her; if naked, clothed her; if wronged or abused in any way, protected her by any means, legal or illegal, within her power; but Araminta, chosen and beloved, was a very very different problem. She didn't want her son to marry a dairymaid who could neither read not write, who had been trained in submission, whose manners would be coarse, and whose only point of contact with him would be the bed they shared.

"Well?" he said, as soon as the wheels began to rumble. She looked at him and saw by the frank, pleased glance that he turned towards her that he expected words of approbation. She said slowly:

"I'm an old woman, Francis." (She had actually borne this longed-for, long-awaited child at the age of thirty-nine, and he was now twenty-two.) "I'm an old woman. I can't expect to see what a young man would. I wish you could tell me exactly what she possesses that, Evelyn, shall we say, lacks." She saw that she had disappointed him, and added hastily, "These things are very difficult for any woman to understand, Francis. Unless they are very pretty, or perhaps very rich, they so seldom have any *choice*. I know I didn't . . ." She spoke with a terrible frankness. "I wasn't very pretty, you see, and my fortune was comparatively small. Your dear father was the one man who wanted to marry me, and I married him gladly. So I can't understand by what means even women choose their mates, much less men. I'm all at sea, Francis. I saw an ordinarily pretty, very pleasantly-mannered little girl. If it had honestly been a question of engaging her to work I should have done so without hesitation, she was neat and healthy and willing. But I must admit that I am completely in the dark as to why you want to marry her, rather than any other girl you know."

"But she isn't ordinary, Mother. I know that, though I can't explain, giving chapter and verse, where she is different from, or better than, any of the others. There are no words." He looked at her a trifle blankly. "Don't women *know* these things. Mother, think back. Was there never any man whom you would have picked before all others. You needn't consider Father . . . you've as good as admitted that you married him because he asked you; and Father, even dead, isn't a sacred subject to me. Was there never anyone else."

"Their name was legion," said Meg Loveless, after an all but imperceptible pause. "To be honest, I must admit that I was in love with one man or another from the time I was twelve until I married your father. But I was only in love with people whom I *hoped* might one day marry me. I haven't made that clear, have I? I mean they were, all them, men who came to the house . . . they were . . ."

"Eligible?" he said abruptly. "That's it, isn't it? Never the groom who brought your horse round? Never the footman who held you a dish? No." He could suddenly see, in one flash of insight, what her life—from the sexual angle—had been; a strict confinement to the acknowledged preserves, never a glance outside; she had fancied herself in love with one man after another, and all of them men who could offer her the kind of home, the kind of background to which she was accustomed. After many disappointments one had done so, and she had married him without a question, without a qualm. In short, she had never known love at all. And so she would never understand; nothing, nothing he could say would ever make her understand. And, in addition, there were so many things about the whole question which could never be explained . . . how knowing Araminta had made him aware of his manhood, had made him understand about things like rape and prostitution, laid the whole world of sexual experience before him like a book. Finally, he said gently, "My dear, for six or seven years now, ever since I began to think about such things, I've thought that I was bound to be a bachelor, like Uncle Edward and Uncle William. Phœbe Carraway, Clovis Dunne, Penelope Drew, Evelyn, I've talked with them, danced with them, taken them rides—you can't say I haven't tried, Mother. But I haven't wanted to marry any one of them, not even for one moment. There is the difference. I do want to marry Araminta—and I should like to do so with your blessing."

Her face took on an expression of distress. She swallowed audibly.

"If you marry her, Francis, it will be with my blessing. But I should be dishonest if I denied that I have great misgivings . . . what, I ask myself, can you have in common with a girl who can neither read nor write; who has spent her whole life in menial toil, very creditable, no doubt, but very hampering to the mind; who probably wouldn't even know what a handkerchief was. Francis, you mustn't mind my saying these things. I'm your mother; I think our previous relationships have been such as to . . . as to lead you to believe that I have your welfare at heart. And I do wonder, my dear—again you must forgive me—whether the very strangeness of her, doesn't make her attractive. Listen . . . I once heard your father's brother, James Loveless, the one who was Governor of somewhere in the West Indies, telling your father that though he wasn't unduly amorous at home, he'd found young negresses utterly irresistible. They didn't know that I could hear them, of course. But it does shed some light on this matter, don't you think? Because you see, he didn't marry a young negress; he came back and married your Aunt Clotilde."

He burst into a roar of laughter which puzzled her, for she had spoken in all seriousness; but which pleased her too, for it showed that he had not taken offence at having his dairymaid compared with the negresses.

"Of all the horrid warnings," he said. "And you bringing it out so innocently. Aunt Clotilde, that whited sepulchre!" The laughter vanished. "In short, my dear Mother, what you're really suggesting, is that I should make Araminta my mistress, not my wife."

"No," she said, with the nimbleness of tongue which had so often confounded Walter Loveless. "I'm not suggesting that you do so. I'm pointing out that it may be possible that you have confused the two desires. You're young and you're idealistic, Francis. I should be sorry, if in your innocence, you married someone simply to go to bed with."

He stared at her, startled. "And five minutes ago, my dear, you said, not in so many words, perhaps, but unmistakably, that you yourself married for the sake of being married. Supposing my motive to be what you imply—which it isn't, by a long way—is it any worse?"

"Not worse, Francis. I'm not talking of ethics. But it would have more unfortunate results. When I married your father I knew just what I was doing. I wanted a man, and a home and a child. And I got them, and was grateful for them. I wasn't dazzled. So I didn't wake up one morning and look at his face on the pillow and think to myself why in the name of God did I ever marry you. That is what I fear for you. I'm so afraid that, once you know her intimately, the spell may be broken and the differences of experience and upbringing will loom very large."

He looked at her, this time with admiration. "You're a very

unusual woman, Mother; not that I haven't known it before. You have the very clearest mind. . . ."

Meg Loveless dabbed at a strand of hair which was tickling her cheek. "It's never done me much good," she said simply. "But sometimes it's a help to talk things over. At least, darling, don't do anything in a hurry."

He said, with a tinge of bitterness in his voice, "Do I show any signs of doing anything in a hurry? I've known my own mind since February, and so far all I've done is to talk about the matter. One doesn't need time to think things over, with you and Uncle Edward for advisers! A fine crop of devilish doubts you two idealist reformers manage to sow between you— Johnson and Walpole between them could hardly have done better."

"You've spoken to Edward?" she asked in some surprise.

"Yes, in February?"

"And what did he say?"

"Exactly what you do. Wait, know my own mind. All the old stodgy things that I suppose are said every time a man wants to marry someone he's picked for himself." He shrugged his shoulders, and his heavy features took on a look of obstinacy. "Well, you've both had your say now, and you've seen her, Mother. It remains for me to see if I am agreeable to *her*. After all, we are the two people concerned, you know. I'm not asking either you or Uncle Edward to marry her."

Meg Loveless put one of her thin, dark-veined hands to her forehead.

"Darling, don't speak as though we were your enemies, please. Perhaps I haven't said the things I mean exactly; but something, the sun, or the jolting, has made my head ache. I think I'll be quiet for a little while."

She leaned back and closed her eyes. Behind their lowered lids she saw a series of little vignettes, all concerned with Araminta taking her own place in the house and the village. Wasn't there something in the Bible about the confusion of the servant reigning? Unkind, she thought—I mustn't think unkindly of her. She is the least to blame; it was plain from her manner that her highest ambition is to work in our dairy. She's as innocent as the day.

Above the rumbling of wheels in her ears she seemed to hear the malicious voices of those whom Francis would call his friends, all saying that of course all the Follesmarks were crazy, was it to be wondered at that the youngest of them should commit this supreme folly? They'd probably all make mocking calls upon the bride, just to see for themselves what she was like . . . then they would go away and make sport of her rustic speech and manners. A fine look-out for Francis; he would be the real sufferer. People never forgave that kind of thing; think of the things that had been said of Lady Hamilton; why, they'd even accused her of subversive political activities, ignoring the fact that there had been a time when her influence with the Queen of Naples had been used to England's advantage. No use denying it, low birth was looked on as a kind of crime. It shouldn't be, cried her honest mind, it shouldn't be . . . but it is, and Francis will suffer. It's like the Game Laws, they're unfair, too; but if Francis wanted to go poaching, I should feel it my duty to point out the penalties he would risk. Partly it's my fault, obviously I erred somewhere in bringing him up. Ought I to speak more frankly, now; take a firmer stand? Not now, I'm too confused.

The aching pulse in her head changed to a vicious thumping, as though someone were beating on her brain with a club. I must lie down, she thought a trifle wildly, I must lie down in the dark and keep calm. She remembered that most Follesmarks died from strokes. Wouldn't it be a crowning irony if she, who had always sided with the working-classes, died of a stroke brought on by the knowledge that Francis wanted to marry a dairymaid. A little gust of laughter, broken by a gasp of pain, for the club struck her in the the middle of it, burst from her lips. Francis looked at her with sudden concern.

"Are you all right, Mother?"

"Oh yes," she said bravely. "It's just that my head aches, and I thought something was funny. It wasn't. Not really."

He raised his voice, "Drive a little faster, Stevens. My mother is feeling unwell."

Under the thumping blows of the clubs Meg Loveless could feel every consciousness, save that of pain, slipping away. She could think only of lying down, in a cool room, with the curtains drawn. She had forgotten Araminta.

PART THREE

Araminta is delivered from evil

T HAT evening Mrs. Stancy decided suddenly to teach Araminta her letters. Perhaps her attention became focussed on her second dairymaid by the report which Nancy gave of the Loveless' visit and the interest they had taken in her; or perhaps she had, all along, saved the sport of giving Araminta lessons until the weather was kind and there were no chilblains to be forced into the mustard ointment, no colds to be dosed with the belly-aching mixture. Anyway, that evening, just before supper, Nancy delivered the message that after the meal Araminta was to present herself in "the room," without cap or apron and with perfectly clean hands. Araminta, who had spent the day since the Loveless' departure in a happy mood compounded of self-congratulation and far-extended anticipation, faced the ordeal nervously. She remembered what Susie had said about the cane; she remembered the snipping of her ear; she remembered the cold yellow stare which did not need displeasure behind it to render it terrifying. She tried to find out from Nancy what lessons were like, and how best she could avoid giving annoyance; but Nancy, to whom the knowledge that Araminta was about to receive instruction was gall and wormwood, refused to give any information at all. She took slight comfort from the thought that Araminta would find out soon enough what lessons were like and what kind of teacher Mrs. Stancy was.

Actually, Caroline Stancy was a gifted teacher. In another age, given full scope for her abilities, and with her cruel tendencies curbed by public opinion, she might have been one of those head-mistresses of whom staffs and pupils move in awed respect, and whose examination results are the envy of their rivals. In all her life she had had but three pupils, of whom Nancy was one, and none of them had been good material, but they had all learned to write a good clear hand and to read with adequate fluency. She worked on a system peculiar to herself, though it had in it the germs of a method which was to become universal a century and a quarter later. And, although she delighted in tormenting her pupils, she was, in an odd way, proud of them too; and although she enjoyed caning, at least during the lessons she caned with motive, consistently, not in blind fury.

It was still light outside the tall mullioned window, the soft, lingering twilight of late May; and as Araminta, with outward calm and inward trepidation, took the seat which Mrs. Stancy indicated, there came into the room the sound of a cuckoo's calling, borne on a breath of lilac perfume from the overgrown bushes in the shrubbery. Inactive of body, for a brief space, and with her mind suspended between the things that she knew and the mysteries which were about to be unfolded, she thought of Jan. The lane in which they had lingered last September would be a dazzling avenue of whiteness this evening, the hedges snowed under, heavy, fragrant with hawthorn blossom, the ditches frothing with cow parsley. Suddenly her heart ached, and warm, dark, nameless tides moved in her body. But she straightened her shoulders and set her mouth firmly. Wasn't she better off here, really? Four pounds a year, a good new job secured only this morning, and now within her very reach, the lessons for which she had always secretly craved. Of course she was. She turned her eyes from the window resolutely and looked at Mrs. Stancy with steadfast attention.

Mrs. Stancy had propped upon the table a large sheet of white paper upon which, in thick black ink, the twenty-six letters of the alphabet had been inscribed; doubly inscribed, for at the heels of each bold capital a corresponding small letter followed. The large white hand of her mistress closed firmly upon a short, thick ebony ruler, and the low, rather pleasant voice said:

"Now, Araminta, these are the letters which you have to learn. Probably you are familiar with some of them. Follow the ruler as I point and repeat their names after me. A . . . B . . . C . . ." Twenty-six times the confident voice fell upon the silence, and twenty-six times Araminta repeated the sound, a faithful, timorous echo.

"But," said Mrs. Stancy—more than a hundred years in advance of her age—"it's no use calling them that when you read or write them. A and B and the rest are only their names, the names by which you remember their shapes. It is the sound that is important. These are their sounds. Listen carefully." Shaping her lips with exaggerated care she read the alphabet phonetically. Then she brought the ruler back to the first letter.

"Now look . . . A is the sound for Ass, and for Apple, and, of course, a great many other words; but if you remember those two you'll have something to go upon. B is for Butter . . . Basket; C, as I told you just now, has two sounds, it can be hard, for Cake, or soft, for Cissie; D is for Dirty . . . and Duster. . . . All the way through, down to X, which hardly ever starts a word in our language; Y for Yellow and Yeast; and Z, which is not much used either, but is used in Zealous—a thing I trust you will be, Araminta."

She paused for just a second or so, and then back went the ruler to the top of the sheet.

"Now, I'll give you the sound, and I want you to think of a word which starts with that sound. Don't use the ones I have just used. Think of some for yourself, and then I shall be able to see if you have understood so far. Now, A . . ."

What words had Mrs. Stancy used herself? Ass and apple. As Ap, As Ap . . . was there another word beginning with those sounds? If there was, Araminta could not think of it! But the mere repetition of the two words hammered the intial sound home, and presently she brought out, very diffidently, "Ankle."

"Good," said Mrs. Stancy. The ruler moved on. "Beast," said Araminta. And remembering cake, cat came easily, so did dark. After that it became rather a strain to remember what words Mrs. Stancy had used herself; a first mistake, shaking her small remaining confidence, led to others. When the ruler halted at X and Mrs. Stancy said, "We needn't bother about those just now," Araminta was hot and confused and convinced that she had done badly. Her cheeks were scarlet, her forehead moist. She rolled her handkerchief between her hands.

"You have an excellent memory, Araminta," Mrs. Stancy said. "You've started very well. Take a deep breath and calm yourself; you have nothing to be agitated about. Put away your handkerchief. Well, now. They are the letters, and their sounds. And words are simply built up of letters. We look at the letters and we remember their sounds and so we can pronounce the word when we are reading, or spell it if we are writing. Now take an easy little word like this."

She put down the ruler and drew towards her a large, wooden-framed slate. There was a pencil fastened to the frame by a length of string. Very plainly she wrote C A T upon the slate.

"Now, Araminta, first of all spell that out. You may look back at the big paper."

"C . . . A . . . T," said Araminta.

"Now give the letters their sounds."

"Kugh Aah Tugh," mouthed Araminta.

"That's right. Now say the three sounds quickly, run them all in together."

"Cat," said Araminta triumphantly. She was excited. Light began to break in suddenly. Mrs. Stancy's early nineteenth version of the "Look-and-Say" method of teaching was working again. Araminta leaned over the slate eagerly. Wasn't it wonderful? Just these three letters, and there you were; the broken egg, the gable-end with the bar across it, and the place where the lane ran into the turnpike; and there was a furry, four-legged animal, stalking a bird or asleep on the mat. Mat! Her eyes flew to the big sheet. Mm . . . which was that, oh, two gables without any bars. She said aloud in her wonderment, "Mat."

"Yes," said Mrs. Stancy, interested. "How would you spell that?".

"M A T," said Araminta breathlessly.

"That's right," said Mrs. Stancy, writing on the slate. The pencil squeaked. "Think of some more."

After rat and fat, Araminta ventured upon flat, which introduced the matter of the following L, so that Mrs. Stancy wrote C A P and then C L A P, S A M and S L A M, B O B and B L O B. Never had she had a pupil so responsive, so alert and so intelligent. Why, at the end of their first lesson the others had still been confusing B with R, E with F, and M with N or W.

But for some reason it was impossible for her to give Araminta more praise than was absolutely necessary in the first few minutes of the lesson in order to give her confidence enough to try. At ten o'clock she wiped the slate with a damp sponge, folded the large sheet and said coolly:

"You have a certain amount of intelligence, Araminta. I shall remember that and in future attribute all your mistakes to carelessness. On your way through the kitchen tell Mrs. Nead that I should like a cup of tea. I feel quite exhausted."

"Good night, ma'am. Thank you very much for the lesson."

"Good night, Araminta. Don't forget anything before you come again."

"No, ma'am."

Mrs. Nead had boiled the kettle in readiness and in less than five minutes plodded in with the tray.

"Oh," said Mrs. Stancy, turning from the window through which she had been looking, unseeing, into the moonrise. "Why didn't you send Bella? Your feet aren't as young as they were, you know."

The words sounded kind; in another mouth they might even have been so. But they called up—as so many of her mistress' words did nowadays—a vision of the Poor Farm, before the little wizened woman's eyes. The missus was always making reference to her age and failing feet nowadays; and that could only mean that she was getting too old for the job. She said meekly:

"My feet'll serve you ma'am, as long as you want them to."

Mrs. Stancy smiled, knowing that the shot had reached its mark. The evening had been, in a way, wasted. Not a tear, even, wrung from Araminta. Somehow she felt frustrated; and must, must, must hurt the creature that was nearest, now that the girl had gone. Why had she let her go, so pleased and smiling?

"I'm afraid their serving day is nearly done, Mrs. Nead," she said softly. The little wizened woman winced and seemed to grow smaller. She would probably cry in the kitchen, and Mrs. Stancy, after swallowing one cup, scalding hot, would carry out the tray and catch her at it. . . .

Sir Edward and his nephew dined alone that evening. Meg Loveless, though she felt better, had kept to her bed, taking refuge in it from the problem, which, as far as she could see, had no solution, apart from a miracle. Remembering that her own Uncle Edward's stroke had been attributed to the amount of food and drink he had consumed at the Mayor of Baildon's banquet to celebrate the victory of Trafalgar, she refused all food save a bowl of chicken broth, and all drink save a glass of cold water.

Edward had peeped into the darkened room during the afternoon to ask how she did, and between the club's vicious thumpings—for her head ached until almost five o'clock—she had managed to say:

"Edward, talk to Francis. Don't let him do anything in a hurry. I've said a lot and done no good, I'm afraid. But please try again."

"You didn't take to her? Didn't think you would," said Sir Edward bluntly.

"It wasn't that I didn't take to *her*," Meg Loveless said, making a desperate effort to be fair. "It's that . . ." Oh, it was all too difficult; more than difficult, impossible to explain. "It makes my head worse to talk, Edward. Just ask him not to do anything in a hurry."

"I'll do what I can," he promised, and withdrew. Poor old Meg, he thought; and was momentarily glad that he had no son. Though why, he demanded, stumping downstairs, why we all take the matter to heart so much, I really can't say.

Throughout dinner he chatted, volubly, amiably and irrelevantly; and when it was over he lifted the port in one hand and his glass in another and said, "Bring your glass, my boy. We'll go to my study. It's cosier."

The shabby, rather dirty room was warm with the stored sunshine of the day. It was in shadow now, but beyond the wide windows the flat rich fields were washed with gold.

"Well," said Sir Edward, "we're back where we were in February. What's the next step?"

"With regard to Araminta? I'm still in the same mind, you know. I took Mother to the Abbey to-day and we saw her. Mother isn't exactly enthusiastic, but . . . but . . ."

"You can do without her enthusiasm?"

"If I must, yes. I've been thinking, since this morning, that I made a mistake in discussing the matter at all. I ought to have asked her to marry me, and if she said 'yes,' married her straight away. I think I shall do that to-morrow."

Sir Edward raised his head from the back of his chair and looked at his nephew with an interest which was only slightly exaggerated.

"You know, Francis, I've been thinking of that too. And do you know, I can't for the life of me imagine it happening. How, and where, and in what words exactly would one make such a sudden proposal?"

"That's bothering me," Francis said gravely. "I suppose . . . I thought . . . well, the best thing I can think of is to take the carriage and ask Mrs. Stancy's permission to take her for a ride and ask her then."

"Suppose Mrs. Stancy refused. She's capable of it, you know."

"Then I'd wait until evening. Good God, sir, do you mean to say they never have any free time at all?"

"None, according to what I hear. But there, I don't suppose Madam would prove so obdurant. So . . . you'll get her in the carriage and say 'Araminta, will you marry me?' By Jove, you're a bold man, Francis."

"What's bold about it?"

For answer Sir Edward reached out to the far end of the untidy table which stood by his elbow and lifted a book from an unsteady pile.

"I thought about you last week when I was reading this. It's Craigie's 'Life of Henry the Eighth,' very interesting." He thumbed

173

over the pages impatiently. "Damn it, I thought I marked the place. Never mind, I remember the gist of it." He threw the book back to the top of the pile which promptly overbalanced. The books thudded to the floor. "No, leave them, leave them. They'll do very well there. Make more room on the table. This was the incident I wanted to tell you about. Henry—and he was a man who knew about women, take notice—was sending an envoy to look over some foreign princess whose reputed charm, or political significance, I forget which, they muddled them so in those days, had commended her to His Majesty's attention. And he told the fellow that above all things he was to take care to get near enough to the lady to ascertain 'Whether her breath be sweet or stinking.' A pretty thought, eh?"

"I don't see what that has to do . . ." Francis looked blank.

"With you? No? Really? Oh well, perhaps you know."

"What?"

"That much about your Araminta . . ."

Francis' face went stony. Above his left eyebrow a vein bulged suddenly. Sir Edward, undeterred, went on smoothly.

"My boy—last time we talked you were disappointed and annoyed by my attitude. I should like to say now that what I said then was said deliberately. I aimed to set you thinking. I take it that you *have* thought, and you're still in the same mind. That's enough for me. Two months is a good time when you're in love, you're a serious-minded fellow and you've proved that this is no idle infatuation. So now I'm going to help you."

Francis stared.

"And to start with, I want you to get into your head, and keep there, the notion that, if you'd fallen in love with a princess, or a nun in a convent, or a houri in the Grand Turk's harem, I'd speak and act exactly as I am about to do over Madam Stancy's dairymaid. Is that clear?"

"It's a bit involved . . ."

"It'll become clear. Now, all the ladies whom I have postulated as being the object of your desires have one thing in common; it would be impossible for you to enter into any kind of social intercourse with them, or to find out about them any of those things—least perhaps, but not last, the thing which bothered his Tudor majesty—in the ordinary way. I don't like this idea of proposing to a girl whom you've seen three times and once exchanged a few words with."

"It isn't what I should wish myself, naturally. But what else can I do?"

"I'll tell you that. Go home and concentrate upon your cottages and cowhouses until the end of August—that won't be long. I'm sorry to make it *that* long, but I've got to go to Cambridgeshire to finish off this Fenland report, and then I'm going North to start a comparison of cottagers' budgets for Whitmore to put with the one he's compiling in the southern counties. It'll take me the whole of two months. In August I shall be back here for the harvest, and I will somehow ingratiate myself with Madam Stancy and *borrow* Araminta. When next you come here you shall find her making butter in my dairy and eating her head off in my kitchen for a change. You can talk to her, walk with her, and work your way gradually towards speaking the momentous words just as you could if she'd been asked to stay at Arbrey Ash for a week. You might also be able to find out whether *she* likes *you*. That aspect seems to have escaped everyone else. Well, what d'you think of the idea?"

"It is . . . sound, I think, Uncle Edward. I'm grateful to you for thinking so . . . constructively. But it's a long time to wait." He rose and began to pace the floor, taking short, nervous strides. When he spoke, the words came jerkily. "You know, I have a kind of funny feeling about the whole affair . . . a kind of doomed feeling . . . as though I hadn't much time and were wasting what I had. I felt so sure. Uncle Edward, I was *so* sure that I could have asked her to marry me the first day I saw her. That's what I should have done. That would have been fitting and right. I came, I saw, and I was conquered. By delaying and talking first to you and then to Mother and now to you again, I've been caught back . . . made to bring my mind to bear upon what shouldn't be a matter for thought. It's feeling. Think it over, you say; take your time, says mother; and then you, kindly, I'm sure, but with the most immortal audacity, as good as suggest that I must sniff her breath. Of course, neither you nor Mother has ever been in love; you're talking and thinking in a medium that you know nothing about. And I've been fool enough to listen to you . . . and be influenced . . ."

"Have you been influenced? By us, Francis? Or by your inner good sense. Love is one thing, living with a woman is another. And rather than see you go off to-morrow to propose marriage to a woman whom you don't, you can't, know, I would restrain you by physical violence."

"I'd like to see you try."

"My physical violence," said Sir Edward sweetly, "would be strictly confined to the young woman. As Justice of the Peace, I have great powers. I haven't the slightest doubt that, given the motive, I could trump up some charge against her. Arrest her as a wanton woman, as a suspected thief, or as a trespasser against some of our delightful laws of settlement. They're far from obsolete, you know. You've no idea how helpless the poor are when it comes to legal business, Francis. I could have her out of your reach to-night if I'd a mind to. There, there, stop glowering at me, and sit down, do. You'll wear a hole in that rug, and it's seen its best days already. Sit down and think over my plan. I thought it was good, because, for one thing, it won't compromise the girl at all; supposing that, on better acquaintance you found that she was . . . well, not what you had thought?"

"You're so damned plausible." He glowered for a moment. "And I'm so damned sensible. All right then, we'll go through all the conventional motions. 'Please call me Francis, and may I call you Araminta?' God, that wasn't how I wanted it to be; it wasn't how it was *meant* to be."

"It is how things are done, Francis. The human race is very old, and in some ways wise. The conventional way of doing things is usually the way which, through a process of trial and error, mankind has found to work smoothly and successfully."

"All right. I'll wait until August. But I shall most likely propose to her on the first day."

"Oh no, Francis. Have your courtship. Those days of cautious advance, coy retreat, shy surrender, are, I have always heard, the sweetest of one's life. I wouldn't have you robbed of them because your lady lives, as it were, in an ivory tower."

"I never know when you're sincere or not, Uncle Edward."

"If you don't know now, you never will, my boy. I've done my best for you."

"I believe you have," Francis said after a pause, his face clearing a little. Only two months, at least only two full months to wait, and those in summer when time went quickly. He would spend them in making the place fit for his bride. He thought of the big room which had never been used since his father's death. He would have the panelling painted white, and the cornices gilded. The carpet should be a deep hyacinth blue, and all the curtains of velvet to match; and although it would be an awkward thing to move, he would turn out the vast ebony and ivory bed with its over-fat cupids, which his grandfather had bought in Venice during his Grand Tour. The bed should be white and gold, too, to match the walls, with hangings of the blue velvet . . . the bed . . . the bed he would make for Araminta. . . .

He rose abruptly and went out of the room.

Araminta went to her second lesson with alacrity; but it was not like the first. Mrs. Stancy was never again surprised out of her sport. Araminta, chided with ferocity for the first simple mistake, lost her nerve and made a number of errors in rapid succession; reprimands, and then punishments came thick and fast.

The height of summer came, with the meadows full of lush grass and great ox-eye daisies and buttercups, and there was more cream and butter and cheeses to handle than at any time during the whole year. The days were long and the weather was hot, and often when Araminta crossed the dim lobby and entered the big bare room she felt as limp as a thread. Soon, when the letters were thoroughly known by shape and sound and word association, they had to be made, first upon the slate, and then upon a sheet of dazzling white paper with a quill cut by Mrs. Stancy's own hand. The ink-pot was big, and made of glass, with a silver lid that lifted backwards, and when the quill had been dipped—not too deeply, or blots would result, and not too shallowly, or it would run dry in the middle of a letter which for some reason annoyed her teacher, it had to be lifted very carefully across a little space of shining table-top before it reached the paper. It wasn't *safe* to make a blot on the paper, but it would be much worse, Araminta knew, to make one on the table. Every time as the quill's point was lifted and started on its short but perilous journey, her heart beat so hard that it jolted her hand. What would happen if she blotted the table? One evening, when the pot had been newly filled and her judgment was at fault, the blot did fall. Mrs. Stancy boxed her ears so that her ears rang and all the letters did a mad dance. But even without the blot to mar the lesson, it was ordeal enough. The quill had to be held just at one angle; it must not squeak nor splutter; the apparently incurable tendency of her first finger to bend itself must be curbed; if she lowered her eyes too close to the paper, or let her elbow stick out, or followed the quill's point with the tip of her tongue, or sat sideways in her chair to get a better purchase on the job, Mrs. Stancy noted the fault at once and corrected it sharply. The short black ruler was no longer used as a pointer; it was, like something they sang in church, "extreme to mark what was done amiss," and it came down sharply, crack, crack, with blows which momentarily paralysed the unsteady toiling fingers.

Every evening after the lesson—and they occurred about twice a week, she went from the room as near tears as she could be. Susie would say, "Was that hard to-night?" her voice and her staring brown eyes full of sympathy. Sometimes, after a particularly bad session, Araminta would admit, yes, it was very hard, and the tears which she could not shed would well higher in her throat; but more usually she felt that there was something a little degrading in being the object of pity from such a pitiable creature as Susie, and she would harden her heart and her face and square her shoulders and say, "Not so bad," or "I'm getting along." Between Nancy and Araminta the lessons were never mentioned; which, since Mrs. Stancy frequently taunted Nancy with her successor's swift progress, and at the same time held Nancy before Araminta as a model pupil, was a pity. Nancy was hurt by the taunts and made jealous; Araminta, at least, escaped that mental torment; for by this time she was quite prepared to admit that Nancy was indeed a wonderful person. She had lived out the lessons, hadn't she; and she had spent three years in this place of torment and could still take her food and sleep at night and do a day's work with the best. Nancy, as a survivor, was entitled to respect.

One evening a dreadful thing happened. It had been close and thundery all day, and at lesson time the sky was a dark purple pall which seemed to hang close to the earth, shutting out air as well as light. Half-way through, Mrs. Stancy rang for the lamp to be brought, and when it was set in the middle of the table Araminta was sickly conscious of the heat and the smell of hot oil radiating from it. Her head felt dull and heavy, and her behaviour was, as a consequence, unusually stupid. She had just had a special lesson upon the use of capital letters, and was, this evening, engaged in copying the following statements: "My name is Araminta Glover. I work at Abbey Farm in the parish of Summerfield, in the county of Essex. My mistress is Mrs. Stancy. Nancy and Susie work in the dairy with me, and Luke helps us to milk. To-day is Thursday."

She placed the last full stop and would have taken a moment to compare the copy with the original and make any correction that was needed, but Mrs. Stancy snatched away the paper and said crossly, "Can't you even copy, you careless girl? A small e for Essex and a small m for Mrs. How dare you?" She smacked her open hand against the upper part of Araminta's arm. It was not, for her, a hard blow, and most of its force was expended upon the bunch of sleeve which Araminta always rolled up before lessons to ensure greater freedom. But, as though the slight force of the impact had released something in Araminta's head, her nose began to bleed, soiling, before she could snatch out her handkerchief, the front of her dress and the clean sheet of paper which had lain beneath that upon which she had been writing. At the same time, she, who never cried, who had come to think of herself as immune from tears, began to sob, noisily, a trifle hysterically.

"Be quiet! Be quiet!" said Mrs. Stancy in a strange voice, low and urgent, almost as though Araminta had been making a noise in church. "Put your head back, against the back of the chair." She went to the cupboard and brought out a large square of soft old linen. "Take this," she said. "That handkerchief is totally inadequate." Then she stood there, close to Araminta's shoulder, watching, watching, watching. Through all the confused emotions of that moment, Araminta became conscious of those watching eyes. And she knew, without turning her eyes that there would be a dusky flush on Mrs. Stancy's pale cheeks and that her eyes would be very brightly yellow. Yet, despite this knowledge, she must look. She moved her eyes above the bunched-up handful of linen and looked sideways. Yes . . . it was with just that face that Mrs. Stancy had watched the bleeding of her ear. She was suddenly frightened beyond the ordinary measure of fear; frightened into calmness and coherence. Still holding the linen to her nose she put her other hand upon the table's edge and stood up. Her knees felt weak and unsteady. But when she spoke her voice was level enough, if a little breathless.

"Ma'am, what you've said to me so often is the truth. I ain't worth teaching. You'd best give me up as a bad job and save wasting your time. I just can't seem to get on with it. Thank you for the lessons I hev had."

"Don't be ridiculous, Araminta." Mrs. Stancy's voice was pleasant again. "I can't let you stop now: a half-finished job is worse than one not started. I should be very much ashamed if in later life you said that I had tried to teach you and failed. Go and have a good wash in cold water and come to me to-morrow. You'll feel very differently by that time. Good night."

There was no escape.

The summer sped away. By the first week in August Araminta was reading, slowly and after some deliberation before the longer words and the people's names out of the big black Bible which Mrs. Stancy had always used as a primer. And in the middle of the month, at the end of the lesson, she closed it with the heavy thumping sound whose finality was always welcome to Araminta's ears, and made an astonishing announcement.

"That'll be the last lesson for a week, Araminta. Try not to forget everything you have learned in that time. I've lent you out for a week."

Araminta sat quite still and quite silent, but excitement began to run in her veins. Lent out. For a week. To whom? Oh, if it were a nice place, with kind people, it would be like a holiday.

"I didn't want to do it," said Mrs. Stancy, moving her thick white fingers across the black cover of the book. "But it isn't often that one is asked to do a favour for a grand gentleman," Her voice rasped. "You're going to Sir Edward Follesmark's place at Sible Havers. I need hardly warn you, Araminta, that you must do your best."

Her yellow eyes fixed themselves upon Araminta's and bored into them.

"I believe you'll be working alone, which is a good thing. You can maintain your own standards better so. And I want you to remember that I have lent you to make Sir Edward's butter and skim his cream, not to indulge in a lot of idle gossip, or go teaching somebody else our little ways. You know what I mean, don't you, Araminta?"

Araminta nodded helplessly.

"You just do your work, say as little as possible, and answer no questions." She held Araminta's eyes for another moment, and then, dropping her gaze, said with a change of voice, almost elaborately casual and careless, "I dare say you will enjoy yourself. Sir Edward has a name for spoiling his servants, which is why, I suspect, he has been left in the lurch and forced to borrow from me. Probably you will be tempted to compare his establishment with mine." Her voice changed again, hardening. "But you will kindly keep such comparisons to yourself, Araminta. I shall be informed in due time of everything you say and everything you do while you are absent. Don't forget that. And remember also, that though you will probably eat beefsteak every day and be free to wallow in your bed by seven o'clock each evening, that is because Sir Edward is a man of means. He isn't a dairy farmer, he's a gentleman who keeps a couple of cows. If everyone were like him there'd be little enough work for such as you."

"When do I go, please? And which way?"

"Sir Edward is sending a conveyance for you to-morrow at ten. Probably it'll be his own carriage," said Mrs. Stancy sarcastically.

But in the morning it was a light farm cart, spattered with mud and filmed over with dust which ambled up at about a quarter past the hour to carry Araminta to Sible Havers. Sir Edward had remembered his own dictates about putting ideas into the heads of innocent maidens; and on her arrival the housekeeper showed her to a room at the head of the back stairs, comfortable, in the way in which the room at Uplands was comfortable, but with nothing about it to suggest that she was anything but a visiting servant.

The dairy was much like Mrs. Pollard's, too, and after a year of the Abbey specklessness, Araminta's eyes found it more than a little dirty. There was some sour milk in several receptacles, the morning's milk stood in buckets just underneath an open window so that dust and bits of dried leaf blew in from the dense shrubbery which darkened the dairy, and the floor was marked all over with the track of heavy nailed boots coming straight in from the cowshed without even a pretence at a wipe.

Araminta, who had brought all her aprons and caps, tied on her sacking and went to the kitchen for some hot water.

"I wus just coming to call you," said the stout housekeeper. "I reckoned you'd like a cuppa tea arter that journey. I've just mashed it. Jenny! Want your tea s'morning or to-morrer?"

Jenny, from some invisible outpost, shouted that she'd be there in a moment, and in her turn yelled to another person out of sight that the tea was made. The stout woman, whom everyone called Liza, or Mrs. Liza, set a great brown teapot and a number of cups on a table which could have done with a good scrubbing, and fetched from the larder a dish of what looked to be (Araminta's mouth watered with hope) meat patties, and the major portion of a currant cake. She began to pour the tea, good brown tea such as Araminta had not seen for a year, and she filled up the cups with thick creamy milk and ladled in sugar with a generous hand. Possibly Araminta's face betrayed her. Mrs. Liza said, half-apologetically, "Sir Edward don't dine till five, and we take ours arterwards. Too much trouble to cook twice in a day. So we make our 'levenses pretty solid. Hev a pie." She pushed the dish forward and Araminta took a pie and bit through the flaky brown pastry crust and into the succulent minced beef within. It was glorious. Two girls, with rosy cheeks and bobbing curls under rather rakish muslin caps with cherry-coloured ribbon round them, came in together, took cups and pies and perched on the edge of the table chattering, looking at Araminta with quite friendly curiosity, and, almost before she knew where she was, were engaging her in conversation and plying her with questions. Where did she come from, how did she like being borrowed, and cheerful nonsense of that kind. They told her that the girl who usually looked after the dairy was called Annie and had been sent home for a week to celebrate the return of her brother who had been a soldier in India for ten years.

"Though why this week, beats me," put in Mrs. Liza, who had shown no sign of minding that, what with chatter and feeding a full twenty minutes had already been wasted. "He been home a good month to my knowledge, and Annie never show no sign of wanting to see him. But Sir Edward, bless his heart, read her a lecture about family ties being sacred, and packed her off with a grut ham what he said would go down well with a chap fresh from Indian grub. Jenny, where's Charlie? If he don't come soon, I'll hev to make a fresh pot."

"He's taking his 'levenses with Mr. Graves."

"Oh, I see. Madeira more to his taste than tea." A mischievous look came over her face. "Well, just for being so haughty they shan't neither of 'em hev pies. Jenny, pop yon dish in the bread bin. He'll never look there. Anybody like another pie afore they're going, going, gone!"

Jenny and the other girl snatched a pie, and Araminta took another, her third. Then Jenny hid the dish away and in about a minute a young man in footman's breeches and waistcoat but with his shirt-sleeves rolled up above his hairy forearms, appeared and said, "Mrs. Liza, what about a bite to eat?"

"There's cake," said the stout woman, pointing to it.

"A little bird whispered something about meat pies, old dear. Where are they. Damme, I believe you've et 'em all. What guzzling pigs women are!"

"They're gone. Thass all I can tell you," said Mrs. Liza, laughing. "You get back to Mr. Graves and the Madeira. And don't forget to spare a moment for that silver. Thass as black as your hat and hev been for a week. And Mr. Francis is arriving this afternoon, don't forget. Sir Edward will want the place looking decent for once."

"The silver, madam, has all been cleaned; and we who have cleaned it feel the need of some solid sustenance. Bring forward the pies."

"Get 'em, Jenny. If they've cleaned *that* silver they've earned a pie. If I kept a footman and a butler I'd hev my silver so you could see your face in it all the time."

"And if *I* kept a cook-housekeeper and a couple of wenches I'd have my bed made before noon."

"Ain't his bed done yet?" Mrs. Liza demanded. "What on earth hev you two been up to. Get off and do it at once. And see that Mr. Francis' room if fit for a human being, do. Daisy, afore you go, get me my board and roller and all I'll need for pastry." She turned to Araminta. "Did you notice if the new milk was in?"

"Yes, it is."

"Bring me a quart, there's a dear. I reckon I'll make a junket. Daisy, time you're there look on the top shelf and see if there's rennet and cochineal. I'll make a pink one, I fancy."

Araminta stood up. She had had three cups of tea, each as good as the first, three meat patties and a thick slice of cake. Her stomach was taut as a drum, and her heart was beating with excitement. This was a lovely place. And somebody had said *Mr. Francis*. . . . Of course, it might not be the same; but at the same time it *might*. And if only he could eat her butter, this very evening and learn somehow that she had made it. Wouldn't that be the most wonderful luck in the world. Ordinarily she would have been pessimistically certain that this Mr. Francis would not be her kind-faced young man. But in this delightful, jolly place a belief in luck and in miracles was very easy to attain.

"Can I have a bucket of hot water, please?" she asked.

"Of course you can, dearie," said Mrs. Liza, beginning to sort out the things which Daisy had carried on to the table. "Help yourself."

In the next four hours Araminta worked as, even under the spur of fear and compulsion, she had seldom worked in her life. She gave the dairy a thorough cleaning, scrubbed the floor and the shelves, tipped the sour milk down the drain, washed all the crocks, flung away five or six stinking floor-cloths, "dwiles" as she called them, and scoured all the shelves. Then she scalded all the wooden tools, churned some butter and made it up. There were no stampers here, so she marked each slab with a cross-pattern with the edge of her patters and made so many shells that her wrist ached.

Mrs. Liza, who was puzzled by this new girl's apparent passion for hot water, ambled in at three o'clock with another cup of tea, and looked round in amazement.

"You'd hardly know the place," she said. "But there, thass a case of a new broom. I reckon if you wus here a fortnight you'd be the same as the rest, fat and saucy. Don't I go to sea I'll hev that Jenny scrub my kitchen table afore I'm a day older." She ambled out again.

When, soon after four o'clock, Araminta, finding nothing else to be done in the dairy, went into the kitchen to ask when she should do the afternoon's milking and which was the way to the cowshed, Mrs. Liza's kitchen table was still unscrubbed; but through the muddle and the apparent purposelessness a certain order and direction became visible, if one looked closely. Plates were warming and trays were being piled, and the scent of cooking and a hissing sound came from the oven. For Sir Edward, in spite of his queerness in the matter of politics, liked his creature comforts very well; and Mrs. Liza would hardly have kept her position if a certain competence had not lurked beneath her easy, haphazard manner. Once, long ago, Sir Edward had suffered the ministrations of the lady housekeeper for whom his establishment seemed to call; but he had denounced that way of life as "bearing all the pains of marriage without the compensating pleasures." The good lady had fussed if he sat down in a damp jacket, she had pounced on him with delight if he showed signs of starting a cold, sent him to bed and obviously gloated at her power over him; she had looked pained when the gun-dog pupped on the library hearth-rug, when Sir Edward took a drop too much, or propped his muddy boots on the marble mantelpiece. When she left, with infinite regret and many tears to rescue the household of a widower brother from complete dissolution, Sir Edward had sighed with relief and straightway engaged Mrs. Liza, who was the widow of one of his keepers, and at whose cottage he had often stopped for a glass of home-brewed and a chunk of cake. Mrs. Liza would sit in the kitchen and know her place, and it would be odd if, with a little help she could not satisfy his simple demands. Several ladies had warned him that a mere village woman would probably have trouble in keeping the staff in order, but there were fewer quarrels and complaints than in the old days; and if the house was dusty, or only superficially cleaned, if the housekeeping bills were out of all proportion to the modesty of his establishment, those matters never worried Sir Edward. His food was well cooked, and Graves saw that it was served properly, and everybody always seemed happy. Mrs. Liza had been in charge of the household now for ten years, and if any fate had called her away the tears would probably have been shed by the baronet himself.

"Ted milk, and he'll bring it in presently," said Mrs. Liza over her shoulder, prodding at something in the oven. "You come and sit by the fire. That get cold in there this time of year. I'm heving to howd the dinner back a bit on account of Mr. Francis. He's come, but Master took him straight out to see summat or other."

Araminta took a low stool by the corner of the fireplace and sat down.

"What Mr. Francis is it?" she asked.

"Mr. Francis Loveless, from Arbrey Ash. He's Sir Edward's

nephew. A nice young man. Dint him and his mother come over to your place, back in May, seeing how to make a dairy run right? I thought I heard summat of the sort," she ran on as Araminta gave a glad confirmatory nod. "Daft, I call it; but then the whole lot is daft-like in some ways. Reckon he'll waste a mint of money giving all his cows silver bracelets and teaching the dairymaids how to dance round a Maypole. Thass the sort he is."

How nice to be able to say . . . I'm going to work at Arbrey Ash come Michaelmas twelvemonth. Discretion sealed her lips. But oh, if only the household there were as happy and carefree and well-treated as here. And she thought that was another thing the Abbey had taught her, she'd know a good home when next she saw one, and it'd be a rare rum fellow who made her run out of a comfortable place again. And then her heart gave a heavy kind of jolt and there was a pain in her throat; she thought of Jan suddenly, thought of him as she hadn't done for months and months, with longing and affection. She hadn't heard so much as a whisper about him in all her time at Summerfield; whom had he married? For whom had the daffodils bloomed in the little garden at Theo's cottage?

"Let me do something. I ain't used to sitting still," she cried, jumping up and speaking in such a cracked queer voice that Mrs. Liza and Jenny looked at her in surprise.

"You can dust them plates," said the cook. "I reckon I heard the South door slam a minnit or two since. Ah, I knew it," she said, as high up one of the bells which hung in a row over the inner door, broke into a cracked jangling. She lifted a black pot from the fire and poured enough soup for a dozen people into a great white and gold tureen with a bad chip in its lid. Araminta dusted and handed over two soup plates so hot that they were only just bearable to handle. Charles, as though he had been waiting the signal, strolled into the kitchen, his neckcloth very white and tight, his shirt-sleeves covered by his jacket. He lifted the first tray and bore it away.

After that there was quite a flurry of activity in the kitchen. The meal was simpler than those Araminta had sometimes assisted in dishing up during her days in the Manor kitchen, but Mrs. Liza made it seem more complicated by keeping everything so piping hot to the very last minute that everyone who touched anything had to scream and shake burnt fingers; and she forgot things, to remember them at the last minute, and she kept up a stream of orders and directions, repeating and contradicting herself continuously.

"Cream," she said suddenly, just as she set a firm pink junket and a dish of jellied fruit on the tray. "I clean forgot about cream. Run quick and fetch some, whass-your-name. And bring plenty. There's junket for us too, do we ever find ourselves sitting down arter all this flurry."

But the flurry was almost over. Already Daisy was clearing the fireside end of the big table and setting it with a crumpled cloth which might have seen a month's service, to judge by its limpness and the stains upon it. And almost at once Mrs. Liza hauled out of the oven a great sizzling joint of pork and a deep brown dish full of roasted potatoes. Jenny said, "Did you remember the onions?" And Mrs. Liza said, "D'you think I'd forget them?" and pointed to a pan drawn aside from the fire. "Just let 'em heat for a minnit."

And Daisy said, "My, I'm something hungry," and Mrs. Liza said, "Hunger's the best sauce, you on't want no onion my girl," and they all laughed. Very soon they were sitting down to what Araminta—forgetful of the momentous Horkey night—considered the best meal she had ever eaten. There was no doubt about it, she thought, peace and plenty did make people nicer. Crunching the crisp crackling between her teeth she wondered what Daisy and Jenny and Mrs. Liza would have been like if they had fallen, not into Sir Edward's employ, but into Mrs. Stancy's. She spent the rest of the meal in slightly morbid speculation, seeing Jenny as spiteful and spying as Nancy, Mrs. Liza as mean and nasty as Mrs. Nead ... and what about herself? Thass made me right greedy, she concluded, as she gladly accepted a second helping. But there she knew that she wronged—if that were possible—the Abbey régime. She had always been greedy, and she would remain so. Even her scrupulous sending home of her wages was a form of greed; she wanted her mother's approval and gratitude; she wanted the contented feeling of a good conscience; she wanted the peace of mind which could think—there I've done my best for them—and dismiss them with a shrug.

She was quite appalled by this self-revelation, and deliberately didn't have two helpings of junket and cream.

Daisy banged on the door in the morning, and when Araminta reached the kitchen she found Charles and the two girls gathered round the brown teapot. Mr. Graves and Mrs. Liza, by virtue of their positions, were taken tea in bed.

For breakfast there was porridge—very different from the Abbey oatmeal—smothered in cream and brown sugar, a choice of eggs boiled or fried, and an apparently limitless supply of bacon rashers. On the previous day Araminta had been dazzled by the sight of such plenty and undisposed to be critical, but now, with slightly clearing vision, she saw that the waste was appalling. Mrs. Liza was apparently so much afraid of not cooking sufficient, either for the Master's table or for the servants', that she made it a rule to cook about twice what was really needed. And all that was not needed went into the fire. Utterly horrified at the sight of good food being *burned*, Araminta, forgetful of her precarious status, blurted out, "Ain't you at least got a swill tub?"

"We did hev," said Jenny, indifferently scraping a dish into the stove. "I reckon Ted took it away time that reeked so and never brung it back."

And there must be, thought Araminta, feeling a little sick, dozens of families like her own, within ten minutes' walk of the back door, to whom the food which Jenny was throwing away would be a feast never to be forgotten.

"Don't you hev no poor people arsting for food?" she demanded.

"Plenty," said Jenny. "And thass a rule nobody's to be turned away."

"Then what do they get?"

"Oh, there's allust heaps in the larder," said Jenny easily.

It was daft, it was wicked, thought Araminta, stamping off to the dairy. In a way it was as wicked as Mrs. Stancy's cheeseparing.

That, at least, didn't take good food and put it out of the reach of everybody. And good luck! Come the day before she went home she'd see if she couldn't make up a good bundle and smuggle a bit to Susie . . . maybe Nancy too. If Nancy knew that it came from outside she might condescend to eat it.

Ted had brought in the morning milk, and once that was set up there was very little to do. She had made enough butter yesterday to last this household, wasteful as it was, until the middle of the week.

The floor was certainly soiled again: for this unknown Ted, although apparently in the habit of putting the milk down in the first place he came to, had wandered all round, dropping bits of straw and cow dung from his boots. That startled young man had, in fact, peeped into every corner and every crock during his visit. He was conducting a violent and illicit love affair with the absent Annie and meant to warn her upon her return that the girl Sir Edward had borrowed had shown her up proper on the very first day.

Araminta set up the milk, scoured and scalded the buckets, and set them in place for the afternoon and then scrubbed the floor. She wondered a little about Annie; what on earth did she find to do all day? It wasn't really even a one-girl dairy. She was a little sorry that she had worked so hard yesterday; because to-day either Sir Edward or Mr. Loveless might peep in, and it wouldn't do for her to be found with idle hands. She knew, she'd make some "quick cheeses," both milk ones and cream. They'd be fit to eat by to-morrow.

She was busily engaged—although taking her time, deliberately making the job last—and happy because she was on her own, out of the fear pall that hung, definite as a cloud over every nook and corner of the Abbey, and because she was full of a good breakfast, when the door opened and two gentlemen came in. She recognized her Mr. Loveless, and his beaming, portly companion could only be Sir Edward. She made two bobs and flashed two of the smiles which made the vagrant dimples dance. They were both gentlemen, and one she knew was nice and the other was old, so it was quite safe to smile at them so.

"Well," said Sir Edward, "here you are then." His manner seemed very cheerful and hearty to Araminta, but Francis could tell that below the habitually bluff manner his uncle was preoccupied.

Edward Follesmark studied Araminta carefully, pretending to inspect the dairy all the time. He had, for some reason, expected a different creature, small, more lusciously curved, fair-haired and pink-cheeked. There was nothing immediately alluring about this thin brown girl, and he thought, with a certain reassurance, that at least Francis hadn't fallen prey to the lust of the eye. And yet . . . there was something, not the voluptuous cuddlesomeness which he had expected and distrusted, but something warm and vivid and vital. By Jove, he thought, I believe the boy was right. Forty years ago I'd . . . nonsense, rubbish, balderdash! All the same there's something even about the way she stands.

"I hope they're treating you properly," he said.

"I'm having a lovely time, sir. It's like a holiday."

"I'm glad of that. Well, Araminta, as you already know, I believe, Mr. Loveless here is interested in dairying, so you won't mind if he comes in now and then and watches you work."

"Not at all, sir. It'll be a great pleasure, sir," she said, using the automatic civility of the lowly to the rich in order to cover the thrilling excitement which flooded over her. Just what she had longed for, a chance to show him what she could do. And oh, what a pity she'd made the shells yesterday!

"Well, I must get on. Are you coming with me Francis, or taking your first lesson now?"

"I'll stay," Francis said, breathless at the thought of being alone with her.

"You can sit on that chair, sir," said Araminta as soon as Sir Edward had gone. "I give it a good scrub yesterday." She was completely, blissfully at her ease. She knew what she was doing, and she knew she was doing it well. She could make cheeses quite confidently in front of anybody except Mrs. Stancy.

Francis took the chair and sat down, staring at her. He cleared his throat once or twice; he must say something. But what? If he'd followed his natural impulses he'd have got up, gone over to her and taken her in his arms. He wanted, most dreadfully, to kiss her. But she'd think he was mad, probably scream out or something. Of course, Uncle Edward had been right—things like that had to be led up to. And how thankful he was that he hadn't plunged in with that carriage drive and the immediate proposal, he'd never have got it out. Dear, dear, little Araminta, how sweet your neck is between your bodice and cap.

Araminta thought he was very quiet. And that might be for two reasons. He might think talk would disturb her, or he might be feeling out of place in a dairy. After all, it wasn't the proper place for a gentleman. Presently she said:

"Thass a good idea of yours, sir, to see the work being done. Then you'll know for yourself how it ought to be. I'm making what they call "quick cheeses" now; they're called that because they don't need to ripen. Would you like me to explain what I do as I go along."

"Yes, I would. Shall I come and sit over there?"

He left the chair and perched himself on the dairy shelf.

"You must tell me if there's anything I can do to help, anything you want lifted or fetched, or reached down."

She smiled at him. As though she were likely to give him any trouble.

She went on with her work, now and then dropping an explanatory word. He liked to hear her talk, but not about cheeses.

"In May," he said, "when I came with my mother, you mentioned some of the jobs you had had, Araminta. I found it interesting. Tell me a little more about them."

"There's nothing very exciting about it," said Araminta. But if he wanted to hear there was no harm in telling him. She could let him see how she had worked her way up, and she could get in a word about wages. The idea of sharing the profits of the dairy was all very well, but she did want him to see that it was important to her to draw a pound at the end of every quarter, for the first year, at least. So, working away at her cheeses and stopping now and then to give him a glance which underlined or explained or apologized, she laid before him, with several shrewd comments, a wealth of untutored observation and more than one brilliant little thumbnail sketch of character, the story of a life which had been hard and monotonous, small in comfort and reward, but never for a moment dull or futile. She did not mention Jan Honeywood.

"So here I am," she concluded, with a final smile. He wanted to leap up and take her hands and promise that never again should she be hungry or cold or overworked.

"You've got a remarkable memory, Araminta," he said. She thought he was looking at her rather queerly. Did he perhaps think she had spoken too freely, especially about her first place.

"Mrs. Stancy said something like that too; when I was learning the letters."

"Oh, have you been learning to read? How are you getting on?"

"I can read. I make mistakes, of course, and there are some hard words in the Bible. And with writing I've got to where you should put capital letters and full stops."

"Last time I saw you you said you couldn't read or write. D'you mean to say you've learned all that since May?"

She nodded.

"Good Heavens; it took me quite a year to master three-letter words. My mother taught me, and she still teases me about how slow I was."

Just at that moment Jenny put her head in at the door and shouted cheerfully, "Whass a matter with you? Don't you want no 'levenses? I called you minnits ago." She took a step into the dairy to see what could be making Araminta deaf to the call of food, and checked herself at the sight of Francis.

"I'm sorry, sir. I din't know you was here."

"That's quite all right," he said. "Araminta has been giving me a practical lesson in cheesemaking—and other things. But I don't want to keep her from her refreshment." He stood up. It was a pity that girl had come bursting in—Araminta and he had at last found a subject upon which they could compare experiences. And he imagined that he had caught a bright knowing look on the girl's face. There'd be kitchen gossip if he weren't careful. Not that it mattered, he would be engaged—perhaps even married to Araminta by the end of the week, then they could talk their silly heads off, but furtive, speculative gossip was distasteful somehow. He said, rather loudly:

"Araminta, do you know as much about cows as you do about cheese?"

"I can tell a doer from a waster," said Araminta confidently.

"Then later on to-day, say at about three o'clock, I'd be obliged if you would come out with me and we'll look at some cows, and you shall show me the difference. It's a thing I should know."

"He's gone daft on his dairy," Jenny said disrespectfully, as they went towards the kitchen. "The master's just the same. Always some bee in his bonnet. D'you know, once he made us all live for a week on boiled potatoes and a gallon loaf apiece, and weighed us at the beginning and the end, to see what we'd lost. He did it hisself, too. That were something to do with some family he'd got to know about."

"And what did you lose?" asked Araminta, to whose mind the matter of diet had a more than academic interest.

Jenny giggled, "The master'd lost most, eight or nine pounds. None of us was more than a pound down; but then, we'd cheated. Mrs. Liza said she worn't going to starve on account of his nonsense, she'd done enough of that when she were young. Ain't that what you said, Mrs. Liza?"

"Aye," said the fat woman with her broad smile. "We had the bread and taters well to the fore all day, and then I used to fix up a mite of something tasty arter he'd gone to bed. I got no patience with fads. Like him now . . ."—her wide gesture of the head indicated Francis in whatever direction he might be—"sitting hisself there in a dairy all morning. Wonder is that just acause he's going to hev a cook he don't want to come in here and watch me at work. Ours is right a rum family."

But such a nice one, Araminta thought, as she sat down to a plate of cold pork and pickles, two slices of buttered bread, three cups of tea and an apple turnover.

When the meal was finished she addressed herself to Mrs. Liza.

"Could you find me a job? I've really finished in there for the day now."

"Ah, that I can," said Mrs. Liza, as appreciative as though she were running the house single-handed. "I'd be right thankful if you'd straighten out that pantry for me. I keep on about it but, to tell you the truth, there ain't time in the day to get round to it."

Araminta was still at work, lost to everything save a mixture of exasperation and wonder, when Mrs. Liza herself called a halt.

"Thass nigh on three; and none of our family can abide being kept waiting," she said.

Araminta looked down at her soiled apron. So many of the receptacles which she had moved and cleaned and rearranged had been dirty on the outside, or leaking a little. What on earth would Mrs. Stancy say if she could see that apron? Araminta finished it off by cleaning her hands on it, and then untied its strings. And a cap looked silly without an apron, so she took that off too.

"I'll just leave these here," she said, "and wash them when I come in."

"You're right a pretty girl without yon cap," said Mrs. Liza, staring at her critically. "Or you'd look better in a cap like Jenny's. Yours is like a pudding bag."

Araminta laughed. "Mrs. Stancy provides our caps," she said. "I don't think she'd fancy muslin with red bows, somehow." She pulled down her sleeves and buttoned them at the wrist and went out into the yard, smoothing the creases from the thin print.

Almost immediately Francis, who had been watching for a long time from a side window, emerged from the South door and joined her. He thought how pretty she looked without her cap and apron and began to plan the clothes he would buy her.

"I've asked about the cows," she said. "They're in the Lower Meadow, and thass over here somewhere."

The country here was prettier than in the flat lands around Summerfield. There were more trees, too. And after the monotony of level green pastures it was a relief to the eye to see a field of standing corn, bronzed in the August sun, climbing gently towards the skyline. In another field close by, the harvesters were busy; a man's blue shirt, a girl's pink sunbonnet, an old woman's red skirt below a white, pinned-up apron, made satisfactory splashes of colour.

"I worked at a harvest last year," said Araminta, taking the conversational lead again. "If you have good weather thass the best job of all."

"My uncle seems to agree with you," he said, smiling and pointing. Following the line of his finger Araminta could see the short tubby figure, coatless and with loose flapping white shirt-sleeves, helping to shock up the sheaves which the women were tying.

"Thass the first time I ever see a gentleman at work," said Araminta.

"We're a funny family," said Francis. "Has no one ever told you that?"

She was a little confused, remembering the number of times that she had heard it said that all the Follesmarks were mad.

"Thass a nice way of being funny."

"I'm delighted to hear you say so. This looks like the Lower Meadow."

They had come to a gateway set in a high, overgrown hedge massed with blackberry brambles. At the far end of the green meadow was a little stream, almost dry now, but with a trickle of water still shining over the rounded pebbles in the middle of the dry cracked-mud bed. There, under the shade of a group of willow trees stood four cows, lazily twitching their tails to keep the flies away.

Araminta studied them carefully, remembering everything she had heard Mr. Pollard, and Jackie, and Luke say about cows. While she was choosing words in which to express her honest, but at the same time tactful opinion of the unimpressive little herd, she became aware that Francis was not looking at the cows at all; he was looking at her again, with that same strange expression on his face. Waiting, of course, to see if she had been boasting when she said she knew about cows. She forgot about being tactful.

"There ain't . . . I mean there's not a *good* cow amongst them," she said boldly. "That browny-white one is the best, but she isn't really a mucher. The two red ones are all beef and no bag as they say, and the one that's quite white is old. Nobody that really thought about milk would keep her. And they're all too fat. Did you know that? The best cows are thin—I don't mean bony, but thin. I expect Mrs. Stancy told you about the way they're fed at the dairy; they get more food when they give more milk, and less when they begin to dry up. So they don't ever get fat, you see. They stay the right size."

"You explain things very well, Araminta. I can see that you're going to be a great help to me." The words sounded extremely fatuous. But everything he said to her was silly. There was only one thing that would sound right . . . Araminta, I love you, and I want you to marry me . . . and really he might almost as well burst out with it at once. These stupid talks about cheeses and cows weren't really making the final words any easier to say; and to say other things, as, for instance, in this sun your hair is the prettiest colour I've ever seen, would simply be to betray himself without doing any good.

"Why, look at that," said Araminta in a startled voice, pointing upwards. "Blackberries, ripe already. Oh, if there is one thing I do dearly love, thass blackberrying." She hesitated for a moment, her face aglow. "I've done the dairy work and cleaned the pantry. And I've said what I know about the cows. Do you think that'd be all right if I blackberried for an hour?"

"Nothing easier," he said. "I like blackberrying, too. I'll fetch a basket."

"Oh no, sir," she said, remembering her place. "I'll fetch one; if you're sure it'll be all right. And a stick with a crook to it. The ripest ones are at the top."

"All right. You sit on this gate in the sun and I'll be back in no time."

"I think I ought to fetch the basket," she persisted.

"No, you do as I tell you. Up you go."

He lifted her and set her on top of the gate. Araminta gave a little gasp of surprise. Of all the queer, familiar, friendly things to do!

He said breathlessly, "Now sit there and don't move, because when I come back I want to talk to you about something very important."

She stared thoughtfully at his back as he ran across the yard and at last vanished around the corner of a building. Something very queer had happened to her in the second during which he had held her in his arms before setting her lightly on top of the gate. An old hunger had stirred; she had thought of Jan and remembered the feeling which had shot through her when she had watched Jan swing Cissie in the dance. But, was it a remembered feeling entirely? Or something new? Sweet Jesus, thought Araminta, not irreverently, but with profound astonishment, what will I think of next? And him so innocent and friendly, lifting me up just as Sir Edward is lifting the sheaves, because of his gay good heart.

She twisted her head and leaned forward so that past the bulge of the overgrown hedge she could stare across into the harvest field. She could no longer discern Sir Edward's short, white-shirted figure. When she turned her head again, Francis had reappeared. He was running, and there was something comic about the sight of a gentleman making such haste and carrying a big reed basket and a crook-headed stick.

He was almost within reach when she slipped from the gate; and the next moment she was glad she had done so, for around the corner of the building between the yard and the house came Sir Edward. He, too, was hurrying, not exactly running, but walking very quickly and taking little short prancing steps now and then to hasten his progress. He was trying to pull on his coat as he came. His face was darkly purple and dripping with sweat.

Araminta said, "I think Sir Edward wants you, sir," and pointed with her hand. Francis stopped and took a step or two backwards to meet his uncle. Sir Edward laid his hand on Francis' shoulder.

"My boy," he said, panting heavily, "I've bad news for you. Latchet's just ridden over. Your mother's very ill."

"Ill? She was all right yesterday when I left. Accident?"

"Stroke I'm afraid."

"Oh God. The one thing she always dreaded. I must get back at once."

"I sent a man from the field to get the horses ready. We can leave now. I'm coming with you, Francis. But I must just get my breath. I was nearly beat when I saw Latchet riding towards the house and called out to him, and the news about finished me."

"Wait, uncle, won't you, and ride over in the cool to-morrow morning," said Francis, surveying Sir Edward's wet, beetroot-coloured countenance with some misgiving.

"No, no. I shall be all right." He struggled with his coat and Francis took it by the collar and eased it on for him. They turned and began to walk quickly towards the house.

Araminta followed slowly, picking up the stick and the basket from the place where Francis had dropped them. She remembered the fortnight, back in the spring, when she reckoned the new baby would be about due, and the sweet relief which she had known when the Uplands carter had made another visit and told her that mum and the baby were both well, and it was a boy and they were calling it George. Poor Mr. Loveless. Strokes were dreadful things; you either died or else lost the use of your legs or arms, or couldn't speak clearly ever again. She called up the stored vision of the untidy, grey-haired lady with the abrupt voice and remembered that she had been kind, and that she had had a pleasant smile. It was very sad.

Suddenly she was reminded, by the stick and the basket, of her intention to pick blackberries. There was no reason why she should change her mind. She turned and walked briskly back to the meadow gate, climbed over it, took a pace or two along the hedge until she saw a promising spray and lifted the crook-stick. Now and then as she loosened the black globes and dropped them into the basket, the memory of the distress on Mr. Loveless' pale face and on Sir Edward's red one, haunted her for a moment. She wondered how far it was to Arbrey Ash and how long they would take to get there, and whether they would be in time. But on the whole she enjoyed her afternoon in the sunshine, and the sense of getting something for nothing which was part of the pleasure of blackberrying, and the peace and quietude of the pretty meadow. She gathered until Ted came to drive up the cows to the afternoon's milking, and then she carried the fruit into the kitchen. Mrs. Liza welcomed it as though there were not already great pans of plums and greengages and early apples rotting in the larder.

"We'll hev a pie," she announced. "With master gone, I've nowt to do. We might as well pleasure ourselves for once." She spoke as though it was only during Sir Edward's absence that the staff had anything to eat. "Jenny, hand me my pastry things."

The party that sat down to eat the pie was a very merry one, and even the lugubrious view which Mrs. Liza took of Mrs. Loveless' state did nothing to mar it. Everyone seemed to enjoy hearing about the strokes which were so prevalent in their employer's family. Mrs. Liza, who had lived in Sible Havers all her life, could remember six fatal ones, and recounted, with a great deal of verve and a wealth of dramatic and tragic detail, each visitation of the family curse.

"They on't see her alive," she finished cosily. "But they'll be in time for the funeral, thass one comfort. Betcha the next thing we know'll be Sir Edward sending for his funeral clothes. Thass so long since he dressed up tidy, I doubt the moths'll hev got 'em. I'd best look them out time thass still light enough."

It was when she had at last actually torn herself out of her chair and lumbered off upstairs on this errand that she remembered one of the things Sir Edward had gasped out just as he was ready to go.

"Araminta," she bellowed from the top of the stairs. "I clean forgot to tell you. Master said you best go back to-morrow. 'Parently your missus made a rare owd to-do about lending you, and he reckoned you'd best got back to-morrow in case he wanted to borrer you again."

"I see," said Araminta glumly from the foot of the stairs. Just my luck, she thought, as she returned to helping Jenny with the dishes; if that had been a worse place than the Abbey, supposing there was one, I'd have had to stay a fortnight. I get in a nice place and go back after two days. But she was glad that Mrs. Liza had told her after the meal, not before. She had enjoyed her supper, and that was something.

She had been sedulously obedient to Mrs. Stancy's order not to gossip about the Abbey; but apparently conditions there were well enough known. Next morning, when the light cart in which she had come was already drawn up by the back door and the driver had wandered across the threshold to share the 'levenses which was early that day out of consideration for Araminta's journey, Mrs. Liza said:

"Maybe you'd like a bit of food to take back with you, Araminta. I'd kind of laid forward, thinking there'd be two gentlemen to feed this week and you extra like. I doubt we shan't get through it all ourselves. Come along of me and pick out what you'd like."

It was a little difficult to evade the danger of returning to meet Mrs. Stancy's eye laden like a packman and at the same time not to offend Mrs. Liza's haphazard generosity. Araminta refused a ham from which only one slice had been cut, on the grounds that it would be difficult to eat on the quiet; and a big meat pie in a dish was rejected because the dish itself would be hard to dispose of; and she argued her way out of accepting a plum pudding, one of a batch which Mrs. Liza had made early so that they could be thoroughly tested beforehand, saying that it would be a shame to eat it cold and so miss the full glory of it. But she received gratefully, and carefully packed in her little bundle a number of the meat patties which had figured in Monday's 'levenses, some small sponge buns each topped with a crystallized cherry and a huge slab of fruit cake. She could just imagine how Susie's face would light at the sight of such food, and also how gladly, after twenty-four hours of the Abbey diet, her own stomach would greet it.

They all came to the door to see her off, waving and shouting that they hoped she'd be borrowed again. Lovely, happy, slovenly, wasteful household, it was with a pang that she left them. And she would never go back. Sir Edward would stay away more than a week and by that time Annie would be back at duty. All the way back to the Abbey she fixed her mind upon Michaelmas twelvemonth and the new place at Arbrey Ash in order to keep from being downhearted.

There was apparently some secret means of communication between Summerfield and Sible Havers; for Mrs. Stancy had already heard about Sir Edward's departure and received Araminta back without surprise.

"If you hadn't come to-day I should have sent for you. One doesn't mind obliging a neighbour, but I see no reason why I should be understaffed while my maid makes butter for his. Let them make their own."

Nancy regarded her return with her usual cold torpor, but Susie was like a puppy whose master had come back after a long absence. Araminta hid the food in her drawer, hoping that Mrs. Nead's round of inspection was not due for a few days, and after the candle was out that night, Susie, previously warned, stretched out her hand and received a hunk of the plum cake which Araminta had taken to bed with her. She had meditated for quite a long time upon the possibility of asking Nancy to share the feast, but during the course of the day's work . . . which seemed endless again after the brief respite, Nancy had reported Susie for breaking an egg, and Araminta's generous impulse had shrivelled.

Susie, who had, as usual, forfeited her breakfast, ate only half the cake in the darkness, and next morning, while feeding the hens, wolfed the remainder in three ravenous mouthfuls. She had forgotten, or, in her lighthearted way chose to ignore, the warning that Araminta had given her about Mrs. Stancy's window overlooking the garden and the fowls, and when Mrs. Stancy opened the window and called clearly:

"What are you eating, Susie?" she was so much surprised that she almost choked.

"Come here? Is it hen meal again, you disgusting girl? Open your mouth."

"Cake, indeed," Mrs. Stancy said accurately after a second's revolted glance. "Where did you get that?"

Susie went dumb, as she could on occasion do, and looked so

profoundly stupid that anyone less familiar with her might have doubted if she really knew the cake's origin. Mrs. Stancy fetched the cane. After six shrewd cuts with it Susie, drowned in tears, blurted out that the cake was give her. Mrs. Stancy pushed her out to the hens and descended in wrath upon the dairy.

Araminta, with weary resignation, said at once that Sir Edward's housekeeper had given her the cake to eat on the journey home, but since she wasn't hungry she had saved it and shared it with Susie.

"I suppose Sir Edward's housekeeper, in common with her master, thinks a carefully balanced diet is the equivalent of starvation. Why all you girls aren't dead is a mystery to me, starved as you are. I suppose you gave them all to understand that you were starved."

"No ma'am. I never said a word about food the whole time I was there. I swear I never. Only they eat so much and they eat so often, they'd want a basket of food to take with them if they went across the road. And since Sir Edward had gone she'd got it to spare and gave me some to eat in the cart like I said."

"Just so . . . to eat in the cart. Not so that you and Susie should go about my premises chewing like cows all day long. Well, Araminta, it may teach you to appreciate the inferior, inadequate food which I do provide, if you abstain from it for a little while. Don't present yourself at breakfast again this week."

And breakfast, with that one cup of hot unsugared tea was the only meal of the day worth eating. Araminta had worked breakfastless on occasion, though not lately, and knew the dreary, gnawing feeling which laid hold of a stomach newly awakened and quite empty. She was sorry for herself and furious with Susie.

"I told you about that window, that silly fool," she said crossly as soon as an opportunity for speaking to Susie alone occurred. "I shan't ever give you a mite of anything again. You've been and lost me my breakfast."

"I never towd her where I got it," Susie protested, her eyes filling again. "Wholly hard she caned me too."

"I never supposed you *told* her, you daft mawther; but that wasn't hard to guess. And I bet she sent old Nead straight up to turn out my drawer. I'd got a lot of stuff, 'nough to keep us going for a week." She was nearly crying herself from mortification and disappointment. Why the devil hadn't they eaten the lot last night; might just as well have done. That was what came of trying to share and trying to make things last.

"I'm sorry, Araminta. I really am sorry," said Susie, all meekness and contrition.

"So you should be. After I'd told you about that window, too. For your own good. You should ought to think what you're doing, Susie. You'd save yourself trouble and other folks too."

"You can bang my head if you like."

"Don't be daft. Your head don't want banging. That want opening and a little sense shoved in."

She had guessed quite rightly about the rest of the food hidden under the clean clothes in her drawer. She was frightened rather than disappointed to find that every crumb had vanished. The story of a casual bite to eat on the road would hardly explain the little hoard, and Araminta wondered drearily what Mrs. Stancy's punishment for proved untruthfulness would be. However, nothing was ever said about the buns and the patties and the remainder of the cake; and after two days Araminta began to wonder whether Mrs. Nead had so far succumbed to appetite to gobble them up and pretend that she had never found them. The thought of the wizened little woman snapping up that amount of food like a hungry mouse lifted the corner of Araminta's mouth.

She had made her peace with Susie, for on the Friday morning— the first upon which she was doomed to lose her breakfast and suffer pangs of genuine hunger till dinner-time, Susie came out from breakfast with a smug, self-satisfied expression upon her face and tried to convey with hideous grimaces that she was concealing some secret or other. As soon as Nancy had left the dairy for her daily conference with Mrs. Stancy before the latter left for market, Susie produced, practically whole, the slice of dry brown bread which had formed half her breakfast.

"Here y'are," she said, with an air of triumph. "They on't starve you while I'm about."

Coming from this starveling creature who so often missed her own breakfast, both the bread and the boast were extremely touching. Araminta, with wonder and scorn, felt the lump in her throat.

"Thass all right, Susie," she said gruffly. "You eat it. You can do with it."

"Go on; get it into you. You done as much for me many a time."

Araminta bit out a mouth-filling semi-circle, and then another, and handed it back.

"Thass all I want, thank you just the same. I don't often miss a meal. I'm better lined than you."

"You sure?" Susie asked dubiously. Her simple mind could hardly entertain the possibility of anyone really hungry not immediately eating anything actually in hand. Araminta nodded.

"But you hev forgive me?" Susie said anxiously.

"Of course. You just din't think. But thass what you should ought to do, Susie. Come Michaelmas twelvemonth I mightn't be here. S'pose you got another like Nancy, always on at you. What'd you do then?"

"Reckon I'd die," Susie said simply.

"You shouldn't talk like that," said Araminta with a superstitious shudder.

On Saturday the lessons began again; and despite the sultry heat of the August evening and the week's break in the educational régime, Araminta succeeded in leaving the presence with nothing more painful than a rapped knuckle.

The weather continued almost unbearably oppressive for the next two days. On Tuesday afternoon Luke, who was weatherwise, lifted his head at the door of the milking-shed and saw the elm trees stir as though from the breath of an oven.

"Brewing up for a storm," he said.

By six o'clock the sky was heavily overcast; it was almost dark in the dairy, but no cooler. The three girls gasped and sweated over the packing of the next day's orders. The butter was oily, despite the application of every cooling device, and in the dimness it was difficult to tell brown eggs from white. Yet they were reluctant to light the lamp—though it was there ready filled, for late August evenings were short—because of the extra heat it would cast out. They heard Mrs. Stancy arrive home from the market and go straight to her room. Thank God, at least there were no stores to unpack this evening.

"A dozen brown eggs in here, Susie," said Nancy, consulting her list. Susie came across with a basin of eggs in her hand. Nancy turned back from the butter slab and looked closely at them.

"They're *white!*" she said, on a snarling note. "You daft, slop-faced, goggling idiot. I know what you're trying to do; get me in trouble with the missus, that's what it is. Half the things you do are done for the same thing; so she can say that I don't manage you like old Grace could. I'll show you if I can manage you or not, you pauper scum; if reporting you don't do it, I know something that will."

She snatched a butter patter and aimed a blow with it at the side of Susie's face. Susie ducked, and at the same time Araminta said sharply, "Mind what you're doing, Nancy. That ain't for you to hit her.".

"Who says so," Nancy demanded, wheeling round. "I'll hit you too, 'less you're careful." But she checked herself before the expression on Araminta's face. She stood stock still for a moment and then hurled the butter-patter across the dairy and said, "No. I'll report you both. Now this minute. Nobody could expect a girl to work with two lazy bad-tempered bitches like you."

She flung herself out of the dairy and Araminta said wearily:

"Now that'll be no breakfast again, just when my week was up. Why couldn't you get the right eggs, for goodness sake?"

Susie looked into the basin and said, "But they are brown."

Araminta looked. And there they were, twelve of the best brown eggs for which the Abbey was so famous that the demand always exceeded the supply by several dozens.

"Nance musta gone mad," she said.

"Owd Grace allust said she would. She towd Nancy so once and said get away afore thass too late. She coulda gone too; she was offered a job over at Cley; but she was set on being head girl here."

"Then she been mad all the time," said Araminta briskly. "Come on, we'd better get on with this."

After a few moments Nancy reappeared, her face calm again, but darkly malevolent.

"Mrs. Stancy wants you, Araminta Glover," she said. And there was considerable menace in her tone, and in the use of the surname.

Araminta's heart fell and began to beat heavily in the region of her stomach. But she drew a deep breath and squared her shoulders. This time, somehow, she'd muster enough pluck to say right out that the row was all of Nancy's making; the eggs had been the right colour, and that wasn't right for one maid, even the head girl, to hit another with a butter-patter. She was a little disturbed in her mind to realize how difficult it would be to say it all in a steady firm voice; and a year ago it would have seemed so right and reasonable. She hadn't the courage now that she had once had.

But she knocked on the dreaded door and entered the room with a tolerable imitation of bravery. Mrs. Stancy had removed her hat and her white apron and was drinking a cup of tea, standing. Apart from the big silver tray there was nothing on the table except a folded paper, oblong and sealed. The room was as dim as the dairy and against the dark polished table the paper looked very white and the seals very black.

Mrs. Stancy, after a glance at her, drained her cup and set it down. She dabbed delicately at her lips with a handkerchief and then picked up the letter. Araminta kept her mind fixed on the statement she was determined to make, the simple, truthful statement which seemed to grow more difficult to say with every minute of waiting. That's why she's keeping me waiting, Araminta thought.

"Have you any idea, Araminta, who this letter is from?"

"No," said Araminta; and the monosyllable quavered from the bumping of her heart. She had no idea, but the only person in all the world who could possibly wish to send her a letter was Jan.

And he couldn't write a word . . . but he might have got Mrs. Pollard to write it for him.

"Yet it is addressed to you," said Mrs. Stancy gently, "and the paper is expensive and it is elaborately sealed. Does that give you any clue?"

"No," said Araminta again, and thought, I could tell in a minute if you'd let me open it, not stand there staring at it in your own hand. If it's my letter, give it to me.

"I think you are lying," Mrs. Stancy said, still in a quiet voice, "because you *must* know who would be likely to send you a letter. For one thing, it must be someone who has heard that you can now read. Think again."

Yes, she'd told Mr. Loveless . . . and the daft fool had written that he liked the way she made cheeses and would keep a place for her next Michaelmas. That would be just the sort of thing he would do, so kind, so silly. Yet, as she thought again, even that explanation seemed hardly likely and she daren't say, "It might be from Mr. Loveless" in case Mrs. Stancy should laugh. Mrs. Stancy didn't know how kind and friendly he was; she wouldn't believe that Sir Edward had worked in the field, or that Mr. Loveless had lifted her up on to the gate. She wouldn't understand how it was just *possible* that the letter might be from him.

"Well?" asked Mrs. Stancy.

"No ma'am, I'm sorry, but I can't even guess."

"Very well, in that case I must insist that you open it here and now and read it aloud to me. This is a situation without precedent. I can't allow any mysterious correspondence to enter this house. Here you are, open it and read. No, no. Use the paper-knife and pry up the seals first."

There were two sheets, the inner one only written upon. Araminta looked at the first words and a feeling of dizzy helplessness came upon her. She couldn't read handwriting, at least not this kind. Mrs. Stancy set the copies in an even, plain round hand . . . this was small and fine, and there seemed rather a lot of loops. But it must be read, now, in this dimness, under the stare of those prying yellow eyes. She pressed her lips into a grim line and frowned ferociously. "My darling Araminta . . ." That was how it began; and it must be from Jan. But if so, Mrs. Pollard hadn't written the letter, she knew Mrs. Pollard's hand, a hearty open scrawl that could hardly get "Damson 1816" cramped on to the top of a pot of jam. But, whoever had done the actual writing, the letter itself must be from Jan, he was the only person who would call her that. Well, one thing was quite certain, Mrs. Stancy wasn't going to read this letter.

"Well, I am waiting," said Mrs. Stancy inexorably.

"I can't read it to you," Araminta said, her face flushing and her eyes growing desperate.

"Do you mean that you can't, or that you won't, Araminta?"

"Thass a private letter," said Araminta, stubbornly, but with some dignity. " 'T'wouldn't be fair to whoever wrote it for me to read it out."

"Ah," Mrs. Stancy's voice had more vigour now. "I thought so. There's something very mysterious about all this, and about your manner most of all. And I'm going to know what it is." She reached out her hand suddenly and tweaked the letter away. Araminta, who had dropped her eyes with the intention of gaining a moment by pretending to be prepared to read aloud, was taken unprepared. The letter was snatched before she knew it.

Fury took the place of fear and confusion. She darted towards Mrs. Stancy like a little vixen. "You give that back to me," she said. "Thass my letter. Thass got my name on it. You got no right to read my letter."

Mrs. Stancy held the letter out of reach and brought her free hand smack, smack, one to the left, one to the right, on Araminta's ears.

"You unruly girl," she said. "Sit down there on the far side of the table, and don't you dare stir until I give you permission."

Araminta's head rang like a bell from the force of the blow and she was glad enough to sit down and rest her brow on her hands. The words came to her through a daze.

Mrs. Stancy began to read in a nasty mocking voice. The opening suggested that it was a love-letter, and she pitched her voice to make the words sound ridiculous. But before she had finished there was nothing but startled incredulity about her tone.

"My Darling Araminta," she read, "when I left you on Tuesday I told you that I should be back in a few minutes and that I had something of importance to say to you. You know what prevented me. I had planned to hold your hand as I said these things, but now I must write them instead. I am so glad that you told me that you could read now, because I have already wasted so much time that unless I could write and make everything plain between us, I should be unhappy and impatient. My mother is very ill, but fully conscious again, and I cannot leave her just now, even to come and tell you what is in my heart.

"I have been in love with you, Araminta, since that long-ago day last February when I found you singing in the field. I want to marry you. I realize that there is no reason why you should love me; you hardly know me, and I have so far done nothing that might win me your affection. I meant, last Tuesday to tell you what I felt for you and to spend the week in trying to make myself acceptable to you, so that at the end of the time you could give me your answer. That plan fell through. So now I must ask you to tell yourself that I love you, as dearly and truly as ever a man loved a woman and to ask yourself whether, with time and opportunity, you could ever feel love for me in return. If you can, I shall know myself the happiest and luckiest man on earth. I would try so hard to make you happy too.

"Latchet is riding over to Sible Havers to pick up my valise and a change of clothes for my uncle. He will leave this on the way. On Wednesday afternoon he will await your reply. Not, my dearest, that I wish you to make a hasty decision, but do, I beg you, send me one line at least so that I may know that you have read and understood and are considering your answer. I shall come to see you myself as soon as I can leave with an easy mind. In the meantime, know that I love you and am, and have been for a full six months, your utterly devoted, Francis Loveless."

The name fell with a slight hiss, and then there was a great silence in the room. Araminta, with all the colour drained out of her face, and great, wondering, blind-looking eyes, sat like a person who had been stunned. Capacity for astonishment, like capacity for pain, is limited; her mind was numbed with surprise. What had happened had not even the half-familiarity of a thing longed for and dreamed of. It was too completely fantastic to be credible. At the back of her mind, pushing forward through the numbness, was the memory of Francis Loveless' physical being; she identified it wonderingly, and thought that's him, that's the person who says he loves me . . . but the thought was formless, soundless in the void of her astonishment; it made no impact, had no reality. Afterwards she remembered with a sense of shock that she was hardly pleased; there was no room in her for anything but surprise.

She became aware that Mrs. Stancy was looking at her, and that the whites around the yellow eyes had darkened so that in the gloom of storm-threatened evening they hardly showed at all. It gave the woman a strange and sinister look.

It was Mrs. Stancy who broke the silence. She said harshly, "All the Follesmarks are mad, and this poor young man must be utterly beside himself. I wonder if he had ever imagined you at table, rootling in a bowl like a hog in a trough; or blowing your nose on your fingers."

Araminta, who prided herself, not without reason, upon her table manners and personal habits, reddened at the cruel words, but neither spoke nor stirred.

"Well, don't sit there looking like a turnip lantern," said Mrs. Stancy harshly. "Until the poor lunatic actually marries you, you're still supposed to be working for me. Get back to your work."

Araminta stood up, and reached out and took the letter from underneath the heavy white hand which was holding it down on the table.

"One thing more," said Mrs. Stancy, "be good enough to refrain from spreading tidings of your conquest throughout my household. A thing like this happens only once in a thousand years, and it would be a pity if Mrs. Nead and Susie got ideas into their heads."

Araminta kept silence, moved to the door, opened it quietly, and shut it gently behind her. Then, in defiance of the rule which forbade the maids to use their bedroom during the daytime, she climbed the stairs, and, after closing the door, carried the letter to the window and read it again. It was quite easy now, and the written words had a substance and a reality which had been lacking in those which Mrs. Stancy had read aloud. Her mind began to work again. The writer of these sweet and oddly humble words was a man, different only from Jan in the possession of wealth and education. He loved her as Jan had loved her; and, given the chance he would act as Jan had acted. It was all very simple really. After all, Jan had chosen her, and he had had all the girls of at least four villages to choose from; and now Francis Loveless, who probably had as wide a choice amongst fine ladies, had chosen her too. But then, nobody had ever said that ladies were, well, *better* for that kind of thing. Why should they be? You couldn't take your money or your grand manners to bed with you.

Of course, there'd be a thousand things to learn, but then she learned quickly, and she never forgot anything. She looked back upon all she had learned and all the hard work she had done in the last eight and a half years. Her superb confidence in herself flooded back. And the corner of her mouth lifted as she thought that she had always wanted a husband that she could make something of; and now she had got one who, instead, was going to make something of her. Dear Mr. Loveless, she'd liked him all along, to love him would be extremely easy, partly because she would always be so grateful to him. It might not be the wild, crazy feeling of the lane and the stackyard at Uplands, but only she would know that.

Thunder began to roll heavily in the distance and a flash of lightning played over the letter in her hands. Reminded of it, she glanced again at the writing and could not read it in the gloom. It was getting late and there was still a lot to do, what with Nancy flying off in a tantrum and now her own absence. She folded the letter small and tucked it into the front of her bodice. Then she went down.

Nancy had lighted the lamp, and by its light Araminta could see the baleful expression on her face, and upon Susie's the sympathy which she dared not express. Susie was working, but Nancy stood with her arms folded, staring out at the shrubbery and watching the flashes of lightning. Her inactivity was so unusual that presently Araminta said:

"Don't you feel well, Nance?"

"I've stopped work," the girl said in a dead voice. "What's the good of it? I've worked like a slave for four years and I'm no further. You and Susie sauce me just as you like. And my legs hurt."

Great generous feelings welled in Araminta's heart. Poor Nancy, poor Susie, whose lives were just as they were an hour ago when she left the dairy. And of the two, perhaps Nancy the more pitiable, because she knew how cheerless her life was; even she must see, at times, that all the work, all the slavish behaviour, all the spiteful little bits of tale-bearing didn't really make Mrs. Stancy like her any better. It was like pouring water into a leaky bucket. She said warmly:

"Cheer up, Nancy. You feel bad because of the thunder. That'll be supper-time in a minute, and then you can rest your legs."

"Shut your face," Nancy said nastily, and went on staring out of the window. Presently some tears slid down over her set, immobile face, and lost themselves in the bib of her apron. Susie nipped Araminta's arm, looked at Nancy and grinned. She was a little disappointed to find that Araminta did not regard the sight of Nancy crying with quite her own relish.

The bell rang for supper. It was oatmeal again, and for the first time in almost a year Araminta's appetite failed before it. Now that her hands were unoccupied and she was free to think she just sat thinking about the future. Plans that were almost delirious flashed through her mind. Mr. Loveless was so kind, he'd surely do something for her family. And maybe, being a gentleman, he could get round the Poor Farm overseers and ask them to move Susie. She could have some easy little job about the place and eat her fill every day. And woven amongst these altruistic thoughts were little flashing ideas, such as that she could now grow her hair and let her hands get white and smooth.

"Are you sickening for something?" asked Mrs. Nead, noticing the untouched bowl.

"I've just lost my appetite," said Araminta in a bolder voice than had been heard at that table for a long time. And she thought, I could tell you why, and wouldn't you be surprised! But, even without Mrs. Stancy's order, she knew that she would be utterly unable to tell of her own good fortune to those who could not share it. The only persons whom she could possibly have told were Susie and Luke. Susie was going to share it . . . and Luke too, if he liked. There would be a place for him in the wonderful dairy Mr. Loveless was planning. But she didn't think he would take it. He was staying at the Abbey for some strange secret reason of his own. Well, perhaps they could send over from Arbrey Ash and buy his medicines and pay him well for them.

But it was a pity, meantime, that the oatmeal should waste in her bowl. (Rootling in a bowl like a hog in a trough! Whose idea was it that they should always have spoon food in bowls, eh?) She lifted her spoon, and after a moment's deliberation slashed across the congealed mass with its edge. One half she conveyed, safely, into Susie's bowl, and the other was on its way into that of Nancy, for, despite her melancholy, the pale girl had fallen upon her share with avidity and a little extra might do something towards making her feel more cheerful. It was on its way, but it never got there. The wobbling mass divided and fell from the spoon on to the cloth. It looked very dirty and sticky against the spotless whiteness. There was a hiss of indrawn breath, a kind of gasp all round the table.

"That'll be sixpence, sixpence! sixpence! sixpence! Oh God, that'll surely be sixpence! sixpence!" said Nancy hysterically, and yet with a glee that was unmistakable.

"You know very well thass forbidden to give your food away," Mrs. Nead said in a voice of ice.

Araminta suddenly burst out laughing. Mrs. Nead cut the laughter short and also curtailed Susie's extra bit of supper by rising to say Grace. She didn't know what was the matter, but there was something curiously wrong in the house to-night. So, "make us truly thankful, Amen." Stick to the routine, pursue the safe ordinary course, combat crazy behaviour, insolent laughter and hysteria alike by saying Grace.

But Araminta was not the only person at the Abbey who had lost all appetite for food. Mrs. Stancy had sent her tray away untouched. She had, to be truthful, not noticed its arrival and had been barely conscious of its removal. Both times when Bella had entered the room she had been sitting at her desk, her chin propped on her hands, her eyes fixed on the storm outside. Bella had said, when, having waited for the exact time, she came to remove the tray, "Shall I take it away, ma'am?" and Mrs. Stancy had said, without turning, "Yes." It was a lovely supper too, Bella thought, looking enviously at the cold, spoiled food.

Immediately after reading Francis' letter Mrs. Stancy had been sufficiently herself to say a few cruel and cutting words to Araminta; but even while she was speaking a high tide of thought and emotion had been gathering for a final assault upon her mind, as a spring-tide, bent upon undermining, beats a threatened cliff. When Araminta had gone and softly closed the door, Mrs. Stancy was left with the realization that the dairymaid, from the boxing of whose ears her fingers still stung, was to be the mistress of a great house and the wife of a man, who, however crazy, was young and personable, of undoubted lineage and great wealth, and one who was, moreover, certainly in love with her. In fact, the shining dreams of the proud, ambitious girl, whom Caroline Stancy had been, were to become actuality for Araminta Glover. And with that realization the door which the woman had, by devious devices, kept shut upon the past, creaked and opened.

In a space of time immeasurable by ordinary standards, she lived again all the gruelling disappointments of her youth. That night of the Ball in the Assembly Rooms across the Abbey Hill when young Mr. Cullum of Hardwycke had danced with her six times, and all the ladies had whispered and the gentlemen had stared and smiled . . . and the day after when he had passed her in the street with a bow so slight that it was almost indetectable. . . . That other evening when Father, after long angling, had succeeded in cajoling Sir

Willoughby Cuthbert to come and inspect his prints. Sir Willoughby was a widower, and musical, and he had come, as though by accident, upon Caroline playing the piano as only she could play . . . and had listened entranced for more than an hour and had praised her execution as it deserved . . . and had gone away and after a week had written to suggest that he would like her to teach his daughter. These were but two of many bitter humiliations. But it could happen you see . . . it had happened to Araminta Glover. Why hadn't it happened to Caroline Bowyer? Then she might have been a loved wife, the mother of strong sons, respected by society, instead of an ageing market woman, driving her gigful of yokel produce to back doors and draughty stalls, wearing an apron to show that she knew her place. Then she would not have been left to marry that vile creature whose only shred of acceptability had been the pale mirage-like reflection of her own dazzling dream. Then there would have been in her life none of these things which could only be forgotten, or whose memory could only be assuaged by two vices, cruelty or alcohol.

Usually she chose the former, it was subtler and cheaper. But to-night, rising at last from her desk, she went to a cupboard that was always locked, and took out a bottle of brandy and a glass. She loathed the very smell of it; it reminded her of the man who had been her husband, and of certain occasions when she had turned to it for strength; but it had been her friend too, on many a sleepless night when all the house was still and she had only memories and ghosts for company. She sat down by the table and poured the liquid with a steady hand and drank it, waiting. The whites of her eyes, already veined with red, darkened, and her heart beat faster, but to-night for her mind there was no relief. Her face was like clay, and the deep lines upon it might have been scored there by the chisel of a sculptor intent upon portraying the ravages that vice and madness can make upon a human countenance. She drank again, steadily, without taste, waiting only for the moment when the passions which tore at her mind so savagely should sheathe their talons and leave her to the emptiness of heart and mind that passed, with her, for peace.

But to-night the tried and trusted ally failed her. The processes of her mind grew swifter and sharper. The ghosts of her old humiliations rose before her, fresh clothed in venom; the memory of her crimes haunted her . . . compelling her, not to remorse, but to self-pity, for to her they were not injuries which she had inflicted upon others, but wrongs which had been done to her. Her warped, distorted mind reeled as it compared the fate which should have been hers with that which had been.

Brandy was no good. Only one thing in the world would have brought her relief from the jealousy and the hatred and the haunting memories and the self-pity; and that would have been to take Araminta's little neck between her hands and rip the life out of her. But Araminta was sacrosanct now; even in her madness Caroline Stancy knew that. Araminta was not a drunken old reprobate, snoring upon a tumbled bed, who could die and cause no one a moment's regret; nor was she an old dairy woman, past all use, who could be dragged from her last bed to die over the making of a butter-cow.

But there were others. There was that idiot girl whose presence was a constant offence.

By this time it was almost ten o'clock. The three girls had come in from the plucking-shed and were working upon the ugly, leggy bodies of the plucked fowls, making them neat, setting them prettily upon the wooden trays. Nancy had been odd and silent all through the evening, working slowly and fumblingly, quite unlike herself. Now Susie, with a lighted taper, was singeing away the delicate fluff which still clung to the pimpled, pinkish flesh, and Araminta, with a little help from Nancy, was pressing the legs close to the bodies in such a way that the breasts looked even plumper, tucking the wings in, and having made all neat, securing the birds in position with lengths of fine white twine.

They were all aware of Mrs. Stancy's entrance, and Araminta, who had worked in Nick Helmar's house during her impressionable youth, recognized the scent of brandy which came with her. She turned from the fowl she was trussing and looked at her mistress, and despite the new confident happiness in her heart, she was frightened. Mrs. Stancy was always fearsome, but to-night there was something else. Araminta stared at the dreadful, glistening pallor, the crazy eyes, and, above all, at the dishevelment of the always tidy black-and-white hair, and felt her mouth go dry.

"I had other things to think of, Nancy, when you came to lay your complaint," Mrs. Stancy began in a voice which, though not unlike her own in moments of anger, was subtly different, a little blurred and with a crack in it. "Now I have come to do you justice. As you say, how can you manage the work with such as these to help you. Whores and idiots. Whores with their minds on their next man, idiots with their minds on their next meal." She lowered her head and glared, like an animal about to charge. Susie, who had turned round and then backed close to the slab as soon as Mrs. Stancy began to speak, seemed to shrink smaller and the nervous twitching which had grown more marked of late, especially in moments of tension, convulsed her green face.

"Ah, you may laugh," the mad woman cried gleefully. Even now, bent upon deliberate brutality, some twist in her made her glad that the victim had offered a technical provocation. "I'll make you laugh on the other side of your face."

Susie gave a shrill squeal of terror as Mrs. Stancy bore down upon her. The big white hands struck her on either side of the face and then fell to her shoulders and shook her until her head wobbled as though her neck were broken. The ugly mouth fell loosely open and out of it came a bubbling cry, shaping itself rhythmically to the shaking, thin, piteous and despairing.

Nancy, after one glance, began to truss a bird briskly. It was all right. Mrs. Stancy was taking her side after all. The perverse despair which had come upon her earlier in the evening when Mrs. Stancy had dismissed her complaint so lightly, so abruptly, melted away and was replaced by exaltation. If Susie's cries were intended to appeal for pity and aid they fell on deaf ears, worse than deaf where Nancy was concerned.

But as soon as Mrs. Stancy laid hands on Susie, Araminta had dropped the length of twine and now she stood irresolute. Behind her the long years of meek submission, poverty and helplessness stretched, heavy with the knowledge gained by experience. Interference was no good; the rule held firm, whether it was a boy tormenting a dog, a man beating a horse, or a mistress bullying a maid; you did yourself harm and made things worse for the victim too. You must learn—indeed you had learned—to hold your tongue and your hand, and then, afterwards, if it could be done safely, you could be kind and apply what comfort was in your power to give. But . . . but there were limits. She'd always known that Mrs. Stancy had a devil in her and to-night the devil was uppermost. And Susie wouldn't be hard to kill. . . .

Her thin red hands shot out suddenly and seized Mrs Stancy just where the thick arms joined the heavy shoulders. It was like grappling with a bull. Feeling the inadequacy of her own wiry lightness she gasped out an appeal to what sanity might remain in Mrs. Stancy's spirit.

"Stop! Stop!" she cried in a high, shaking voice. "You'll kill her. There ain't much of Susie!"

Mrs. Stancy flung Susie away from her as she might have thrown a sack, and like a sack Susie seemed to fly through the air and strike the stone floor and lie still. Then the mad woman turned—beyond thought now, beyond caring what she did or whom she hurt, and twisted her shoulders free and brought both fists together and with them struck a great blow at Araminta's chest, just where her neck joined her collar bone. Araminta went backwards and sat down, suddenly, ridiculously and helplessly in the basket used for carrying the plucked fowls from the shed to the dairy. For a moment, wedged in it she saw Mrs. Stancy looming above her, and thought, with sharp despair, this is the end of me, I'll never be married now. But even as she thought it she was struggling free, pressing against the edge of the basket with both hands, her eyes tight shut against the blow she knew to be coming. Then she was free, out of the basket, stumbling to her feet. She opened her eyes and saw Susie, still on the floor, hauling Mrs. Stancy backwards by gripping the full black skirt with both hands.

Nancy, leaning back against the slate slab was laughing, hysterical and helpless.

"Fetch somebody," Araminta screamed. "Can't you see she's crazy. Fetch somebody, Nancy, before she kills the lot of us."

Nancy said, and the words came oddly through the laughter, "He-he-he, you both deserved a good hiding, he-he-he, and you're going to get it, he-he-he."

Mrs. Stancy seemed to notice Nancy for the first time, and then everything happened so quickly that afterwards it was difficult to describe exactly what did take place. Mrs. Stancy kicked herself free of Susie and lurched forward towards Nancy, whose laughter changed abruptly into a stifled scream. Araminta clung dizzily to the raised right arm of the mad woman, and shrieked as well, "Susie, help me! Mrs. Nead. Bella!" Susie got up dizzily and hauled again at the back of Mrs. Stancy's skirt; the gathers at the waist tore out with a noise very like the screaming. Then the great powerful body gave a heave and Araminta fell backwards again, fell upon Susie, so that they reeled together, and the big white hands closed upon Nancy. Three times the white-capped head went crack, crack, crack, against the whitewashed wall. Nancy crumpled at the knees, at the waist, and fell forward, held only by the murderous hands, and then suddenly free of them. The red sacrifice which Caroline Stancy's demon had demanded began to flow.

Mrs. Stancy stood still for a moment looking down at the blood on the white cap; then she turned without a word and walked out of the dairy, leaving the door open.

Luke was brewing something in his little brown saucepan over a smouldering fire in the harness-room when Araminta, with a face as white as her apron, burst in. He turned his head at the sound of the door opening, and, after a glance at her face, carefully lifted the saucepan aside and straightened himself.

"Well, lass, whass up?"

It was difficult to speak, she was shaking all over and her chattering teeth nipped her tongue.

"Luke, she've killed Nancy."

The hunchback did not inquire who She might be.

"You sure?" he said, quite calmly.

Araminta nodded. "I know death when I see it. Mrs. Nead said so, too."

"Where's *she?*"

"She went into the Room and locked herself in. And I turned the key in the lobby door as well. I had to do that before Mrs. Nead and Bella dared come in the dairy to look.'

"Thass right," said Luke calmly, "you done well. He spoke as though Araminta had been acting under orders. And he behaved as though he himself had had orders too. Quickly but deliberately he reached down his old jacket and put it on; then he lifted the lantern from the hook in the middle of the ceiling.

"I'll get Doctor Wesley," he said.

"That ain't no good, Luke. She's dead, I tell you. And Mrs. Stancy did it deliberate. She ought to hang."

"Maybe she will," said Luke, pushing his arms into the sleeves of the jacket. "I bin waiting for this. Bessie was owd and there worn't a mark on her. Natural causes the crowner said. But Doctor Wesley listened to what I towd him, and he'll listen again. This may be the end of it." He sighed heavily. "I allust feared that'd be Susie. But thass better this way. Nancy were that poisoned she'd hev been no good in another place. That devil had her by the soul." He took the lantern in his hand and moved to the door. "Thass bin a long time coming," he said. "But you mind what I said to you about the mills of God, Araminta? They're grinding this minute."

There was something a little frightening about the calm, impersonal words. And Araminta had been frightened enough.

"I ain't going to stay here, Luke," she said tremulously. "I'm going to fetch Susie out of that house and we ain't going back there, never."

"Now don't you be a silly girl," Luke said. "Thass too late for you to get to Minsham to-night. And that door is good and strong. 'Sides, I shall be back with the doctor presently."

221

"I ain't going to Minsham," Araminta said. And as she said the words a little of the horror of the last hour fell away. "Let me just get Susie, and then we can all go together. Susie and me'll go to Sible Havers. There's chap there I've got a message for . . ." The message, upon whose form she had had no time to brood, flashed suddenly bright and whole into her mind, 'Yes, with all my heart.' "They'll take us in, I reckon." She put her shaky hand to her bosom, and from within her bodice came the faint crackle of the death warrant which had been a love-letter. And at the touch it became a love-letter again.